Sovereignty

Sovereignty

A NOVEL

ANJENIQUE HUGHES

New York

Sovereignty
A NOVEL

Published in New York, New York, by Morgan James Publishing. Morgan James and The Entrepreneurial Publisher are trademarks of Morgan James, LLC.
www.MorganJamesPublishing.com

The Morgan James Speakers Group can bring authors to your live event. For more information or to book an event visit The Morgan James Speakers Group at www.TheMorganJamesSpeakersGroup.com.

ISBN 978-1-63047-818-6 paperback
ISBN 978-1-63047-819-3 eBook
ISBN 978-1-63047-820-9 hardcover
Library of Congress Control Number:
2015916057

Cover Design by:
Rachel Lopez
www.r2cdesign.com

Interior Design by:
Bonnie Bushman
The Whole Caboodle Graphic Design

For my sweet cousin Mariah Nicole Swingley,
who will forever be loved . . . .
10/18/1997–8/27/2015

Prologue

I used to think I knew all the answers; now, I no longer even know the questions. One of my wise-ass professors at the Hall of Academics once told my sociology class that technology was limitless, and he wasn't kidding. The world is so far gone technologically that some days I wish I had never been born.

Fact: Every baby born in the twenty-third century is implanted with a one-zettabyte microchip in his or her wrist ensuring that everything that is done, seen, or experienced is recorded for all eternity. One glance at a computer panel, and they know where you are and what you are doing, and the rest is history, as they say. Paperwork? Gone. Computers? Gone. Smart phones? History. They originally wanted to implant the chip in the frontal lobe of the brain, but that proved to be too time consuming and costly. They didn't want to spend any more money than they absolutely had to, and they didn't want any idiot robots walking around causing a ruckus from possible brain injuries.

"They" used to be referred to as the government in twenty-first century terms, but today they are known as the Sovereign Regime, or SR: Sovereign, because they frickin' know everything about everyone at any time; Regime, because they arbitrarily and systematically override a person's life through dominion and authority. Earth has come a long way, baby. And it ain't pretty.

Chapter 1

"It has become appallingly obvious that our technology has exceeded our humanity."

—Albert Einstein

Goro!" My five-year-old brother Josiah yelped in the distance behind me. I turned in my sprinting and caught a glimpse of him struggling to keep up on his scrawny little scraped-up legs, his backpack banging against his side. He wasn't in distress, not at all; he had a crap-eating grin on his face in anticipation of the contraband we were about to explode.

Josiah and I were tearing across a barren dirt field toward a small hill along with my best friend Alex. We clutched ancient, old-fashioned firecrackers in our hands. Our cargo was precious; it had taken months to locate and stash our spoils. It was dusk, so we would wait for the cover of night when it was as black as coal on the horizon to launch our operation. Not only did we want to light up the sky; we were damn near attempting to do the impossible—evade the SR. I didn't want to dwell on the magnitude of our audacious mission. I was sure I was going to end up barfing up my generic tuna fish sandwich I had eaten earlier for lunch.

Alex, eighteen, legit technological genius, had designed the steel sleeve cuffs that we wore tightly wrapped around our right wrists. The million-dollar question was whether they would deflect any chip activity. Would we remain hidden from surveillance? This was our anticipated test run. I wanted to see if we could avoid detection by having our identity chips masked with titanium.

Alex also devised a way to detonate our mini bombs from a distance with a device that didn't require scanning our wrists, since nobody pushed buttons anymore in our world. For this experiment, we would just touch a panel on the detonator and voila. I had to give my man props for his ingenuity. Whether we would all crash and burn remained to be seen.

I slowed my pace, allowing Alex and Josiah to catch up with me.

"You douche, you always outrun everyone." Alex bent over at the waist breathing hard, dropping his rucksack filled with ammo on the brown grass. Water was a luxury, and it hadn't rained in months, save but a rare sprinkle or two.

"Yeah, well . . . not SR goons." I stretched my arms over my head and gave him a wink and a smile.

Alex is 100 percent Latino and proud of it. He is my always cocky, sometimes insecure best friend. He tends to question everything, and is always paranoid about committing infractions, but that must mean he believes in his "chip slip" invention enough to take the risk we were about to make. I have known him since we were six years old, and I would take a laser hit for the guy. I glanced at him, dressed in his signature cargo shorts, his eyes fixed on the vast expanse of what was remaining of our city, once known eons ago as Los Angeles.

"Goro's king Khal," My little bro interrupted the quiet ambience to defend me. "Call my bruh a douche again, and I will end you." He had on such a pouty look that Alex and I both burst out laughing. I tossed my bag down. Several roman candles spewed out as the bag opened upon impact.

"Wrecked." I slapped Alex on the shoulder. "R. I. P." He tackled me and we both crashed to the ground. Josiah chanted my name over and over, ad nauseum.

"Get off me, ya derp!" I laugh-shouted as we jumped to our feet, and he waved some ridiculous martial arts moves in my face. "Where's Cory already?" I staved off Alex's mock fighting moves, which Josiah was now mimicking. His steel cuff was too large, and it kept catapulting off his wrist toward our heads.

"Ahhh!" I yelled grabbing his cuff from the ground after it careened past my nose. I crammed it back on Josiah's wrist before Alex and I began organizing our gear.

Cory is the third homie in my squad and the voice of reason; he is always keeping Alex and me from getting into trouble. I think he is Polish or Scandinavian, or something European. He is non-emotional, a real pragmatic thinker. I don't ever remember a time when he lost his cool or wigged out about . . . well, anything. He watches Alex's and my back. If anyone insults me in the slightest or appears to be scorning me with an attitude, he gives them a death look, and they immediately back down. Sometimes they even feel remorseful in the end. I don't know how he does it, to be honest. He's shorter than Alex and I are, but he is squat and compact, low to the ground and beefier than either of us. I may be able to run fast, but Cory could lay me out flat on my back if he wanted to.

"His elderly, senior citizen grandmamma prolly needed some soup heated up or something." Alex collapsed onto the ground, crossing his legs under him. "I can't believe that old lady is still alive."

"Alex . . . ." I reprimanded him, giving him a look as I separated the explosives into specific firepower intensity piles. I paused every now and then, squinting into the distance for Cory. I covered my eyes in the glare of the setting sun and thought I saw him ambling toward us. Sure enough, Cory came into closer view wearing fatigues and camo boots.

"Ahahaha!" I laughed out loud at Cory's choice of garments. Alex looked up at the source of my amusement as Cory came to a halt in front of us. Josiah just raised his eyebrows.

"Hey, girls." Cory grinned, both his dimples perking up.

"What the heck is that getup?" Alex stared, climbing to his feet. Cory's disposition turned sarcastically sour. He stared Alex down.

"You never can be too cautious, man . . . too many SR goons, not enough bros, too many posers, not enough pros." He smiled, straightening his button-down camo shirt. He put his hands on his hips as if to say 'go ahead, hate me . . . but I'll pummel ya if you do.'

"Do you hear yourself? What is that?" I snickered. "Relax, buddy." I patted his shoulder in an affectionate manner. "It's all good."

Cory changed the subject. "Watcha got? Did you bring the Hail Marys, bub?"

"Pshhh . . . of course, idiot." Dude hadn't shut up about the potent mother of all firecrackers when he got wind of Alex's invention and our ensuing adventure. I pointed to the arsenal we had finished setting up a few feet away. We started collecting these antique fireworks as soon as Alex had the schematics of a prototype worked out. Now that his design had come to fruition, it was the perfect opportunity to kill two birds with one stone: blow these suckers sky high in a beautiful display of rebellious angst and see if we could evade the almighty SR to boot.

"Yeah, ya know . . . as soon as these moh fohs go off, we need to be safely ensconced in our so-called hiding place. The SR will show up before you can say Geronimo!"

I fake scowled at him, smirking at his Geronimo comment. He looked a little leery at the sheer amount of booty we had managed to haul up the hill.

I caught Josiah fingering one of the larger crackers and told him to leave it alone. I had only agreed to let him come with us as long as he listened to me and did everything I said.

"Don't be a fuddy-duddy," Josiah marched in place, addressing Cory and saluting all of us stiffly. "Oh-h-h, say can you see!" he said, and he threw his hand down from his forehead salute so hard that his metal cuff flew off yet again. We both stared.

"Yo! Give me that, ya little twerp." Alex scooped it up off the ground and threw it toward our bags. "Where'd you learn that song, little man?"

"Don't diss my brother." I addressed Alex with mock anger—half serious, half not.

"No one is going to be suspecting a five-year-old of any illegal goings on." Alex rolled his eyes. "Don't even trip."

"You sure about this?" Cory glanced at our hoard of supplies. "Last thing I want to do is bail out your two asses from Camp."

Camp is where the SR sends young unruly street rabble, of which we are not. Legend has it that it is a brutal boot camp in which SR rookies rule with an iron fist. It was created post War, because the Sovereign Regime won't tolerate any delinquency. They send juveniles there to make them "soldiers." Last thing anyone wants is to be dragged there, where havoc runs rampant and torture sessions are just a part of the daily scheduled happy hour.

"This is the best way to test my invention," Alex argued, yet still managed to preen his ego feathers at his ingenuity.

"Yeah, but the SR will still see what's up regardless of whether or not our chips show up on their grid," Cory protested.

"Which is why we haul ass as soon as we have set everything up." Regardless of the outcome, I was looking forward to the prospect of seeing the spectacular colorful display of unlawful explosives. I was antsy with the heightened excitement that comes with taking dangerous risks.

"Meh," Alex replied.

"Aw, don't be a party pooper; this will be super-duper!" Josiah giggled at his own dumb rhyme. Cory held out his fist for a bump. Josiah reciprocated then grabbed Cory's raised bicep with his two hands and hung there like a monkey making high pitched "ooh ooh ahh ahh" monkey sounds. I had no idea where he learned monkey sounds, as they had been extinct for centuries. He must have seen some old animal history film in the Hall of Digital Archives.

Alex and I began prepping the sophisticated lighting system of wires that would allow us to ignite every single firecracker at the same time. We arranged each firework according to the map we had configured and drawn out earlier. Everything was meticulously planned and executed. Even though the curfew alarm was still over an hour away from blaring, we still needed to stampede back down the hill to our designated cover location, and soon. Once everything was detonated, the remaining paraphernalia was rigged to self-destruct, destroying all evidence while we watched the panorama from a safe distance. The sun was descending, bringing a chill to the air. I rubbed my hands together to keep warm. Cory stood off to the side, entertaining Josiah with his alternating pec dance.

"Show off," I muttered at Cory's pulsing chest pectorals.

"D'awwww, butt hurt much?" Alex chuckled. "You could pump some proverbial iron yourself, stupid."

"Okay!" Alex announced. "Let's bounce." He grabbed both our backpacks, which carried our remaining supplies.

"Wait! Now?" Cory yelled, stricken with fake panic. Josiah turned to me, eyes wide. I punched Cory on the arm for scaring my kid brother.

Alex held up a hand to Cory's overreaction. "Calm down—I will give the signal when we need to start hoofing it down the hill. We are detonating from the bottom. Easy peasy." He held up a small portable device he had dug out of his front pocket in order to reassure us all. I stood still for a second, ruminating over our little excursion once again, counting the costs, hoping against hell that we would not be caught. I could be so indecisive sometimes. *Maybe we shouldn't do this*, I thought as I glanced at Josiah's small frame dancing around Alex. He was trying to grab the detonator out of Alex's raised hand.

"I wanna do it!" Josiah yelled like a two-year-old. "Me! Me!"

"Um, H E double hockey sticks, NO." I scooped him up from the ground and put him on my shoulders so I could hold onto him when we jettisoned down the hill.

"Who says that?" Alex shook his head, making fun of me.

"Do I sense some hesitation?" Cory mimicked the fake enthusiasm of an SR recruiter. "Because we can pull the plug on this at any . . . ."

"Cory!" I cut him off. "Let's get this joyride started." I gave him a quasi-stern look, which Cory ignored. My friends knew most of my talk was BS. I loved to be an obnoxious ass. We all started down the hill, me grasping Josiah's small hands and legs in my own hands.

When we reached the bottom of the knobby hill, we cut across the dry field toward an old Catholic cathedral that had been rotting since before the war. I marveled at how some of the stained glass windows had managed to survive all these years. Some of the tall spires on the roof had collapsed in on themselves in one corner of the building. When we entered the broken side doors leading into the vestibule, something scurried into the darkness. Josiah clung to my neck, grabbing under my chin for a firmer hold. My brat pack skidded through dust and wiped spider webs from our clothes and faces.

I refused to climb the sketchy staircase to the back balcony, so we hunkered down near one of the larger windows that contained some remaining colored shards of glass that still displayed faded blues and reds, dirty with age. This perspective gave us a bird's eye view of the field arena, which was about to erupt in a glorious display of pandemonium. My heart fluttered with nervous energy. *God, I hope we don't end up shrouded in SR body bags over this.*

Alex took the small scanner from his bag as I lowered Josiah to the floor; he immediately started jumping up and down with glee.

"Let's rock and roll!"

Cory laughed at Josiah's innocent excitement.

I put my hand on top of Josiah's head.

"When I say it's time to go, we have to go," I stated, staring down into his eager eyes. He nodded his head in obedience.

"Can I scan the detonator?" he asked in a timid voice, tugging on the leg of Alex's shorts.

"Why not?" He glanced in my direction for confirmation, and I shrugged my shoulders, changing my mind on the spot to let him do it. "Okey dokey stokey . . . wait for my word." Alex handed Josiah the panel. "We're not scanning this time; you just touch this circle."

Josiah gripped the detonator in his hands, his eyes centered on the far-off hill. I held my breath for so long that I finally kicked the heel of Alex's boot with my toe to get his attention.

"C'mon," I whispered. "Enough pissing in the wind." I wanted to get this whole ordeal over with.

Alex, Cory, and I looked at one another as if we were getting ready to dive out of a heliplane. "Ready?" Cory breathed in the still silence, prolonging the agony.

I spread my hands wide. "Yes!" I blurted, keeping my eyes on Josiah.

"Here goes . . . everything," Alex turned to Josiah. "Now."

Josiah lifted a tentative finger and without looking, jabbed the touch panel on the face of the detonator screen. The knowledge of what he was about to unleash dawned on all of us.

Nothing happened.

I looked at Alex.

"A little slower than that, buddy." Alex guided Josiah's finger back toward the device again.

This time Josiah watched where he was pressing as he touched the circle on the panel.

A low rumble preceded the deafening boom in the distance accompanied by a chorus of shrill whistles. Josiah dropped the detonator when he heard the resounding thunder.

Holy crap.

We stood mesmerized as the brilliant display of firepower waned, forgetting the fact that we would be in danger in about two seconds. In the wake of the last sparkle, I saw six bright lights in the distance, the all too familiar sight of heliplanes heading fast toward the carnage. *Didn't take them long*, I grudgingly surmised. I grabbed Josiah by the hand as Alex, Cory, and I sprinted for the nearest exit. When we were outside, we slowed our pace, sticking to the route in the shadows we had mapped out.

"And . . . split now." Cory ordered, with Alex going straight, Cory turning right, and Josiah and me going left. Breaking up gave us an obvious advantage. We would regroup in a few days to debrief, but my vision was tunneled on getting Josiah somewhere safe.

I heard the ghetto vultures circling the smoky hill as high wattage spotlights scanned the entire area. They should know that whoever was responsible for this little stunt would be long gone by now, but the SR would send out air and ground reinforcements to investigate in an all too common show of power.

Josiah and I kept close to the walls of the various buildings we passed. We were all to head to our prospective homes and meet up at a later time. All communication between us would cease so as not to arouse suspicion of any collaborative activity among us. I groaned when I heard the heliplanes abandon the hill and head toward the dilapidated city. Josiah and I were still some distance away from our family's dwelling, so I surveyed my options. I could shuttle us into the nearest eating establishment or bar, which was the only thing open at 8:30 at night, but people would raise eyebrows at seeing a five-year-old kid in a bar. Plus, we only had thirty minutes left until curfew.

Screw it. I pulled Josiah into a crappy looking old movie theater that had been converted into a restaurant, and I scanned the room with shrewd eyes. I dropped down into a chair at a small table with Josiah sitting across from me.

"Curfew is soon, Goro." Josiah looked at me with a flicker of fear in his eyes. I was pissed at myself for letting him come after all and for cutting it too close.

"I know, buddy. We'll be okay," I glanced around, noting that several patrons were finishing their meals or putting on their coats to leave.

A waitress sauntered over to us with a bored look on her face. "Curfew will be upon us, folks, and we close in, like, fifteen minutes."

I gritted my teeth. "I know—just bring two sodas." I held out my wrist for her scanner.

"That'll be ten credits."

"Um . . . ." I heard her tentative pause. "Classy new bracelet?"

I looked up at the smirk in her eyes and noticed that in our hasty retreat, I had forgotten to take off my metal cuff. Damn. I pushed it off into my pocket and scanned for the bill.

"We're in a hurry." Josiah's wide eyes were looking back and forth between the waitress and me. He looked nervous.

"Ya think? That'd be good." Our waitress turned in a huff and stalked off.

"Josiah, it's going to be all right." I ignored the waitress's snarky comments. "As soon as our drinks come, we'll down them fast and head out with some other people, as if we have been here eating supper the whole time." I put my hand over his and squeezed. "Behebik, habibi?"

"Behebik, habibi," he answered back in a small voice, using our favorite Arabic phrase for one another. His brown eyes darted to and fro throughout the restaurant. He'd never been out this late, ever. Our waitress brought our sodas and plunked them down on the table in front of us. Suddenly, the doors banged open, and four SR soldiers entered, their fingers on the triggers of their raised rifles, causing me to jump in my seat. Everyone halted what they were doing. The waitress froze in place next to our table. I could see Josiah shivering in fear. My hand was still atop his, and I gripped it tightly, whispering for him to look at me. He turned his frightened eyes toward mine.

"Don't say anything," I whispered. "I won't let them hurt you in any way."

He nodded his head hard up and down, sitting stock-still.

The soldiers made their way into the establishment, their eyes shifting and assessing the environment, not once lowering their weapons. I attempted to look as casual as I could, for my little brother's sake, actually picking up my glass to take a sip. It didn't work.

Two of the four men stalked over to our table. I silently cursed myself for drawing attention to us. What, did they think that quenching my thirst at that very moment was offensive, or an act of hostile insubordination? I almost wanted to chuckle in disgust, but knew I didn't dare.

The waitress backed up and gave them a wide berth. One of the men stopped right at my elbow. I could smell the chill night air radiating off his clothes, the scent that someone carries when he has just walked in from the cold. He tapped the side of my forehead with the muzzle of his rifle.

"You," he addressed me in a low voice. "Stand."

I stood up, refusing to take my eyes off Josiah's terrified stare. I tried with all my being to reassure him with a look. *Be strong. I will protect you no matter what happens.*

"Look at me!" The mercenary screamed into my right ear, leaving me momentarily deaf. I turned to face him, seeing a man not much older than myself. His head was shaved and he had a pockmarked face. He was dressed in the regulation black SR uniform, his eyes fierce and savage but vacant. Dead.

"Let's go!" He shoved me backward so hard with his rifle that I staggered, just managing to stay upright.

"No!" Josiah launched out of his seat at that moment and lunged for me in a desperate but futile attempt. The second SR soldier, who had been standing behind Josiah's chair, grabbed him mid-air and pinned his arms behind his back. Something snapped inside me and I rushed him, yelling at him to let go of my brother. They could accost me all they wanted, but not my family.

My own personal mercenary jammed the butt of his rifle into the back of my head, slamming me to the floor. I saw stars that were brighter than the fireworks we had just witnessed earlier.

"Goro!" Josiah sobbed, "Leave him alone!" I could hear Josiah struggling in his captor's hold as I picked my sad self off the floor. The SR soldier shoved his boot down on my backside, pinning me face first for another bite of concrete.

It was so quiet; the only thing I could hear was the loud ringing in my ears. I lost all sense of time, direction, and space. Adrenaline kicked in, and I scrambled to my feet, furious, facing him head on. Even though I was without a weapon, I would fight as long as I could. This was it.

He advanced on me when another SR soldier thrust his head into the restaurant.

"We need to go," he barked to the other men. Everything stopped, and I felt like I was in some surreal daydream.

"This one goes with us," my adversary ordered, jabbing his rifle into my chest.

"Leave it. Command wants us back." This SR soldier seemed to have seniority; he spoke with such an arbitrary air of death that the rest of the men headed toward the exit without a word.

The man on the other end of the rifle reluctantly lowered his weapon and followed the other soldiers, but he was taking his sweet time. I could tell he was beyond pissed. What just happened?

Josiah let out the air he had been holding and ran to me. He grabbed me around the waist, burying his face in my shirt. He was crying so hard he was hyperventilating. I stooped to pick him up in my arms. The pain in my heart at putting him through this ordeal overruled the pain in my head.

Everyone else had quickly departed the restaurant in a mass exodus as soon as the SR had vacated. Just then the curfew alarm blew. Dammit. I carried Josiah outside and headed in the direction of our dwelling, knowing full well that there would still be SR out and about dealing with curfew infractions. At this point, I didn't give a damn; I moved as fast as I could down alleys, staying as hidden as possible, which wasn't much.

I was going to have a hell of a time explaining all of this to my parents. I could already feel a bump forming on the back of my head, which I gingerly touched in confirmation. The next day was our sister's graduation. Who knows what shape I would be in tomorrow. I wasn't sure if I should be exhilarated that I had managed to escape an encounter with the SR or concerned about how my family would react. Probably both.

Chapter 2

"We must rediscover the distinction between hope and expectation . . . ."

—Ivan Illich

Today, one swipe of your wrist pays for everything, shows what you got on your most recent college term paper, pulls up the date of your last speeding ticket, going all the way back to three days after you were born. They wait three days just in case the baby dies; that way, they don't have to waste a precious chip. A removed chip is worthless because it loses power, and no one has been able to replicate the neural interface, the connection to a human nervous system. It's good that not just anyone can see your whole life; they would need your entire passcode to do that, and the twenty-digit code is surprisingly difficult to hack. The first six alphanumeric digits, however, are cake if someone really digs deep enough. Heck, the black market for passcodes brings in some pretty decent money.

When you scan your wrist, only the information that is pertinent for that transaction is displayed. When Dad applied for a vehicle loan last month, he scanned his wrist, and his entire credit history, bank statements for the last three years, jobs held, addresses going back ten years, and so on was displayed. *Cuts back on time and red tape, I guess.* I could say that luckily, it is illegal to program a scanner for anything other than the intended purpose, but there is nothing lucky about it. People do it all the time, though the SR cracks down pretty deftly and swiftly. Fact: The SR is the only entity that holds the entire 20 digit codes for each and every human being on what is left of planet Earth. Bastards.

I'm not sure when the Sovereign Regime took over the planet; scanners in the Hall of History say that many moons ago, governments all over the world failed and then ultimately fell, and what was left sort of merged into one world government they called the New World Order. Despite the hokey name, this was a peaceful government that bred prosperity and harmony. Too bad I didn't live then . . . this all happened before I was born, of course.

Comprised of ten nations, the New World Order lasted for over a hundred years and eventually collapsed under one of the most brutal and barbaric world wars ever to occur in human history. Billions of people died due to the advanced weapons technology unleashed on the planet that harnessed the heat and power of the sun, vaporizing everything in its path. I don't understand it all, to be honest, and it's never taught very clearly in history class. Anyhow, the world's population ended up clocking in at just under three billion, with the SR making up at least two billion.

I just know I used to badger my late grandfather Howard with a plethora of enthusiastic questions about the history of our society. He liked to lounge in his favorite easy chair eating peppermint candies with me at his feet listening enraptured to his every word. He regaled me with stories from long ago of him and his younger buddy Mitchell storming this or that "fortress." He always had a far-off look in his eyes when he recounted his glory days. He could always surprise me with some juicy bit of information that wasn't in our history scanners at the Hall of Academics.

"Lasers," grandpa would say. "It all came down to lasers, but also biological and technological warfare—Ebola, the Caldera plague, extreme radiation. When computer-guided tactical lasers were invented, missiles and air power became irrelevant, as well as conventional ordinance like bullets, of course. The instantaneous targeting and destruction of anything larger than a football became the norm. We were back to a conventional ground war, and there was no way to deliver nukes at all. At least it saved us from the big boom."

Yes, there were the obvious initial revolts and uprisings, but those attempts were squashed in nanoseconds, leaving no question in anyone's mind that additional protests would be dealt with harshly. Mom always yelled how "damn grateful I should be that I wasn't alive during the war" in my general direction whenever she was pissed at me.

My grandfather actually fought in that war. I begged him to relive every moment of it with me whenever I had the opportunity. He has since expired, and I still have his identity chip; it's worthless, just more of a sentimental trinket than anything else. My mom made the undertaker cut it out of grandpa's wrist, even though removing identity chips from human beings, alive or dead, is strictly against the law of the Sovereign Regime. We didn't care. It hangs around my neck like antiquated army tags, and it never comes off.

My younger sister Stephanie was graduating from the Hall of Academics today, and the sky was a dull, swarthy gray. I was so *not* into attending the drab ceremony. I had suffered through the same snoozer last year for my own graduation, and my recollection of the event was far from thrilling. The pompous headmaster gets up and says a rather long yawning speech; plaques are handed out, pictures taken, yada yada yada. Very uneventful. My parents, however, acted like it was a party celebrating the end of the SR's reign, seeming to forget the events of the previous night, thank God. I received a heavy lecture about breaking curfew and putting Josiah at risk, but for the most part, it blew over. They had no idea we were a part of the "explosion debacle" that had made the news that evening. The words of the SR media, which promised Camp to the perps who most certainly would be apprehended, still rang in my ears. I was probably on their watch list now, which was so not good, and my head hurt from getting clocked, but at least my injuries weren't visible. I knew I should be grateful and just let it go.

The Hall of Academics is an institution throughout the world for children aged four to seventeen. Much like the way schools were set up back in the twenty-first century, denominations zero through thirteen are similar to grades levels, but students must pass a content heavy exam before moving on to the next denomination. If they don't pass, it's SOL for them, and they must either repeat the denomination all over again or study like a mad demon over the summer months and hope to pass the exam on re-take status prior to the first day of the new school year.

Josiah and I had made Stephanie a graduation present awhile back, and he was bouncing around in Dad's new helicraft with excitement in anticipation of giving it to her. My family's tradition was to make presents that were unique and suited for the recipient rather than buy anything. Mom said that was way more sentimental. I had to agree, as I still have the present my sister and parents gave me from my Hall of Academics commencement. It was a model airplane of one of the first aircraft ever designed in history, something akin to what the Wright brothers constructed. They know how much I love flying.

Josiah was annoying me with his jack-in-the-box behavior, but what the heck, he was only five. I gazed down at him spazzing out in the helicraft, gripping the gift on his lap. He had wrapped the gift himself in shiny pink metallic wrap he had found around the house, and he had also come up with what we would make for our sister, being quite proud of his creation. My sister loves miniatures of any kind. She has a small collection of tiny chairs and dishes and whatnot that she has gathered over the years, so my brother decided to build her a house to hold all of it. Stephanie is not really a girly girl, but she does allow herself the one indulgence of collecting teeny tiny objects. Josiah took one of Dad's old boot boxes and brought it to me with the idea of making the thing, which ended up being more of a room actually. We spent two afternoons and evenings cutting out windows and gluing bits of colored paper on the walls. We had us some quality bro time.

Stephanie had to be at the Hall of Convocation early for rehearsal, so my parents and brother and I didn't have to leave for the commencement until later. My girlfriend, Angelica, was supposed to attend with me, but she had dumped my ass a few days prior—something about me being too self-absorbed or not communicating enough . . . typical girl grief. I was still a little wounded from our parting, but I am a very strong person, so I knew that overall I would be just fine.

When we showed up, Stephanie walked over to us and gave a slight nod of thanks for our attendance. Any sort of hugs or PDA was forbidden by you know who, and we had to rely on our excellent acting skills portrayed through our eyes alone. Josiah was not so subtle, however. His exuberance was making my parents nervous. Their eyes flitted around the gardens of the Hall of Convocation, and they decided to usher us all inside. I got the feeling that Josiah was going to get nagged about social etiquette later at home.

"Picture?" my dad whispered before we entered the building. He looked smart in his one blue suit with matching tie.

"Later," my sister whispered. She looked happy, for a minute, having accomplished something that was hers alone and that no one could take away from her, not even the almighty SR. I was proud of her. She was most likely looking forward to the very prestigious award for highest marks in the Academy. She had only been talking about earning it since she was thirteen years old.

My sister was stunning in the traditional Hall of Convocation garb, her long blonde hair lying sleek and smooth down her back. My buddy Cory never ceases to flap his jaws about how legit she is—whatevs. I had to admit she was all that and a bag of chips, with her fair blue eyes popping against her red satin robe. She and my father had the same coloring, whereas Josiah, mother, and I have brown eyes and darker characteristics. Males in my world cannot have any semblance of long hair, but *le mom* joked that I would be her twin if my hair grew out naturally curly like hers. That's not gonna be happening, I always toss back at her.

We sat in uniform rows, with the graduates in the front three rows and the guests seated in the back. It was business as usual, absolute silence, while we were waiting for the presiding officer to make his appearance and begin the program. He emerged from the eaves and climbed onto the platform. *Psshh, finally.* He sauntered to the podium, also dressed in a red robe, but he was rounder and heavier than anyone else in the building, looking like he was about to bust open like some overstuffed burrito. Thank God the SR can't read thoughts, or I would be arrested on sight for the crude humor that rolled through my mind at a steady clip. Hehehe.

"I expect all of you to carry out your lives in a manner of integrity and morality," he spoke in melodious tones, "not causing disunity or division in any way." I immediately tuned him out. Yawn. I occupied myself by scanning the room and observing what everyone else was doing. I wanted to pull my buzz cut out from boredom. Everyone looked like robotic mannequins with deadpan eyes focused straight ahead at nothing. No smiling, and God forbid any bantering from the peanut gallery. No whispered side comments or glances to one another, and no expressions of any kind. Good, the dude was gearing up for some thunderous conclusion and would eventually introduce the headmaster, who would only reiterate everything the presiding officer had already said, and add some mundane tidbits that nobody cared about. I suppose I was committing an infraction by looking around, but I didn't care, not even when Alex, who was sitting next to me, punched me on the arm.

"Cut it out," he mouthed to me.

All at once, I caught the eye of a somewhat elderly gentleman standing in the back. Whoopsay. Why was he looking around so much? He looked familiar for some reason. I glanced toward the front again, pretending to be enraptured by what the headmaster was droning on about. Curiosity pinched me in ass, though, and I glanced back in his direction. The creepy dude was still staring at me. What did this geezer want? We're supposed to be focused on the nonsense in front. I decided to make it a stare-down, just for amusement. He stared right back at me and even smirked! What the . . . ? I broke contact, a little unnerved. When I peered back at him once again, he was gone. *Okay . . . not sure what to make of that*. Mercifully, the headmaster was wrapping up. Thank God. Next was the handing out of the plaques and the highest marks award, which would be given to my sister or the headmaster's daughter. Alex, Cory, and Zan—our friend who lived in the Backlands—had a bet going on as to who would get it.

When the headmaster finished reading all the names of the graduates, no one clapped or cheered. You would think we were at someone's funeral or something, but instead of watching the casserole parade, we were staring at the passing of plaques. He picked up what looked like a glass trophy of some sort, and I assumed it was the award Stephanie had worked so hard for all these years. I waited with bated breath, expecting him to call her name and present it to Stephanie.

"Stephanie!" he called out as I let my breath out in a rush of relief. She jumped up a little too quickly in her excitement and started toward the stage. She was almost to the stairs when the headmaster cleared his throat, taking to the mic once again with his scratchy voice.

"Oh . . . " he chuckled maliciously, "I'm sorry, I read that wrong. My apologies!" He smirked as he read his daughter's name loud and clear from the podium. I clenched my fists. Another slap in the face; just what I didn't need.

I watched as Stephanie, red faced, spun around and made her way back to her seat. The mortified look on her face pierced my heart. The headmaster's daughter flounced toward the stage, and when she passed Stephanie, she bumped her hard out of the way. In that moment, I knew that the headmaster had planned this. It had all been choreographed to humiliate Stephanie, as the headmaster wouldn't dare have any competition win over his daughter. Blood boiled in my veins.

I needed some air, and fast.

I ran out of the Hall of Convocation pissed off and breathing hard. I knew I could get fired up, and I slowed my heart rate down by taking long, deep breaths. I ignored the SR soldiers that were standing nearby, rifles at the ready and watching me. Let them watch. If they wanted to arrest me, I would put up a hell of a fight knowing full well it would end badly, but I didn't give a damn that I was making a spectacle of myself. I hated life, I hated the SR, I hated everything; I wanted to shove the award down the headmaster's throat until he crapped glass. I looked down at my right wrist where a vein was pulsing in anger, and I secretly hoped the vein would burst, flooding my chip red within.

Chapter 3

"The biggest guru-mantra is: never share your secrets with anybody. It will destroy you."

—Chanakya

The first time I was aware of my implantation was when I was about five years old. My mom had always waved my right wrist in front of the scanners at the doctor's office, of course, but I had never really understood what that meant until I had my first school picture taken. When I got home that day, my mom grabbed my hand and held my wrist in front of the scanner, and up popped my holographic photo in mid-air.

"Goro!" shrieked my mother. "You look presh!"

She always abbreviated all her words in our family. Adorable became adorbs, and precious became presh. To be honest, I looked so goofy with one of my front teeth missing, and my hair high and tight for a six year old (a regulation haircut), but my mom and dad whooped and hollered. My dad circled my image and remarked that I was looking more and more like a little young man. I rolled my eyes. I didn't get what all the hoopla was about, but I guess when the world sucks swamp water, your parents find joy in even the mundane things.

I distinctly remember being fascinated with my 3D face projected from the data stored in the small piece of technology in my wrist. It was all downhill from there, as "secret" was no longer a word the Sovereign Regime recognized. Nothing was secret anymore. Nothing was sacred. Nothing was private. Little did I know that years from that day, I would embark on a very treacherous, appointed, and sovereign path of my own that didn't invite the SR to the party.

I could hear my buddy Alex jogging up to where I was standing in front of the Hall. He caught my arm and said, "Dude, slow down." Funny how some vernacular remains the same over centuries.

"Ya know, Alex, if there is any one thing that I have learned over the years, it is that human nature *never* changes."

"How's that? Look, let's get out of here before we're hit up with some loitering infraction." Alex shifted his eyes from side to side, panning our surroundings, catching sight of the nearby SR soldiers. "Here, over here," he said under his breath, and led me to a little dive a block down the street that was falling apart, of course, sort of like my life. People I really cared about were always somehow exiting my life, and I had the sinking feeling that it had mostly to do with me.

We shuffled inside and took a seat in a dingy back booth before checking to see if it was covered by any cameras. It didn't look like it, but I was more worried about the camera's internal microphone anyway.

"Ugh, gross." I grimaced as I ran my forefinger across the tabletop. "This probably hasn't been wiped down since the war." I looked down at my hands. "Stephanie should have gotten that award," I said through gritted teeth after a pause. "But that jerk gave it to his daughter just because he could. Just because Stephanie isn't some hotshot's kid doesn't mean she didn't deserve it. She had way better marks than that other total waste of time."

"Whoa, simmer down, bro." Alex patted my bicep.

I noticed two SR mercenaries sitting at a table near the front of the restaurant, their rifles resting on their laps and aimed outward. Most alcohol was illegal, but it sure looked like they were drinking beer. The SR was above the law anyway. *Must be nice, evoking fear all the time*, I thought. The so-called waiter came over to our table and hovered, as there were very few other customers in the joint. I say so-called because he looked more like a dockworker than a server.

He grunted at us. I just stared straight at him, but Alex peered at him from the corners of his eyes before he said, "Two Neerbeers . . . please." Neerbeer is the non-alcohol that most people my age drink in these types of places. The waiter halfheartedly held up his scanner, and we held out our wrists to be scanned.

He started to shuffle off when Alex grabbed a corner of his grimy apron. "Yo, pardner, how much for the crappy fake beer?"

"Twenty credits each," he answered in what sounded like a mouth full of gravel before yanking himself free and moving off.

"Twenty credits?" Alex's eyes bugged out of his head. "What is this world coming to?"

He shook his head in amazement.

"We need to get rid of the SR," I threw out to Alex as if talking about the weather. "I'm actually serious," I said in answer to his stunned expression.

He stared at me hard for a second. "Hah!" he scoffed. "Uh yeah, I'll get right on that."

"Look, I am frickin' sick and tired of this oppression. I'm *not* doing this anymore," I said quietly. "I mean, why do some people have to live in the Backlands? Even though it lists my ethnicity as Caucasian on my chip, I am actually half Russian and half Arab. I am not cool with segregation!" I stopped to let my venting simmer, but something else came to mind.

"Remember when my mom went into labor with my little brother? She 'bout didn't make it inside the Hall of Dispensary in time because the SR guards bitched about her not having the proper clearance to deliver him. He was almost born out on the curb! If she'd been refused admittance and something had gone wrong . . . you know what happens to dead babies." I didn't want to mentally vacation in that past incident. My family never brought it up. Alex just lowered his eyes.

"I know; you're preaching to the choir, man." I could tell his mind was churning because he tapped the table, as was his habit. "The rap sheet of SR brutality is absurd, but do they ever get slapped with infractions? Psshh."

"This is no way to live. I'm done." I stabbed the table with my forefinger on the word *done*. He looked up at me, the wheels turning as he decided how he was going to respond to me.

"And last night? You don't even wanna know, man." I stared back at him, a challenging look in my eyes, until he squirmed a bit in his seat.

"Goro, not possible," he finally offered. He thought I had bought the farm. "That is a thrown-together idea that is completely unrealistic. However, I applaud you." He raised his fist in triumph at me.

"All we need to do is be recruited by the SR, infiltrate the Dominion, and find a weakness. They have to have at least one." I looked past his shoulder at the two SR mercenaries to make sure no one was eavesdropping. "You know those fake ass recruitment plugs they always add to the end of Sunday night announcements? We'd be shoo-ins."

"We?" Alex queried. "Whose this we stuff? I do *not* want to be recruited by the SR, least of all on a volunteer basis. Are you out of your mind? Besides, the age of conscription has passed already," he said, his mouth barely moving.

Everyone in the world has to convene around the family viewing panel every Sunday night at 8:00 p.m., in whatever time zone they live in, and watch as the Sovereign Regime's administration bores us to tears with the SR news of the week. Then they BS about how they are making the world a better place, always ending the mandatory half-hour public announcement with some shameless, beefed-up SR recruitment commercial. I felt empowered with my idea of a coup.

"Abraham Lincoln said, 'Am I not destroying my enemies when I make friends of them'? Where there's a will, there's a way, my mom always says."

"Yeah, well, John F. Kennedy said, 'Conformity is the jailer of freedom and the enemy of growth'," Alex countered.

"We wouldn't be conforming. Haven't you seen any old spy movies from the Hall of Digital Archives? Good one, though," I added, congratulating his comeback.

"The crappy ones, yeah, but they monitor and censor the hell out of everything; you know that."

He frowned and paused for a minute before starting back up again.

"Dude, I would rather have dental surgery than go deep under as a mole within the SR," Alex said under his breath. "I don't even want to have this conversation." He tried to look casual as he glanced around before returning to me. "You're not even listening."

I thought about his response for a second. "Dental surgery is not that far off with their brain washing technology. You know what they say, be careful what you wish for . . . ." I smiled. Alex just snorted, shaking his head.

Chapter 4

"He that is kind is free, though he is a slave; he that is evil is a slave, though he be a king."

—Saint Augustine

I have never met the *capo* of the SR, whose name is Davio, nor do I wish to. He initially came in "peace" to restore order and appease the masses with flowery speech suggesting everything would be just fine. He made all kinds of soothing promises, offering solutions after the war. Hah. Last rumor I overheard was that he hung some dude by his hair for six days because the guy showed up unannounced wanting to meet him or have a word with him, or whatever. The dude must have had longer hair than regulations allow. Who knows? Fact: The only reason anyone goes to see Davio is because they are about to be executed. The devil incarnate lures his prey to his lair under false pretenses, and that person never walks out alive.

He also has a multitude of sycophants eager to prove themselves, forever at his beck and call. His second in command, Ash Sheitan, is just as nefarious; no one wants to have the misfortune of encountering him alone in a dark alley, as the cliché goes, let alone anyone else in the SR.

Davio considers himself the supreme leader of the Sovereign Regime. No one really knows how old he is. In fact, he should be long dead by now. I don't really know how he came to power or how he became the *el presidente* of the SR. Legend has it that he was once among the leadership of the New World Order before all hell broke loose. In that arena, he was cast out of the powers that be because he believed himself to be more intelligent, more powerful, more handsome (puke) than any of the others, and he ultimately butted heads with the New World Order's leader at that time. He did not agree with how the government should be created after that fateful war, or how it should be run, and he openly despised human beings in general, so yeah- he was kicked to the curb, and rather unceremoniously, I might add. This is just from stories that I read and heard growing up. He was excommunicated and ousted from any and all government positions from that day forward. Despite being disgraced and cut off from his former community, he decided to carry on with his own agenda, hence creating the Sovereign Regime in a grand, middle finger gesture.

Nevertheless, the SR's expeditious rise to power was easy; they trampled any other attempts at forming an alternative government. I guess people were just so shell-shocked following the chaos of the war that they were ready to have anyone take over and lead them in some manner. I don't fully know all the details, as my grandfather would never go there, despite my pestering. He would just shake his head, and with a far-off look in his eye, say that it was too heinous to talk about.

~

Our drinks came in dirty glass bottles, lukewarm. I took a sip and put it back down on the table at once. Alex scrutinized his bottle first, smelled it, wiped off the rim with the hem of his shirt, and relented, taking a long pull. He swallowed, his lips tight.

"Ugh . . . twenty credits for this," he choked out.

"Never mind the crappy beer, I am serious about this. I have been mulling over the draft of a plan for a long time now." I put air quotes around the word draft.

"Yeah, well, this draft tastes like cow piss." He waited for me to laugh at his humor. "Goro," he moved on, "there is one thing about wanting the SR eradicated, hell—we all do, but it's another trip entirely when you go running off at the mouth about taking them down." Alex lowered his voice to a whisper. "You've heard what has happened to rebels in the past; everyone has. I mean—you remember what happened to my neighbor Talbert? All he did was give some SR goon the gnarly stink-eye, and they ended up nailing his eyelids to his forehead." He sighed out loud. We sat in silence for a moment, each with our own thoughts. "Please don't jump off the deep end trying to be some sort of world hero or something," Alex pleaded.

""God, no, I mean—who the hell am I? You're starting to sound like Cory," I complained. "How do you know that about your neighbor?" I asked, fingering my drink bottle.

"What, Talbert? He showed me." Alex answered as if citizens got nailed to the wall every day.

"Ick, he didn't die?" I replied. "How is that even done? And why would someone do that?" I leaned back against the booth, horrified.

Alex shrugged his shoulders. "Because Davio's a prick." He mouthed the words in silence, throwing his arm up across the back of the booth as if we were having a chat about nothing important.

I nodded in silent agreement as I gazed out across the dim smoky bar at nothing in particular. "You know, the last thing on this earth I ever want to do is to lie down and settle for mediocrity."

"Nah, not even! What, you think our lives are monotonous? Where the hell you going to go?" Alex spread his hands wide. "But, I love ya, bro!" He said this a little too loud.

"Shh!" I looked up at him with deadpan eyes.

Alex nodded, trying another go at his Neerbeer. "I get it—you want some sort of purpose or meaning with the life you've been given, blah blah blah. But, don't do anything impetuous."

"Since when did you start using fifty-cent words?" I picked up my Neerbeer for another swig.

"Dude, your little bro. I tell ya, he is a genius." Alex laughed, causing the two SR dudes to whip their heads in our direction.

"Shut up," I whispered. "Let's bounce."

We left the bar heads down, walking fast in the direction of my dwelling in silence. Fortunate for us, the SR did not follow us out of the bar. Phew. The sky had turned dark, and a cold breeze chilled my almost hairless head. I spent the walk back fantasizing about how it would feel to actually go out to a restaurant to celebrate your sister's convocation without looking over your shoulder to see who was listening, or what throwing a party with your friends would be like. The restrictions placed on us by the SR really sucked. This caused me to think back to the man who'd been watching me during my sister's convocation. What was that about? Was he SR? What did he want?

Chapter 5

"The Party seeks power entirely for its own sake. We are not interested in the good of others; we are interested solely in power, pure power."
—George Orwell in the book *1984*

The Sovereign Regime sees human beings as trite, trivial peons who are seriously lacking in intelligence. Come to think of it, they believe they are superior to the human race, not even considering us in the same category as they are, as if we weren't human at all. Fact: All jobs and work assignments are handed out by the SR whenever they have a need. And forget about job security. A person can be transferred, moved, fired, and/or excommunicated for any reason whatsoever. My father labored in the meatpacking industry for about seven years when he was abruptly given his walking papers one day. He had to scrounge for work assignments on the down low with the help of a few friends until he was reassigned by the SR. He said he didn't really mind; as he put it, he was not super excited about getting up every morning and wrapping dead animal carcasses, but I could tell it took a toll on him regardless. He was the head of our family, and wanted and needed to provide for us; it was a livelihood for him and essential to his wellbeing. When the SR decided to remember him, he was moved on to laboring for the Department of Water and Electric, and things seemed to go well for a while. If you mind your own business, keep your head down, and don't rock the boat, you can pray and hope that you will hold on to the crappy work assignment the SR doles out.

Besides everything else about us, our identity chip contains our daily movements for every second of our day. If anyone wants to know what I am doing at any given moment, or what I was doing two years ago on March 7, they just key in the first six digits of my passcode, and the information pops up on their scanner, whether it be sleeping, driving, taking a piss, whatever. All scanners are programmed for a person's historical agenda. However, if you don't have their passcode, then you won't know. Only the omnipotent SR knows where everyone is and what everyone is doing without needing any codes.

When I was in eighth denomination (or eighth grade back in the stone age), when puberty was running rampant, a guy named Mickey ran a small-time passcode business out of the custodian's closet on the second floor of the Hall of Academics. Come to think of it, he *was* the custodian. Whenever I saw a pack of twittering girls blushing and dance-running from the closet, I knew what was up with that. Some tweenie girl had spent a week's allowance credits on a crush's passcode so she could keep tabs on him 24/7.

Mickey could get just about anyone's passcode; he even got the headmaster's at one point. I remember flirting with the idea of getting the passcode of the chick I was whipped over, but I just couldn't bring myself to muster up the oomph to buy it. The problem wasn't Mickey's asking prices or a lack of money; it just seemed intrusive for some reason, even at that somewhat innocent age. I could wind up with a busted heart after finding out that she was French kissing some other dude. Sometimes ignorance really is bliss.

You can't actually *see* what people are doing, thank God; all you can see is just a list of daily movements, including timeframes, on any scanner, with the current activity listed at the top. Only the omniscient SR can see everyone all the time; they don't care about ignorance.

When we got to my domicile, my mom was cooking dinner and my sister was braiding her hair. "Mmm . . . smells delish." I kissed Mom on the cheek. "The freeloading moocher is eating with us again." I hooked a thumb over my shoulder in Alex's direction. "Hope that's cool."

"Of course." My mom smiled. She noticed the wicked gleam in my eyes at once and quipped, "Who are you trying to annoy now?"

I avoided her question and glanced over at Alex, who was watching my sister intricately braid her golden hair into a crown atop her head. I'd seen that dopey look before. My sister was gorgeous.

"Dude, let's convene in my room." I gestured for him to follow me, ignoring my mom's question. He threw me a cocky grin, knowing I had noticed his drooling over my sister, and he even did a little skip hop on the way to my room. I mock skipped and kicked the door shut with my heel, rolling my eyes at Alex and shaking my head in mock disdain.

He threw himself down on my bunk while I dropped into my rolling black desk chair. The camera in the ceiling corner of my room had a pair of plaid boxer shorts thrown over it, and the SR hadn't broken down my door yet, so they stayed put.

"What you gonna do with all our cuffs?" Alex motioned to his inventions piled on the corner of my desk.

"I dunno. I just want them in case . . . ya know?" I grabbed the three cuffs that I had asked my buddies to give me after our adventure the other night and threw them in my center desk drawer.

"Paranoid much?" He grabbed my pillow and folded it under his head.

"They worked, didn't they, foo?" I pointed out. "You and Cory were in the clear, unlike Josiah and me . . . ."

Before he could challenge me, I said, "If we're gonna do this, I need you, Cory, and Zander," ticking each off on my fingers. "You and Cory are the brainiacs with the tech side—you know I am technologically challenged—and Zan . . . well, Zan is Zan." I folded my hands behind my head.

Alex just laughed, long, drawn out, and tired. I felt he was just humoring me at this point. "Right, mm hmmm. I'll just comlink them now and have their asses hauled over here to this clandestine pow-wow."

I was starting to doubt myself, and was feeling a little loopy (was it the Neerbeer?). Without thinking, I glanced at the boxer shorts over the camera.

"I am dead serious about this, Alex." He sat up so fast it caused me to jump.

"What planet do you live on?" He cut me off with a sharp edge to his voice that I had never heard before. "Can we stay in reality, dude? Cuz I am getting weirded out by your revolution banter." He flopped back on my bed, staring at the ceiling and pulling his lower lip. He softened his tone. "It's not that I am an SR sympathizer—psssh, I *hate* them, but we can't just march into their base camp and sign up. You and I have family, man. Well, you do, not me," he corrected himself, "but I consider your folks to be my parents, ya know. I know Cory only lives with his super old Grandma, but Zan definitely has fam."

"I help you d'feat the SR," a small voice said from my doorway. Alex and I whipped our heads around to see Josiah peeking out from behind the doorjamb. He had opened my door all quiet-like and had been listening without either of us hearing him.

"C'mere, buddy." I kicked Alex's big size twelves out of the way and sat down on the edge of the bed. Josiah ambled over to me, and I enveloped him in a bear hug. "You certainly have the 'encroaching upon enemy territory undetected' training mastered," I complimented him with a smile. "You sure you don't have any Native American blood running through your veins? All you need is a pair of moccasins, and you will be dead silent when you sneak up on the SR."

"Tru dat!" He grinned. He had been studying about Native Americans at the Hall of Academics. "Will you help me later with my math homework?"

"Of course, after dinner." I held out my fist for a bump. "What are they having you slave away at these days?"

"Profits," Josiah answered.

"Wasn't that like, Mohammed?" Alex had my model airplane in his hands and was doing loop de loops over his head, making *vroom, vroom* sounds.

"That's history, idiot. Give me that, ya derp." I grabbed the dusty plane from him and put it back on my shelf. He spread his hands wide with an expression of "And?"

Josiah repeated in a low, menacing voice, "I will help you defeat the SR . . . ." I covered his mouth, grinning.

Alex laughed. "Persistent little bugger." He sat up on my bunk.

"Mom and Dad need you around, but tell ya what," I said, "I will keep you in the mix with all my covert plans, how's that?" He nodded his head enthusiastically, fingering the brass bracelet on my wrist that he had made me for my birthday last year.

"Yo, stop tantalizing the poor kid." Alex slapped the back of my head.

"Mom says you and Alex have to come eat now," Josiah ordered over his shoulder as he marched like an SR soldier out of my room. I smacked Alex back.

Alex is an orphan; his dad was a known SR rebel who died in Camp back when Alex was a baby. I'm not sure what happened to his mom. I don't ask, and he doesn't talk about her. He and I have been blood brothers since we met in first denomination. He has eaten evening meals at our house several times a week for as long as I can remember, even though he always crashes at Cory's dwelling. Yeah, he thinks he's tough, a know-it-all, loud, and an occasionally sentimental guy who questions everything, but he is very loyal to his close friends. I wanna burn the cargo shorts he always wears, and he could wash his hair more often instead of hiding it under a vintage Dodgers baseball cap, but I would move mountains for the guy. Loyalty is the unwritten code that governs friendships in my generation. It is unspoken, but it always stands at attention, front and center. And my world needs more of it, no question about it.

Chapter 6

"Destroy the seed of evil, or it will grow up to your ruin."
—Aesop

Free speech in public is nonexistent. Fact: There are mandatory cameras with internal microphones in every structure, residential or business. This doesn't mean that a particular family or person is being watched 24/7. It just means that the SR *can* observe someone with the swipe of a finger if they choose to do so. The creepy thing is that there is no warning: no red light comes on, and nothing alerts the person or persons that they are being listened to or recorded. You just never know when it starts or stops, or if something you said three weeks ago is going to come back and bite you in the butt. It's happened before—trust me. Just yesterday, my sister's best friend Emmaline spouted off about how sickening humanity was in her book, and she got reported somehow.

It's impossible to know the number of narcs the SR has running around ready to tip them off. True to form, the SR marched over to her family's dwelling and told her to put a cork in it—her first official infraction, because she is over sixteen years of age. I am painting a very mild and pleasant picture here, but the realities of the SR's warnings are rather daunting. I've heard enough stories . . . .

Families may feel they can loosen up a bit more when they're at home. They get comfortable and end up not censoring their words as much as they would on the outside, and some activities are under watch no matter where you are. The SR does "random" checks in all homes and businesses at their discretion. For example, I heard of one boy whose family was heavily penalized for his playing some military video game. Any 3D video warfare play is strictly forbidden. The SR doesn't want anyone working out any sort of defeating strategies, even in play. Children who play war games are reprimanded by their parents when a notification from the SR arrives, outlining a warning of penalties should another infraction occur. God, you'd think they had better things to do, or get a life or something. That is the problem with power hungry overlords; they have such extreme paranoia surrounding *everything* that if something happens outside of their control, they freak out on a monumental scale.

Curfew for all is 9:00 p.m., no exceptions. We call the SR tanks that appear near curfew time "wagons." They are ready and willing to impose infractions on anyone who breaks regulations. In addition, all men must wear their hair cut short, either in a crew cut or a buzz cut. All women must have their hair pulled back from their face at all times, and neither gender is allowed to wear glasses of any kind. If they are blind without them, well then they have to wear antique contacts (if they can find them) or have their eyes lasered or find an eye donor (if they can afford it). Clothing must be conservative. If men wear shorts, they must be knee length. No short skirts or low-cut tops are allowed for women.

Skirts must be no shorter than two finger widths above the knee. Believe me, I have seen the SR do the ol' finger test on a teenage girl in the street in broad daylight when they suspected her skirt was too short. And I can guarantee that she never wore a short skirt again.

Everyone was at the table, candles lit, just like I love it, with the savory smell of my mother's home cooked food making our mouths water. We are fortunate because, during his meat packing assignment, Dad had managed to accumulate enough meat to last us at least six months.

One thing that was out of place, however, was the troubled look on my dad's face that night, which I picked up on right away when I sat down in my usual spot. Dishes were passed back and forth, with Alex taking huge portions as always. The guy was a porker.

"What's crack-a-lackin, Dad?" I hoped I sounded light and casual. He glanced at me with a knowing look that told me he had noticed that *I* had noticed his demeanor, and my question wasn't casual at all.

"Meh, I don't wanna bore y'all with any more . . . work stuff." He waved his hands around as if to punctuate his words. I got the all too familiar pang in my gut that I hated. What now?

I threw him a look that said I'd get the deets later, period. He returned my look with a no-worries nod, reassuring me a bit that I would find out soon enough.

"Okey dokey . . . ." I answered, not wanting to push it.

"What do you guys have planned for tonight?" Mom chimed in.

"Oh, we're just gonna go over our coup plans for taking out the head honchos," I tossed out. Alex jabbed me under the table with the heel of his boot, his eyes flying to the camera in the corner of the ceiling. We tried to talk in code in my dwelling, as if it would be too hard for the SR to figure out what we were discussing. But then sometimes, things just volcanically erupted from my mouth without me stopping to think.

Stephanie was the first to recover from the stunned silence that followed. "Rock on! Count me in."

Alex erupted in a phony laugh. "He's just joshing you!" He said this loud and clear, and put his arm around my shoulders, squeezing a little too hard. Switching gears, Alex asked Stephanie, "How does it feel to be a Hall of Academics graduate?" Mom's light demeanor had turned stony, and she shot a glance at Josiah, who was pushing his rice into neat little stacks on his plate.

"Whatevs . . . it's not all that," Stephanie replied. "I'm going to comlink Emmy, but don't start your evil plotting without me," Stephanie yelled at us as she ran into the living room. I could tell she was still bummed about the award. Alex just laughed again with a loud snort.

Mom glanced at me, shaking her head, her eyes sharp. I looked at her with love, and smiled. "No worries, Mom."

"Is the sky blue?" was her response.

"No, it's a pukey yellow smog color," I quipped, "but it's all good." Her expression did not change, and I felt a small twinge of guilt at inadvertently making her feel apprehensive.

Dinner wrapped up, and Alex ended up splitting right after, so no more SR overthrow talk followed, much to Stephanie's soon to be disappointment. When the table was cleared and Stephanie still had not made an appearance, I stuck my head in the living room. "Go help your mother with the dishes," I said.

"Yes, sir, Dad," she replied sarcastically, but the firm look on my face said I wasn't playing. She sighed, signing off with her best friend Emmy while I went in search of Dad. I found him in his shed out back, tinkering on an old comlink unit that he had scrapped from somewhere. In this present day, we comlink our peeps, as cell phones, snapchat, skype, what's up, and any other form of Internet social media no longer exist.

I sat down on the stool across from his bench and just watched him messing with the touch panel for a while, a comfortable silence forming between us.

I waited a few beats before I threw out, "What's goin' on, Dad?"

He turned to look at me and gave a short laugh, heading over to his rather ancient LP record player that amazingly still operated. He sure loves his antiques. He pulled an old Frank Sinatra record out of its wrinkled sleeve and put it on to spin. Soon, "I've Got You under My Skin" was playing a little too loud for the tiny shed. It's not that my dad is deaf; it's a cover to muffle our conversation, just in case the SR is listening in. Like I said, you never know.

Dad went back to his workbench and continued splicing wires and checking this and that. He spoke to me softly out of the corner of his mouth, but I could still hear and understand him. This is our regular routine if we need to talk about prohibited matters.

"I came across something at work that was, well . . . alarming, to say the least," he murmured in my direction. My stomach clenched. I jerked my head in an upward motion that indicated *"What?"*

"Are they poisoning our water supply now, or hiking the prices on electricity? It wouldn't surprise me," I said while covering my mouth with my hand to conceal any possible SR lip reading. I hoped they were not recording or watching, but we never could be too careful. We carried on, all the while not looking at each other.

"No." He sighed. "I discovered . . . ." I could tell he was weighing the cost of sharing this information with me. "The SR has been pumping water from the Backlands' own wells and selling it back to them at *three times* the cost, and they have been doing this for God knows how long. That's three hundred percent," he emphasized with a frown.

I let this marinate for a few minutes, watching him work with his tools. He kept his head down so no one could lip read, and added, "I found this out quite by accident, but I know now, fortunately, or . . . I dunno, maybe it's unfortunate?"

I answered him in a rush. "It's not right. What they are doing is abominable. But, by accident, Dad? How? No, forget it, I don't wanna know. Oh, man, this doesn't sound good."

"Yeah, no shit, Sherlock, but what can anyone do about it?" He slammed his soldering tool onto the bench a little too hard. He abandoned his project and put his head in his hands. I surreptitiously glanced up at the camera in the corner of the shed, listening to Frank sing his heart out. I thought about my friend Zan, whose family lived in the Backlands.

"If anyone gets wind of you knowing anything about this, you know full well what could happen or will happen," I said through clenched teeth.

"It happened, Goro. It is what it is." He headed over to the record player again. I shook my head and slid off the stool, exiting the shed without saying "see ya later" or even paying attention to where I was going. I decided to go for a short jog to process what he had just revealed to me. What the heck, I still had twenty minutes before the curfew alarm sounded. It would feel good to run off the day's stress and angst. As I started out at a slow run, I caught sight of the SR wagons rolling out, getting ready to hit people with curfew infractions. I thought about my family. If this knowledge got out, what would that mean for us? I ran faster, and from what, I already knew.

Chapter 7

"Make the lie big, make it simple, keep saying it, and eventually they will believe it."

—Adolf Hitler

Every several years or so, the Sovereign Regime comes up with some absurd plan to eradicate everything "harmful" from the face of the earth, whether it be a grassroots protest group or some ethnic group that is pissing them off at the moment. Population control is an understatement with the SR. Extreme times call for extreme measures is the MO of the SR, with a motto of "Rule all, and if it serves no purpose, it needs to be eliminated." There is no such thing as vagrant people in our society.

Fact: Back when the SR first took power, they rounded up all the homeless people, all the disabled or crippled people, the obese, or anyone with a mental illness of any kind, and made them "disappear." God only knows what happened to them, but I suspect it was something akin to what Adolf Hitler did back in the day. The problem with my world is that no one questions or cares. Life spins around on a rat wheel, and if anyone dares to inquire as to why the SR does this or that, well, let's just say they get flattened underneath the SR's black steel-toed boot. End of discussion.

Everyone in my society just does what he or she is told. No one loiters or wanders around in an aimless manner. Everyone has a particular destination or task appointed daily. I remember when Grandpa used to tell me stories of his great grandfather going to the park with his dad when he was a small child, and watching some mechanical ducks swimming around the lake. We don't have lakes anymore, and today most animals are extinct, except for cows and chickens for human consumption. Only the filthy rich (the SR) have a spattering of real birds or the occasional rare cat as pets. We don't really have parks any longer either, come to think of it.

It is normal to have your eyes downcast when out in public as everyone pushes past one another; there are no greetings or smiles, just quick, furtive glances at someone's face every so often. An undercurrent of fear runs on a steady hum, permeating the atmosphere anywhere and everywhere. Small talk is non-existent. If someone is attempting to engage in some sort of conversation on the way to his work assignment, he is regarded with suspicion. Of course, the omnipresent SR knows when someone is attempting such radical behavior. They intervene and cease whatever is happening, immediately and unpleasantly.

Even if you are not born into the SR, that doesn't stop them from recruiting new blood. They went heavy with me, trying to recruit me when I graduated from the Hall of Academics, but I played airhead and they eventually left me alone. Probably thought I was too thick to be a member of the SR, which was just the image I was trying to convey. Let them think I am a witless wonder; all the better for my family and me.

I made it back to my dwelling at exactly 8:59 p.m. The curfew alarm sounded as the front door slid shut.

"You have nine lives, Goro, I swear." Stephanie smirked from her perch on the sofa as I headed for the bathroom.

During my shower, I watched the water run off my body in rivulets toward the drain as I thought about the people living in the Backlands. How did they survive? How did they ever make ends meet? I closed my eyes, resting my forehead against the shower wall and thinking about my friend Zan and his family. It more than saddened me that I lived in an increasingly evil world that stooped to such lows. My conversation with Alex earlier at the pub replayed over and over in my head like clothes toppling over one another in an antique dryer. I felt like everything that was happening lately was converging on a path that was headed toward something ominous. What was really unsettling was that I couldn't decide if I was thrilled or scared about that realization.

I could hear my mom's cadent voice reading to Josiah in the next room when I crashed in the sack around ten o'clock. He tends to pick the same stories every night; doesn't matter if he's heard them a hundred times. *He's a good kid*, I thought as I got comfortable on my bunk. I fell into a troubled sleep, but woke several hours later in a sweat, the perilous feeling stronger than ever.

I sat up in bed, wiping my face with my hands. *This bites*, I thought. I threw back my covers and walked into the kitchenette for a glass of water.

Even though it was the middle of the night, I will forever clearly remember that moment when I stood with my back to the sink, drinking my water, and the decision I made then and there. I pledged to myself, my family, to everyone and anyone else, without even knowing the cost, to do everything in my power to obliterate and bring down the rule and reign of the Sovereign Regime.

Chapter 8

"The tattoo is the mark of the soul. It can act as a window through which we can see inside, or it can be a shield to protect us from those who cannot see past the surface."

—Anonymous

Everyone involved with the SR has the following symbol branded on the back of the neck:

Some have it lasered onto their right upper arm as well, which I think is overkill. But, psshhh, do they listen to me? Tattoos are so twenty-first century, I guess. Hardcore members have it branded on their foreheads.

Fact: Babies that are born to SR members have the symbol automatically branded onto one of their little arms so that there is no question as to what career choice the baby will embark on when older. Some even have the logo shaved into the back of their crew cuts. When someone is recruited later in life, the brand ends up on the back of their neck, with new members attempting to look like badass soldiers or something. My sister says in secret that dudes with numerous visual reminders of their SR membership are just super insecure about the size of their genitalia. Hehe.

Like I said, the survival of the fittest during the New World Order War graced our presence as the one and only Sovereign Regime, with Davio in particular rising to fast stardom. The SR decided long ago to always know what its subordinates were doing at any given time. They *never* wanted to be caught unaware again, even though the SR had kicked the New World Order in the ass. In their heightened state of hypervigilance, they made it mandatory for everyone to have an identity chip implanted, no matter who the person was. That way, any threat, however so subtle, could be thwarted immediately.

Back in the old days, Washington, DC, was the capital of the United States of America, with a leader living in something called a White House. Seven plus billion people roamed the earth. Well, today the capital is located in what used to be known as Los Angeles, and now the world's population has dwindled to less than three billion. The aforenamed United States has ten domains under one Dominion, the capital. It is in the Dominion that the SR leadership resides. The lesser known political "wannabes" run the individual domains, which all report to the Dominion. It's so convoluted it's ridiculous; the bottom line is that normal society is a pack of marionettes on strings which the SR pulls. There are more domains located all over the world, in other countries of course, from Tel Aviv to Paris to Cartagena to Tokyo, but there are no longer individual countries. The world is separated into four quadrants of sorts; it's hard to explain, but then I never excelled in geography.

I woke up the next morning with a groggy headache that felt like a semi-truck had parked on my face overnight. My alarm clock was Josiah busting through my door at oh-dark-thirty clutching a bagel in each hand. He ran one lap around my bunk before sitting down and giving me one of the bagels.

"Yalla," he said with a grin, which means "let's go" in Arabic. He shot back out the door. I pulled my ass out of bed and grabbed a pair of jeans off the back of a chair. I smelled a black T-shirt that had been lying on the floor, decided it had another day's wear in it before the stink got too bad, and put it on. Lucky for me, the bosses at my work assignment did not concern themselves with proper work attire. I ran my fingers through my unkempt hair, looked in the mirror, decided I looked presentable enough, and headed into the kitchenette. Josiah was raring to go, my sister wasn't even up yet, and both my parents were already long gone to their work assignments. "Ahright, aight," I said frowning, still mid-sleep and checking to see if there was any black coffee left in the panel in the wall, of which there was none.

Josiah and I made our way to the nearest light rail train, finding seats in the back. The train stopped repeatedly to let more and more sad, decrepit people on until it became jammed. It was downright depressing. As my eyes glanced over their drab colorless clothes and settled on their vacant faces, my decision of the previous night came to mind as clearly and defiantly as ever.

Josiah noticed an older lady struggling to keep her balance, clinging to the center pole for dear life. He immediately bolted out of my lap and asked the lady to sit down, pointing in my direction. That kid is a saint; I shook my head in wonder. She gave him a small furtive smile and sat down after I stood up. He grabbed my knees to steady himself, preparing to stand with me the rest of the ride. He looked up into my face and sang, "Rise and shine and time to go to worky, worky, rise and shine and time to go to schooly, schooly," some dumb child's song.

"Ssshh." I put my finger to my lips. "Did you clean your teeth this morning?" I mock-waved my hand back and forth in front of my nose. "How do you have this much enthusiasm this early?" I looked at him, furrowing my brow. He pulled me down by the hem of my T-shirt until I was face to face with him. He took his thumbs and put them on my forehead, attempting to smooth out the crinkles I had formed.

"Don't carry the weight of the world, Goro," he said in a small, serious voice. I just stared at him, biting my lower lip. Kid was beyond his years, I marveled, but it worried me what type of future he would be left with.

We exited the train at his stop, Josiah holding tight to my hand as we headed down the stairs, with me watching him get through the Hall of Academic's doors without incident. When I was back on the platform waiting to catch the next train, my eyes caught sight of a man staring at me; I had seen him before, but where? He looked to be about mid-thirties with blond hair and a weathered look about his face. He was wearing a nondescript tan suit and half standing behind a light rail scanner surrounded by other people. Was it the same guy who had been watching me at my sister's convocation? No, that guy was a senior citizen. *What's this dude's problem?* I thought, frustrated. He made his way in my direction, weaving through the pack of people, with me tensing up instinctively. I stood my ground, preparing for the unknown. Was this guy gonna talk to me or fight me? When he came within about ten feet of me, I braced myself as he tossed something at me high in the air. Muscle memory took over, causing me to reach up and catch whatever it was.

"Find us," the guy said through cupped hands. I frowned. When I held the thing he had thrown at me, I looked down and saw an ancient key. You know, one of those old iron skeleton keys that no longer exist. I turned it over in my hand and saw a number stamped onto the side, but when I looked up again, the guy was already gone. *What the hell am I supposed to do with this? And why did he take it upon himself to give it to me?* I glanced down at the key again. *Am I supposed to be a detective and play what's behind door number 3?* I suppressed half an urge to hurl the key out over the edge of the platform, but curiosity halted me. I jogged over to the edge of the guardrail to scan the street below for any sign of the man, just as the train whooshed past me, coming to a stop. I didn't see any sign of him as I followed the masses onto the train. Nobody that had been waiting with me seemed to see or acknowledge the interaction between the two of us. Nobody cared, as usual.

I scrutinized the key once again, looking for some sort of clue, or anything. Just the numbers 20:10 stamped into the iron key—damn confusing. How was that supposed to help me find them, whoever they were? I shoved the key into the front pocket of my jeans and tried to forget about it. But as the train picked up speed, I looked out the back window, and a strong foreboding feeling ran through my body, making my fingers tingle. I had caught sight of the man again, standing on the platform watching me disappear from his sight.

Chapter 9

"Poverty is not an accident. Like slavery and apartheid, it is man-made and can be removed by the actions of human beings."
—Nelson Mandela

There is a stretch of land just south of the remains of downtown Los Angeles called the Backlands that most of us steer clear of. I say most of us because only the very impoverished people live there. It is a long narrow strip of land that snakes along what is left of what was once the Los Angeles River. Trust me, no one really wants to venture over there at all unless trying to prove some stupid bravery following a bet or a dare or unless you have kin living there. In some areas it is a disgusting pit of filth that reeks to high heaven; it is a wonder there is any foliage growing there, let alone people actually living there. There is a constant sweet smoky scent in the air because they burn all their garbage.

The SR allows them to live because even though they are so fricking poor, they are not physically impaired in any way, and they can still be utilized to do the most menial of tasks that no one else would touch with a ten-foot pole. They figure that since these folks pretty much live in the sewer, they won't have any problems cleaning it, right?

The SR keeps a tight leash on them. The thick twelve-foot-tall cement walls surrounding the backlands have only three entries/exits guarded 24/7 by newbie SR recruits. Those who reside in the Backlands can only leave to report directly to their work assignments, and they must go straight home at the end of their slave shifts. I know it sucks to be under the thumb of the SR, but it royally pissed me off that my friend Zan and his family were forced to live in the Backlands simply because they were poor.

Three and a half years ago, Davio wanted this area demolished, but somehow his underlings ended up having him create a pact with the Backlands that lasted seven years. After the seven-year mark, the lower levels of the SR would assist those living there to find suitable housing. Uh huh, right . . . that'll be happening. Not.

I was early for my work assignment, so I decided to go visit my buddy Zan. Alex and I became friends with him about seven years ago at the Hall of Academics, and his family had fallen on hard times the last few years, something about the SR constantly letting his dad go from his work assignments, but then I don't ask.

When I arrived at one of the three entrance checkpoints, I went through the drill on autopilot. Fall in line, raise right wrist to be scanned, and wait in the detection booth for clearance. It could take anywhere from ten to thirty minutes, depending on how many people were going through the checkpoint, but most of the time it was pretty fast. The ironic thing was that the people who had to wait the longest were those who actually *lived* here.

While I was in line, I observed one woman being berated by an SR soldier because of what she was wearing. It was hard not to overhear; he was making enough of a clamor to raise the spirits of the dead. It looked like she had some sort of a religious symbol pinned to her shirt. She looked fine to me; she was regulation by all accounts. The SR goon wasn't having it though. He grabbed her by the arm and yanked her out of line so hard that she fell forward onto her knees. She was begging the officer for mercy while still on her knees. I turned away, disgusted. I couldn't watch. I tuned out the officer's shouting that followed. I saw her being dragged back toward the entrance by her hands. Denied entry, I imagined was the ludicrous result. Didn't want to know what followed after that. I wanted to rush the SR guy and throw him down on *his* knees. I heard my name called, snapping me back to reality, but I just poker-faced the guard while he waved me through instead of giving him the finger.

Zan's two little sisters came running at me when I got close to his dwelling. They threw their arms around me, making it hard to keep walking. "Uncle Goro! Uncle Goro!" they yelled in unison.

"Whoa, kidlets!" I picked them up, one in each arm, carrying them the rest of the way. "How is Nana Mares?" I pinched Meagan, the younger one, on her leg. Zan's grandmother's name was Marilyn, but she got the nickname Mares years ago from her seven younger siblings. "How's Sylvie?"

"Okey dokey," they chorused through smiles.

"Coolio," I responded, setting them on the ground. "Where's Zan?"

"He's stressing in the back." Morgan pointed to the back of their dwelling where Zan often lounged around in a hammock drinking a cold Neerbeer.

"Stressing?" I surmised. Usually hammocks were for relaxation.

"I wouldn't go back there if I were you," Meagan said, rolling her eyes.

"You girls gotta git to school," I heard Sylvia yell from inside their dwelling. "For land's sake!"

"Yes, Momma!" The two girls went running back into the tiny dwelling, smiling at me the whole way. I followed them into the living area and glanced around. It was still the same, much smaller than my domicile, but comfortable, except for the additional camera in the far corner of the room. I frowned.

"Goro!" Sylvia grabbed my shoulder and gave me a side hug, making me momentarily forget the camera. "What a nice surprise this morning!" I handed her the tin of ginger muffins my mother had baked last night in case I would be seeing them today.

"Oh my stars and garters! My favorite!" She shrieked in delight when she opened the lid. "Your momma—really!" She hugged the tin in her arms. "That woman—honestly!" She always tut tuts, but I know she really appreciates the things that my family does for her and her family. She put the muffins on a plate and offered me one before taking one herself.

"I had about ten last night," I said, shaking my head and patting my stomach. Meagan had latched herself onto my leg and was not letting go.

"Of course you did, honey." She passed one to each of her daughters as she declawed Meagan from my leg. "Now, git to school!" She pointed at the front door. They went, giggling as they left.

"Bye, Goro!" Meagan yelled in retreat. "When Morgan gets older, she wants to marry you!" She laughed as she rushed out the front door. I heard Morgan yelling at her in the distance.

"Bye, my cherubs," I answered using my most common term of endearment, knowing they probably hadn't heard me.

"Now, how you doin?" Sylvia settled herself on the divan, oblivious to her daughter's outburst, and patted the seat next to her. I just chuckled.

I sat down next to her and said, "Same ole, same ole."

"Is the SR giving you lip? Now, you tell those SR guards to blow it out their boney butts!"

I laughed. "I love that you are easily amused, even in these crappy times."

"Well, honey, ya know . . . I quickly count my number of kids every morning, and when it comes up three, then I know I'm blessed." Just then, Zan made an appearance.

"Well, look who decided to join the land of the living!" Sylvia mock marveled.

"Hey Goro," he murmured. One thing about Zan: he is so transparent that his attitude is always stamped on his forehead. It is obvious how he is feeling at any given moment: a real wear-your-heart-on-your-sleeve kinda guy. At least with him, what you see is what you get.

"What's up, buddy?" I asked, getting up and slapping him on the back in a hug.

"Yeah, well, if I start talking about it, I'll just get pissed again," he said interlocking his hands behind his head. "I swear to God I am cursed."

"Funemployed?" I ventured, raising one eyebrow. He nodded his head, rolling his eyes. "Come hang out with me today."

"Are you on crack?" he moped. "I haven't applied for any permits to leave, and you know it takes a week at least, depending on their mood."

"I meant later, douche . . . I'll head over here again, and we can throw darts or something. I glanced at the digital wall clock. "I better head out, or I won't have a work assignment anymore either."

I kissed Sylvia on the cheek as I got up and then noticed Nana Mares wasn't around.

"Where's Nana Mares?" I ventured, hesitant.

"Now don't you go worrying your handsome head; she is down the road visiting with Muriel," Sylvie replied happily. "Nana Mares needed some advice is all."

Muriel was the Backlands medicine woman, so to speak. "Muriel always does have good advice," I agreed. I said adieu and took off toward the exit. I walked past the poisoned iron spikes and electric barbed wire atop the wall, thinking the Backlands resembled a penitentiary more than a cluster of homes where people actually lived. As I scanned through the sensored steel turnstile, I glanced up at the SR dude in his booth, his rifle aimed right at my head. I shook my head slowly . . . same shit, different diaper.

Chapter 10

"There are no secrets that time does not reveal . . . ."
—Jean Racine

Years ago, the SR decided that humankind had too many choices, so they abolished anything in excess. Fact: We all live a meager existence, but not because we want to. It is just the controlling nature of the SR. The only things really bargained for or purchased are the necessities, such as food, clothing, and cleaning supplies. "Want" is not in the vocabulary of the SR. There is no such thing as competing brands. If you want a loaf of bread, there is one generic bag you buy. "Monopoly" *is* in the vocabulary of the SR. They provide society with goods and services.

Mom's work assignment is that of seamstress. She spends every day sewing and repairing the ugly drab uniforms worn by those in the lower echelons of the SR. The same logo that is branded on their skin is embroidered in silver on the arm of their standard-issue dark gray uniforms. When they graduate to the higher levels of the SR, they don't have to wear uniforms anymore. However, they do often wear black sleeveless shirts to show off their logo-lasered arms to represent themselves as SR, as if they would be hard to miss.

I was commissioned by the SR to be an emissary for their smaller businesses, which I do more or less in an obedient manner. I was curious as to what they would assign my sister Stephanie, now that she had graduated. Hopefully, she wouldn't be called upon to be some SR stooge's wife or something.

~

When I finally showed up to my work assignment, the work alarm sounded throughout the city. "Damn, Goro, you always cut it too close." My buddy Cory handed me a hot cup of black coffee.

"You da man," I said as a way of thanking him. A few swallows of coffee set my mind straight and I forgot all about the suspicious man, the key, and Zan. I love Cory because he's got me when I need him. "What needs to be gophered today?" I joked.

"Well, let's see what we have on the SR's agenda." Cory touched a panel in front of him. "One industrial sized scanner needs to be delivered to DWE, and . . . ." He ticked off several items on the emissary schedule, but I had stopped listening as soon as I heard the acronym for Division of Water and Electricity—my father's work assignment. I'd never been to his work area, much less inside the DWE before.

"Why the DWE?" I inquired, trying to sound nonchalant.

"Why what?" Cory asked, a perplexed look on his face. "Why does the SR ever do anything that isn't logical? Who the eff knows." He went back to perusing the list of deliveries.

"I'll take that one," I answered. Perfect opportunity to snoop, I irrationally considered.

"Cool, be my guest." Cory scanned the panel in front of him. "Check."

Sometime later, I parked the helivan in front of my dad's building. I sat and watched the location for a minute. There were very few people out and about; one guy was programming a reader board screen on the wall of a building down the block, and three SR soldiers carrying rifles were ambling down the street looking bored but trying to look important. I watched them for a minute. They didn't seem to have any solid destination. Two men and one woman, wearing standard uniforms, were walking away from my location, talking together. One of the men guffawed loudly and smacked the woman on the back. She smiled at him, gesticulating with her free hand, and the other guy joined in the laughter.

What do they have to joke about? I marveled incredulously. *Stupid drones.*

I got out of the helivan and went around to the side. I scanned the panel on the side of the door, and it slid open silently. I assessed the industrial sized scanner, not looking forward to hauling it into the DWE. I had a half-hysterical funny thought of running after the SR soldiers and asking them to give me a hand. I scanned a panel inside the van, and the bulky scanner slid out on the side ramp. Luckily, it was already on the hand truck as it lowered to the ground. *Thanks, Cory, my buddy.*

Going through security took a whole thirty minutes, even after scanning my wrist, because they wanted to inspect the scanner ad infinitum. *Nope guys—no nuclear devices*, I thought. On top of that, they wanted to do a DNA spot scan on me. I dunno, because they didn't like the way I sniffed at them?

When I made it to the portal lift, I said, "Collections," for my father's division. We stopped a couple times for other people to get in the lift while I drummed my thumbs on the top of the scanner, trying to make it look like I belonged there.

When I reached the floor for Collections, I pushed my cargo in front of me slowly so that I could survey the land. I found myself walking down a shiny steel-lined hallway with only a single solitary steel door at the end. Sheesh. There were more cameras than I had ever seen in my life. It was unlike any building I had ever been inside. When I got to the door, I scoped around for some sort of scanning device or microphone or something. All I saw were two cameras, one in either ceiling corner facing down at me.

"Yes?" came a stern voice out of nowhere. I jumped and looked behind me, but saw nothing. "Um, I have a scanner," I replied in a lame tone.

"Obviously," the voice stated. "Leave it there and we'll take care of it."

"I need to take the hand truck back with me," I said to the door.

"You can bill us for it," came the answer, which didn't surprise me.

"Um, except I have another order just down the street that I need the hand truck for, and I'm on the clock," I lied.

A long silence ensued. Then I heard a small whoosh and the door popped open a couple of inches. A tall slender woman with her jet-black hair pulled back in an immaculate ponytail stepped into the hallway. She was dressed in a light gray skirt and matching suit jacket.

I fake-smiled at her and held out my portable scanner. She glowered at me, visibly annoyed, and held up her right wrist for me to scan, all the while looking into my eyes like she wanted to slice open my liver. *Don't kill the messenger, lady.*

She grabbed the hand truck controls and pushed it through the open door. I attempted to help her, but she held up a hand, barking, "I got it." I told her retreating back that I would be fine waiting here for the hand truck. She ignored me. *Okay, I guess I'll just hang out here in the surgically sterilized hallway picking my nose.* However, when I glanced at the cameras in the ceiling corners, I saw that there was actually a red light shining above each one (what?), letting me know that they probably *were* watching me, no question. Weird. I thought cameras had no recording indicators, though it seemed these two definitely did. Had the DWE upgraded to new cameras?

The door began to close, and I had a fleeting reckless thought of tossing my brass bracelet into the doorway to stop it from closing. It would hold. I could just say I needed to talk to my father.

I don't know if I was fed up or finished, because on a sudden impulse I grabbed the bracelet off my wrist and did just that. I flattened myself against the wall, breathing a little heavier, praying they hadn't noticed. What did I just do? My mind raced. I braced myself for SR goons with guns, but nothing happened—no invisible wizard's voice giving me a lecture about protocol or the tall lady returning to smack me across the face. I inched toward the door. Who knew if anyone was *really* watching me? At that point, I said "screw it" and pushed through the door, snatching up my bracelet.

I scanned my surroundings, surveying any possible threats, and shoved my bracelet back on my wrist. All I saw were more hallways with doors. Weird. The one difference was that the cameras were few and far between on the inside of this creepy vault, which was good. I had no idea how many hallways branched off this one, but I knew I needed to keep moving in case a door burst open.

The chick had gone left, so I treaded softly down the hallway to the right. I had learned long ago that if you act like you know what you are doing and where you are going, people seldom question you. I paused every ten steps or so to listen, but I never heard anything. When I came to the end of the hall, it only went left, and I saw a door partway down that was open a crack. I approached the doorway preparing to say I was looking for my father when I heard the faint sound of two people talking.

"This is above your concern, Joel," an unidentified male's firm voice said. "You are not commissioned for this."

I tensed at hearing my dad's name. Sheer luck had driven me in this direction.

"Oh, yes, understood," my dad replied in a subservient tone. "I had no intention of following up on any of this, sir." I could hear a slight tremor in his voice. "Like I mentioned, it was a completely incidental discovery."

Oh God . . . they found out he knows about the filching of the Backlands water supply. I felt a hot flash beginning at the crown of my head and moving all the way down my body. I was rooted to the ground, unable to move.

"Granted, but that matter will be expunged soon enough," the man replied.

"Oh . . . ?" my dad inquired. "The discrepancies? Or . . . ."

A pause followed, and I couldn't hear anything.

"Let's just say that in due time we will no longer have a need to supply water to this region," came the stern answer. "Now, continue with your obligations."

I froze, waiting for the man to walk out and discover he had an eavesdropping peeping Tom outside, but I heard a door whoosh open and then close from somewhere inside the room. I breathed normally again and waited, clenching my fists for a few seconds before pushing open the door. I felt like a complete hoodlum.

I saw my dad then, sitting at a desk, looking at a computer panel in front of him. By some miracle, he was alone. As I approached him, he turned fast and let out a small shriek when he saw me.

"Oh, my God, what are you doing here?" He looked panic stricken, taking off his glasses as if he could get a better look that it was really me. The SR allowed him to wear glasses at work, God bless them (I snorted inwardly in derision), because my family couldn't afford eye surgery. However, long gone were the "take your son to work" days. I doubt they would allow this intrusion.

"Hey, Dad, I delivered a scanner here today and heard your voice, so . . . I mean, I've never been here, so I thought I'd come see you." I looked around, my hands on my hips with my eyes coming to rest on him. I could tell I was failing to come across as wanting to just stop by and say hi. He saw right through me.

He sighed long and loud and looked down at the glasses in his hands. He abruptly straightened up in his chair. "What did you hear?" he inquired, his eyes wide with trepidation. I put a finger to my lips and indicated we would talk about it later. At that point we both just stared at one another, the realization sinking in that he, and now I, knew far more than we both wanted.

"You need to go . . . now." He got up and ushered me to the door, sliding it open a smidge to look down the corridor. No one was around.

"Dad . . . ."

"Sssshh!" He was clearly flustered. "Go out this way." He pointed in the opposite direction that I had come, pushing me out the door. Just then, we heard several loud footsteps marching in the corridors, heading our way.

"Damn," said my dad who never swears. Adrenaline pumping, I took off down the hall, no longer caring if I was loud. I was wearing rubber-soled camo boots, so I didn't think I made too much noise, but just as I rounded the corner at the end of the hall, someone screamed.

"Hey!"

Then all hell broke loose. I launched into a full run, trying doors along the way for an exit. All that mattered now was getting out. All were locked except for the second door from the end of yet another hallway. I threw the door open and flew down the steps, taking them three at a time to gain some distance. I forgot what floor I had been on. Three stairways down, I heard the door bang open above me and footsteps thundering down the stairs.

"Halt!" a man shouted.

Great, I thought, pissed at myself. Why did I run? I could have just told them I was visiting my father. We would both be pummeled for sure, but now they would question my dad. There was no telling what they would do to him while I was fleeing for my life. I hit the end of the staircase, silently willing the door at the bottom to be unlocked, and by some miracle, it flew open, with me racing down the alley like a crazy person. I turned the corner and ran to the helivan hovering in front. Should I just leave the van?

I scanned open the door panel and jumped in the seat, scanning the panel on the dash to start the van. I took off too fast and looked behind me as I sped to the corner. The DWE men had just emerged from the alley as I turned the corner. Well, the good news was they never really got a look at my face, but the bad news was that they would be drilling my dad pretty hard. He would be blamed for my visit. Dammit, the hand truck! I slammed my hand down on the steering controls. Now it would be cake for them to put two and two together and realize I was the delivery guy. It wouldn't be long before the DWE notified the SR; all they would have to do is punch in my passcode, or hell, all twenty digits and they would find out not only my life history, but where I was at this exact moment.

Chapter 11

"There are two kinds of heroes: heroes who shine in the face of great adversity, who perform an amazing feat in a difficult situation, and heroes who live among us, who do their work unceremoniously, unnoticed by many of us, but who make a difference in the lives of others."

—Susilo Bambang Yudhoyono

My grandfather Howard and his buddy Mitchell, whom he referred to as his surrogate son, saw the tail end of the very last revolution against the SR, and chemical warfare was just bush-league compared to what transpired during *that* riot. Some of what occurred Grandpa wouldn't even touch, no matter how much I cajoled him into telling me the details, even when I bribed him with peppermint candies. Someday I might try to get it off his identity chip, if future technology allows, but

I didn't get his passcode or have the chance to interface with him before he died. I know a handful of peeps that could hack his passcode, but that screams sacrilege to me, and illegally extracted chips are unusable as well. So no, I will just visit the Hall of Repository someday to ask about that one.

Oh, "interfacing" is when two people decide to share their entire identity chip content with one another. It is not illegal, but it is seriously frowned upon by the Sovereign Regime, because of course, they don't want anyone knowing any more about anything or anyone than they need to know. The SR is what my buddies and I refer to as a knowledge whore. Fact: They get jealous and downright violent when people go poking around in any type of "intel," or when a person attempts to retrieve any new information from anyone, even if it is just banal information such as what a person ate during his last meal.

I slowed down and was getting ready to turn into my lot and pull into the portal bay when I saw something that made me slam on the brake controls. Four SR soldiers had convened outside the back door of my work assignment. *Of course—bastards are fast,* I recognized with a heavy sigh. They carried their usual weapons, and they were chatting among themselves as if killing civilians was just all in a day's work.

The weight of my choices today settled on me like an iron blanket. I may have started a chain of events that would not end well. I put my head down on the steering controls in sober thought. Luckily, I had halted under a bridge, so the SR had either not noticed me yet or were too dumb to look around.

I couldn't drive home or even leave on foot, but I needed to stay mobile. I jumped up and rummaged around in the back of the helivan. I pulled out a crumpled, dirty white uniform from underneath a container in the back that had been left in the van for who knows how long. I stepped into it and zipped it up over my clothes. It smelled like stale puke. I then opened a compartment near the ceiling of the van and found a red cap and a white cap. I grabbed the white one and thrust it onto my head. It didn't really matter what I wore; the SR would find me, but it was a start, and white was less noticeable than red. I opened the side door and stepped out, not running, but walking casually away from my work assignment. I aimed for the light rail, but my destination alluded me.

I made it onto the next light rail train with no SR fanfare, to my surprise, and I grabbed a seat in the very last section. Either the SR was sleeping on the job or my guardian angel was providing an escape plan for me. I was hoping it was both.

I couldn't go to the Backlands, as I would be snatched as soon as I attempted to enter. I definitely was not going to my dwelling; that's as good as being a sitting duck. I marveled at how calm I was since putting myself in this predicament. My thoughts wandered from my family to Alex and Cory then to the Backlands, and I remembered the key. I unzipped the uniform and took it out of my jeans pocket, inspecting it again. What was it for? I didn't have a clue; I mean, the key was archaic. Nobody used keys anymore. Who was that man? I racked my brain for any recollection of where I may have seen him before. I gave up and put the key back in my pocket. Rubbing my face with my hands, I went over the day's events in my mind. Mom was going to freak. Cory was no doubt being interrogated back at work, and he was a "by the book" kind of guy. *Don't buckle under pressure, Cory!* I thought, breaking out in a sweat. I looked down at my wrist. I recoiled as I realized my chip was going to have to come out, and soon, but once out, it would be useless. I was not looking forward to the inevitable pain of digging around in my wrist for it.

The light rail train screeched and jerked to a stop. Uh-oh. Did we even stop at a platform? I ducked down, glancing all around me, and then I peeked out the windows. I saw about fifty SR mercenaries advancing in a steady stream from all directions, laser rifles raised. *Oh God, I'm dead.* I was frozen, not sure of what to do, when I heard the sound of inevitable heliplanes approaching. *Maybe I should just give up. Surrender. Get it over with and endure whatever affliction they employ and hopefully go back to a complacent, placid life. Say I had a temporary moment of insanity.*

I found I didn't have to make that decision.

Chapter 12

"Be the change you wish to see in the world."
—Mahatma Gandhi

I grabbed my ears as I heard a deafening explosion, and I was yanked backward by strong arms through what was left of the back of the light rail. My ears ringing, I peered up in my flailing to see who was grabbing me and saw the man from this morning, the giver of the key. He pulled me toward a single heliplane that looked just like one of the SR's, which was hovering above the raised light rails. He shoved me into the seat just as the SR let their ammunition fly.

Everything was moving so fast. I sat numb in the seat and watched dazedly as the guy hopped in and we ascended into the sky. I braced myself as the SR's numerous pursuing heliplanes fired lasers at our aircraft. The man flew haphazardly in a crazy zigzag pattern, circling and then doubling back, intending to confuse the other planes into not knowing who was who.

"We aren't being hit," was my first startling sentence when I found my voice. "Is this thing weapon proof? Who are you?" All came tumbling out in an incoherent mess. My heart was pounding so hard I thought it was going to fracture my ribs.

"This belongs to the SR," was his reply. "It can't be penetrated by any of their own weapons. If I confuse them enough, they will back off. These heliplanes all look the same. And they're all equipped with one-way mirrored windows."

I let that sink in for a second before blurting out, "Are you SR?" My eyes bugged out of their sockets. He raised his shirtsleeve to show no lasered or branded symbol of the SR.

He put the heliplane on autopilot and turned around to face me. "I am with a group of individuals known as the Alliance Defense Force, or ADF for short. I have been watching you for the last few weeks, and I just saved your ass." He looked into my eyes, waiting for a response.

"Thank you," was all I could come up with.

"What were you doing today?" he drilled me heatedly. "What were you thinking, trying to run from the SR?" He held up a finger. "It is impossible to elude the SR," he said, enunciating every word as if I was a three-year-old. "Unless . . . ."

"I know that," I enunciated right back. "I–"

"Stop talking!" He reached into a compartment in the front of the heliplane and took out a black kit, popping it open. While taking out a long and slender metal instrument, he simultaneously grabbed my right wrist and slammed it down on the armrest. Instinct kicked in, and I tried to wrench my hand free. I was pretty strong, but he was much stronger. The guy looked like he could bench press a semi-truck.

"What are you doing?" I didn't even have time to protest when he jammed the instrument down onto my wrist. The most excruciating pain I have ever felt shocked me into a stupor. My heart was banging inside my ribcage. I screamed when he lifted the instrument off my wrist. I sat shaking in a cold sweat, breathing hard and hoping to recover from the pain and *fast*. I wanted to kill the guy.

He held the instrument over his open palm and out dropped my bloody chip. I glanced down at my wrist and saw a neat incision that had been lasered shut in a thin line. He wiped the residual blood off my wrist and applied a pain patch to my lower arm. I shook my head as if to clear my now impending migraine.

By some miracle, it looked as if the SR's heliplanes had retreated. I didn't hear or feel any oncoming firepower. Amazing, I had to admit. It didn't seem possible. The SR were relentless leeches. When I gazed out the window in a pain-induced haze, I saw that it appeared we were now following the herd. The guy relaxed a little and studied me. I glared at him through hooded eyes, contemplating murderous thoughts.

"Who are you?" I was done playing doctor, and didn't give a damn anymore. I wanted answers.

"I'm Luc, a luminary of the ADF, the only underground SR resistance." He said this as if we were watching the morning news.

"Huh? How come no one has ever heard of this ADF before?" I put air quotes around ADF.

"The Alliance Defense Force is relatively new, but we are invisible. We don't exist. We keep it that way. And thank God, the SR doesn't want anyone knowing about us either."

"What do you want with me?" I asked while massaging my wrist and arm, letting the painkillers kick in.

"You'll know soon enough," he said, and then he took the controls again.

I looked down at my wrist again; I was now off the grid. I was taken aback that I didn't know how I felt about that. I should be elated.

Now they wouldn't be able to electrocute me with their torture talking methods. Psshh, waterboarding was child's play with the SR.

And then it hit me: *they could no longer find me.*

Chapter 13

"I alone cannot change the world, but I can cast a stone across the waters to create many ripples."
—Mother Theresa

Three days after my baby sister Stephanie was born, I could hear her screaming cries in my sleep. Sure, I was really little at the time, but it is traumatizing when you realize what happened on the third day of your life. It's good that babies can't remember the chip implantation, because I'm sure it hurt like a biznitch. Years later, my brother Josiah arrived as a "blessing" when I was almost thirteen, and I was old enough to know exactly what was happening on his third day of life, and old enough to want to stop it.

I knew today's events were irreversible, but it only strengthened my resolve to do whatever I could to put the SR out of its misery, regardless of what path I had now embarked upon. Maybe I had a prayer with this ADF outfit.

We continued following the SR's pack of heliplanes deeper into the city when Luc jerked the heliplane to the left just as we were passing a tall skyscraper. We descended low to the ground behind another building, idling to make sure no other heliplanes followed suit. I didn't know what type of pain patch he had given me, but I was feeling rummy by this point. My life was in this dude's hands, and all I wanted to do was sleep. My head lolled forward, and I jerked it upright. "What did you give me?" I slurred.

I was about to ask him where we were going, but I couldn't compete with my drowsiness, and my head flopped back against the seat. I closed my eyes to the silent whirring sounds around me and succumbed to the wonderful feeling of slipping into a deep sleep.

When I woke up, I peeked open my eyes to find myself lying on a bunk in a small, ten-by-ten-foot cement cell. All that had happened today came rushing back at me. My head was cloudy and my right wrist throbbed. I heard voices through the open doorway in front of me. Well at least I wasn't jailed. I pushed myself to a sitting position, my hand on my head. I just sat for a few minutes, letting myself get my bearings. My eyes swept around the room, seeing a wooden chair in one corner, a poster with some sort of symbol on the wall, and no windows. I slid my feet to the floor and took a few shaky steps toward the sound of talking. I stood in the doorway, surveying the scene.

Three men were sitting at a table in the center of what looked like a large kitchen. They all stopped talking and looked up at me. I recognized my abductor, Luc, but I didn't know the other two men. However, one looked very familiar, sort of like Luc, and I racked my brain as to where I had seen him before.

"Mickey?" I asked in wonder. Was it the custodian from eighth denomination?

He laughed and got up out of his seat to come give me a man hug. "You have a good memory, kid. This is my cousin Luc, and this is Robbie." No wonder I had mixed up Luc and Mickey; they were cousins, though Mickey was much older. He was the one who had been watching me at my sister's convocation. Robbie was muscular, shirtless, and he looked to be about Luc's age, in his thirties, with dark scraggly hair. He also had that same strange symbol lasered on his upper chest that I had seen on the poster in my cell.

Luc flashed me the peace sign. I shook hands with Robbie and just nodded at Luc. I was still pissed at the dude. "Goro," I introduced myself.

"We know." Robbie nodded his head. I glanced around at everyone with caution.

"Wanna tell me where we are?" I raised my eyebrows, massaging my temples.

"Welcome to the ADF's compound," Mickey answered me.

I collapsed into the one empty chair at the table, watching Mickey.

"I am sure you have a multitude of questions." Mickey began.

"Why don't you just give him the penny tour," Luc interrupted, looking over at me and twirling some sort of metal instrument in his hand. Maybe he was miffed I hadn't shaken his hand too. His eyes never left mine.

"Tour?" I said, not sure I wanted to know.

Mickey shot a reluctant glance at Luc, who seemed to resign to the idea, shrugging his shoulders.

"Okey dokey." Mickey waved for me to follow him.

I rose from the table, eyes still on Luc, and finally broke contact, having to jog to catch up with Mickey. For an older guy, he was walking fast.

"How long have I been out?" I asked him when I caught up to him.

"Oh, about eight hours," Mickey replied.

"Eight hours?" I was flabbergasted, stopping in my tracks. "What time is it?"

"Kid, you are off the SR's radar, so it might as well be Christmas." Holidays were not acknowledged anymore, but I got his point. He was walking with a purposeful stride, and my mind flew to my family. They must be worried sick. I felt like a PTSD survivor experiencing some sort of real live surreal dream, but while wide awake.

"My family!" I yelled in Mickey's direction. "My friends!" I stood still.

I couldn't believe this. One minute I was waking up to my little brother running circles around my bed and the next, I was being held hostage in some cave. I started walking again, but it felt like I was running through quicksand.

We stopped in another large dimly lit room where it looked like thirty men or so in neat orderly rows were doing some sort of martial arts moves. They were oblivious to the two of us. Their movements were perfectly in sync.

"What is this?" I inquired, not really caring.

"Krav Maga." Mickey observed them in silence for a moment. "Contact combat."

"Awesome. I have to go—I have family . . . I mean, they don't know where I am . . . ." I stammered. "I need . . . ." I turned to head back to the kitchen. I needed Luc get me back to the heliplane or show me the door or something. "This is all fabulous, but . . . ." I protested.

Mickey cut me off and grabbed my arm, looking me straight in the eyes. "Kid, life as you know it is *over.* Period. We can get a message to them, but . . . you can't go back. I'm sorry." He swept his other hand wide as if to say, *Oh well.*

My blood started to boil. I wrenched my arm free, stalking back to the kitchen, ready to square off with Luc. He looked up surprised when I came marching back.

"Find us?" I reminded him of our little dance on the helirail platform.

"Aww, you bummed 'cause you didn't get to interface with anyone? Oh, and I found you."

"Where's the exit? I need to bolt."

"Son, wake up and take a whiff of the garbage burning outside. This is your new crib."

Crib? "I'm leaving." I glared at Luc.

Luc shook his head back and forth, not budging. He shoved back his chair and kicked his feet up, resting them on the edge of the table.

"What, son, you think I should have left you to fend for yourself?" Luc's question had sharp points.

"Let the Sovereign Regime have their way with you?" He said the full name of the SR as if to make his point loud and clear. He pointed in my direction the metal instrument he had been twirling. "You wouldn't have lasted a nanosecond, studhorse." He got up to refill his cup from the coffee panel behind him. Guy had the chip to end all chips on his shoulder.

"Wow." I nodded. "Do I need to pack a suitcase—for the *guilt* trip?" I retorted, indignant as hell.

"Do you think Davio gives a rat's ass about your puny little life?" He leaned against the counter, cup in hand. Mickey had returned to the kitchen and was surveying our little rumble.

The mention of the SR leader's name gave everyone pause, and an eerie silence settled around us. I blinked a few times before I lit into Luc again.

"Why me?" I shouted. "I appreciate the cavalry rescue, but you said I would know soon enough." I stabbed the table with my finger emphatically. "Now is good."

Robbie, Luc, and Mickey just looked at me for several seconds.

Luc broke the silence. "It's you," he said, looking down into his coffee.

Pardon me? My mind raced.

"Didn't I just ask that? It's me, what?" I blurted out, my hands on my hips.

"You have it—what we need," Luc said all calm, ignoring my outbursts and nodding at my chest.

"I have officially boarded the good ship Lollipop." I was sarcastic, quoting an old Shirley Temple movie Josiah and I had watched a while back at the Hall of Digital Archives. Everyone looked at me with furrowed expressions as if they were thinking *huh?*

Nevertheless, my hand shot up and mechanically patted my chest, then stiffened. That's when it clicked.

My grandfather's identity chip.

I reached into my shirt and pulled out the chain that I never removed, twisting the chip with my fingers. All three of them stared at the chip like it was the Hope Diamond, which I had seen on a Hall of Relics field trip when I was still attending the Hall of Academics.

"This," my voice cracked as I said it more as a statement than a question. My vision became unfocused.

Luc nodded. "That."

"Removed chips are worthless," I whispered, staring into space.

"Wrong. Mickey has developed a program to retrieve data from withdrawn and even damaged chips," Robbie chimed in. "He has also figured out how to use harvested chips, which are reprogrammed by yours truly, to simulate a connection with the nervous system; it functions the same as a genuine identity chip. Mickey figured out the technology a while ago, and it has been kept on the down low. We have a modest stash of these repurposed chips here in the compound in a secured location." Robbie paused in his explanation, "We need them to move around the city at times, acquire food, scan equipment so that it works properly, etcetera. But, the fake chips are not on the SR's grid." He emphasized that point with a raised finger. Not that it mattered, though. I'm sure an outfit like the ADF was on the SR's radar regardless.

"Harvested from where?"

"We need the chip, son," Mickey responded, letting my question go. "It holds the key."

"The key to what?" I was not sure I wanted to know. "And what's this key for?" I broke out of my reverie and pulled the ancient key out of my pocket, holding it up.

"It's the key to the door of this compound. We all have one." Luc said this as if it was obvious, and I was the only dummy here.

I found my resolve again. "Was I supposed to find your secret hideout by Braille, or selective telemetry or something? Nobody uses keys anymore! Whatever . . . ." I held my hands up. "This is where I get off. I need to go."

"We can't keep him against his will, Luc," Mickey said softly. "Let him leave."

Luc shot a defiant glance at his cousin, and then he slammed his coffee cup onto the counter, making us all jump. He marched out of the kitchen.

"It was good seeing you again, kid," Mickey spoke to me. "Ciao." He motioned for me to follow Luc.

I ran after him, following him down an opposite corridor and up some stairs to a large, rusty iron door. He took a key from his front pocket that was identical to the one he had given me and inserted it into a lock. He twisted and then pushed the door open wide, still heated from our exchange. I would've laughed out loud at the antiquated door with its keyed lock if I hadn't been so enraged. He stopped me once with a hand on my chest.

"You'll return, son." I shrugged off his hand and didn't answer as I walked out into the darkness of night.

Chapter 14

"That which does not kill us makes us stronger."
—Friedrich Nietzsche

My sister and I have always tried to make things as easy for our parents as possible. Mom comes home drained on most days, but she ends up cheerful once she sees our faces. I know they have tremendous responsibilities they have to shoulder, and it makes me hate the SR all that much more. My father is strong and wise, keeping it together as best as he can under the circumstances in our world today.

Besides my own work assignment, I often run the daily errands needed to obtain my family's supplies. Josiah also insists on doing his fair share; the noble little guy takes out the trash and has been known to wash a dish or two. Stephanie in turn keeps up with all the cleaning so that Mom doesn't have to even think about that stuff when she comes home in the evening. I know it sounds very stereotypical and gender specific, but Stephanie has offered to run errands in my place, and I have offered to clean. Stephanie, however, has reprimanded me for my cleaning methods. Hey, if it looks clean, it *is* clean, in my world. We switch it up sometimes, but being the big brother that I am, I'm not super red hot about her being out and about with the SR lurking in the alleys. Besides, the last time she went to the commissary, her chip was acting wonky, and she had to scan her wrist seven times before it registered credits. This made the personnel suspicious, as usual, and a supervisor was called over to inspect her wrist for any abnormalities or evidence of tampering. They scanned her credit account activity for the last twelve months, scrutinizing every transaction before they finally let her leave two hours later. I mean, give me a break; she was still in the Hall of Academics then . . . .

When I busted out of the ADF's lair, I discovered I had been in the basement of an old rundown building that wasn't far from the Hall of Academics. The door was located in what looked like the huge tunnel of a drainage ditch underneath a bridge. From here, it was less than five miles to my family's dwelling. Suddenly, I was eager to see my family and put the whole day in the rearview mirror.

I started jogging in the direction of home, keeping to the shadows. I caught sight of plenty of SR mercenaries walking around all stiff and moronic, probing the area. Man, why were there so many out and about right now? It couldn't really be because of the little stunt I had pulled this morning, could it? Regardless, as much as I hated to admit it, Luc's little outpatient surgery on me gave me a huge advantage, as the SR could no longer monitor my whereabouts.

When I got to my family's dwelling, I knew the SR would be watching it, so I hid out of sight behind some bushes across the street. The house was completely dark. Where could they be? It wasn't curfew yet; did the SR have them? My mind ran through various unpleasant scenarios as I crept as close to the dwelling as I dared, confirming that no one was home. The Backlands. Could they be visiting Zan's family? It was worth a try.

I jogged to the Backlands until I came to the first entrance, stopping abruptly just out of sight of the SR night guards. Ugh. They would be ready for me if I attempted to enter. I forfeited the entrance and jogged along until I could find some area of the wall that I could scale. I found a patch of wall that had a tree growing up against the side, with the nearest guard tower a good thirty-five feet to the left, so I hoped it would provide good cover. I grabbed the lower branch of the tree and hauled myself up, climbing higher as quickly and quietly as possible. I was just barely able to grab the top of the wall with my fingertips, and it took every ounce of strength I could muster to pull myself up and onto the top of the wall, taking care to step around the poisoned spikes. I peered down. Damn, there was nothing on the other side. Getting down would be tricky. I decided to just slide down the inside of the wall feet first and hope I didn't twist an ankle upon landing. I turned my body facing the wall and hung by my hands, finally letting go. I hugged the wall as best I could, scraping my palms on the way down, but when I landed, I fell back hard onto my ass. Ouch.

I got up, brushing the seat of my pants, and raced toward Zan's dwelling. I screeched to a halt. What was I doing? No. The SR would be watching Zan's family as well. Who could I go to that the SR could not link me with? Muriel. I had never been inside the medicine woman's dwelling, nor had I ever really talked to her, but I knew where she lived. I changed directions and jogged over to her small hut. When I arrived, the windows and front door of her little shack were wide open, and I could hear her singing inside. I stopped fast at her front door and knocked hard on the doorjamb.

"Muriel!" I whispered.

She jumped at the sink where she was washing dishes, and whipped around when it registered that someone had spoken her name.

"Goro!" she half whispered, half yelled. "What are you doing here?"

"Where's my family?" I whisper-shouted, putting a finger to my lips.

"They're at Sylvia's," she answered. "Your father . . . " She didn't finish the sentence.

"Can you get a message to him for me? I need him to meet me here in the back."

"No, I'll have him meet you at the health clinic. That way if anyone is watching, I can say I was treating him." She gave me the address and then left.

"Okay," I muttered to her retreating back, dreading what she meant by that.

I jogged over to the clinic and waited outside in the dark. Where were they? The ten minutes that passed seemed like an eternity, and then I saw her approaching with someone, but it was too dark to make out who it was. She came to the door and opened the clinic, with me following behind my father. When we got inside, she led us to a back room and then scanned the lights on with her right wrist.

"The camera in here is broken, and I think the SR has forgotten about it," she said with a sardonic grin. "I will give you two some privacy."

When I turned to face my father, my heart lodged in my throat and I choked back a cry.

His face was swollen to twice the normal size, and his left eye was blackened. His lower lip was puffed up from being split open, and he leaned oddly to one side.

"Dammit!" I punched the wall next to me as hard as I could, not concerned with the pain. "What did those bastards do to you?" It took all my emotional strength not to burst into tears at that moment.

"Son, it's okay. All that matters is that you are all right," he said in his usual calm demeanor, putting a reassuring hand on my shoulder.

"I'll kill them!" I spat out, not caring who heard me.

"Son, please, revenge is not the way." He switched tactics. "Your mother and siblings are fine; they are with Nana Mares."

That's when we heard it.

A deafening explosion rattled the windowpanes. We both started, looking at each other, with me running to stand next to the window and taking a quick look out. I didn't want to stand directly in front of it for fear of being seen, and because I knew the glass could explode inward if an explosion hit nearby. I could see approaching heliplanes, and I heard another explosion somewhere farther away. *Oh, God.* Dad and I ran to the front of the clinic and grabbed Muriel; she was peeking out the front door, which she had opened a crack.

"What is it?" Her eyes were wide and scared.

"The SR is bombing the Backlands," my dad said in a resigned tone, as if he had known all along. I just looked at him, meeting his sad eyes with a certain realization setting in. The conversation I had overheard at DWE earlier today flashed through my mind.

"What?" she wailed in disbelief. "How can they do this? What about the Pact?"

I grabbed her and Dad by the arms, not bothering to answer her, and yelled, "We have to get out of here!"

We made a mad dash for Zan's house, covering our heads and ears on the way. People were running in the streets, shouting. More missiles were launched, and I saw some dwellings in the distance blazing with fire.

"Mom!" I screamed when I got to Zan's doorway ahead of Dad and Muriel. "Where are you?" My wild eyes swept the front room. I found her and Stephanie huddling under a bunk in the only other back room.

"Goro!" Stephanie choked out a cry. "Where have you been? What's happening?"

They both crawled out from under the bunk, with Stephanie hugging me hard.

"Where's Josiah?" I yelled in fear, my heart stopping.

"I thought he was with Nana Mares!" exclaimed Mom, looking frantic and grabbing Dad's arm.

I left her and Stephanie and ran to the front living area, searching. A note scribbled on a control panel on the wall caught my eye. I would recognize that handwriting anywhere. Josiah had written in small print, "I will distract the SR so you can get away." NO! I ran to the kitchenette and grabbed a knife. I was improvising, but it was better than nothing, and I didn't know what to expect anymore. I could hear more explosions from outside.

"Josiah!" I screamed out the front door, heading into the street.

"Goro, what are you doing?" Muriel yelled after me.

My eyes scanned both directions. I finally caught sight of him and Nana Mares making their way down the street, heading in the direction of Muriel's dwelling. Sylvia and Zan's sisters had run up ahead. I halted, turning the opposite direction, and saw SR mercenaries advancing on foot with raised rifles, moving toward the people who were running out of their dwellings. I wanted to frickin' kill those SR a-holes, but the only person I was concerned about was my brother. Just then, Nana Mares tripped and fell, and Josiah bent down to help her up.

That's when I saw him.

I saw the one solitary SR mercenary before they did. Some little girl running near Josiah and Nana Mares had obtusely thrown a rock at this soldier, and he had broken rank, approaching the two of them, thinking they were responsible. He raised his rifle upon reaching them, aiming it at Nana Mare's head. Just then, everything moved in slow motion before my eyes.

"No!" Josiah shouted, now seeing the soldier. He boldly stood up straight in front of Nana Mares and raised his arms. I raced toward Josiah, screaming the whole way, hoping to distract the SR soldier in my direction. The mercenary's mouth broke into a wide wicked grin as he switched his aim from Nana Mares's head to Josiah's. *He would kill a child?* I thought, horrified. *Oh, my God!*

Josiah heard me and turned. I saw his eyes light up with relief when he saw me coming for him. "Goro!" He reached out his arms toward me. Adrenaline kicked in, and I ran as fast as I could toward his arms.

Nana Mares screamed, "Josiah, no! I have lived my life!" I could vaguely hear people screaming in the distant background behind me. She tried to push him to the side, but the soldier squeezed the trigger, the rifle laser hitting its target point-blank. Josiah's head whiplashed back, and he crumpled to the ground in a heap, just as I reached him.

"NO-O-O-O-O!"

I heard screaming and realized it was coming from me. I was screaming Josiah's name at the top of my lungs, burning my throat. I slid to the ground feet first, throwing the SR murderer off balance. I kicked the SR's rifle out of his hand, knocking him to the ground. I threw Josiah over my shoulder. The SR soldier scrambled to his feet and turned his attention to me, but I buried the knife up to the handle in the side of his neck. He fell to the ground, bleeding profusely.

That was the very first SR coward whose life I took.

"Go!" I shouted to Nana Mares, snatching the soldier's rifle. Nana Mares was still sitting on the ground, crying in hysterics. I helped her to her feet, and she limped toward Muriel's house. More explosions went off. The SR was firing at men, women, children, chickens, anything that moved. I saw more people fall, slain by the SR laser fire. It was an all-out siege, and I was horrified that it was happening. It didn't seem real.

Stone-faced and working on autopilot, I carried Josiah's lifeless body back into Zan's dwelling. Mom had been screaming out the front door to me, but when she took one look at her little boy close up, she collapsed to her knees with an anguished cry. A mother knew. Stephanie burst into sobs and tried to take him from me. My dad just stared, dumbstruck. Muriel had covered her mouth and was crying softly. I laid him on the couch, and my mother grabbed him and cradled him in her arms, wailing incoherently. I snapped back to reality.

"Mom, we have to go!" I yelled, trying to pull her to her feet.

"I'm not leaving my baby!" she screamed, tears streaming down her cheeks.

"Dad!" I looked at him with desperation in my eyes.

"I'm staying with your mother," he said with resignation, and lowered himself next to her, putting his hand on Josiah's head and looking up at me with sad eyes.

"We have to go," I repeated, pleading with them both. "Please, I'm begging you. Bring him!" I tugged at both of them to get up.

Several more loud explosions erupted, too close for comfort. At that point, Mom and Dad got to their feet and followed me like zombies, with Dad carrying Josiah. I led them to a section of the wall that had been destroyed by a bomb, aiming the rifle ahead of me the entire time. Two SR soldiers saw us and started toward us. I aimed my rifle and fired. Both went down. I would not hesitate to kill any other bastard who touched my family. We climbed over the rubble up the wall and back down to the street, with Dad carrying Josiah. I kept looking over my shoulder to see if any soldiers were following us. I guess they were only concerned with obliterating the Backlands.

"You have to head home!" I said to my dad and mom. "They are only bombing the Backlands. SR scum wouldn't dare kill everyone in the city."

"Goro?" My dad looked at me with a stunned expression.

"The SR is looking for me," I stated the obvious, handing him the rifle I had confiscated.

"Why?" he screamed, finally snapping out of his daze.

"I don't know!" I screamed back. "I have stuff they want from me, or something. You should be safe at home until I can come for you!"

I spoke fast, saying the first reassuring thing that came to my mind. I wasn't sure if it was true, but I didn't know what else to tell them.

"No. We'll head to a safe house I know about."

I thought of something and quickly blurted out, "Dad, go into the center desk drawer in my room and get the three metal cuffs there; wear them on your right wrists. Alex designed them. They will cover your chips and deflect any grid activity. You, Mom, and Stephanie will theoretically be missing in action. I need to go get help." I placed a hand on Josiah's cheek. It was still warm. I dropped my head in sorrow. My dad just blinked at me, but he nodded his head, not asking me any further questions. My mother was numb.

Stephanie grabbed my arm. "Take me with you! I wanna go with you!"

"Go with Mom and Dad." I tried shrugging her off, but she clung to me in a vice grip, crying. "You're safe if I am not with you," I added. I ended up having to pry her fingers off my arm.

"Goro!" she screamed after me.

I jogged back to the tunnel in a blur and located the same door I had left through earlier. I found the makeshift lock. I halted for just a second, my eyes drawn to something engraved over the top of the door: RV 20:10. I put the iron key from my pocket into the lock, turned it, and let myself in. Luc and Mickey were still where I had left them in the kitchen. Not that much time had passed since I had stormed out of the compound, but it felt like an eternity. They looked up from their work when I burst into the kitchen, but after one look at me, they didn't say anything.

"The SR is attacking the Backlands! They are killing every human being on sight," I finished, out of breath. No one moved. "Is everyone deaf? Did you hear me?"

"No. We are not deaf. We hear you," Luc leveled at me.

"Sit down, son," Mickey said to me in a quiet voice.

I slumped into the nearest chair, depleted of all energy, and sat in silence, breathing hard.

"They killed my little brother," I choked out after several minutes, pinching the bridge of my nose and scrunching my eyes. I currently had no idea what was happening with my parents and sister. Now I understood why people turned to narcotics or alcohol and became addicts; they did it to numb the pain . . . to not want to experience it anymore . . . to escape into oblivion.

"The SR is bombing the Backlands," I reiterated, as if they had been half-asleep before. "They are slaughtering every living thing," I said to the floor, defeated. I was living a nightmare, with the SR as a horrific tour guide.

Mickey just slowly nodded his head, compassion filling his eyes. Luc looked away.

"I'm sorry, Goro," Mickey said, his head bent toward the table. I barely heard him.

"Let's go," Luc ordered as he got to his feet.

"For God's sake, Luc, give the boy a minute. He just lost his brother!" Mickey yelled, stumbling over his words.

"I'll give him ten; then it's show time," Luc announced, leaving the kitchen.

Mickey shook his head in Luc's direction.

I glanced at the table, my mind empty. Two hand-held micro panels were there, with what looked like schematics displayed on each of them. "What's this?" I asked, not really listening for an answer.

"I have a surprise for you," Mickey said quietly. I looked up at him with dead eyes.

Huh? I did not care.

He just got up and motioned for me to come with him. Even though I didn't want to, I willed myself to get up and go with him. He stood in the doorway of the cell I had woken up in just hours earlier.

I peered in and saw Alex and Cory crashed out on the single bed in the room, both with pain patches on their lower arms. My mouth flew open in surprise. Cory looked like he had had the crap beaten out of him, though. I turned my head toward Mickey with a question in my eyes.

"We thought you could use some familiar faces in this war." He patted me on the back. "We're gonna need everyone we can get."

"What?" I was stunned. "How did you get . . . how did you find them?"

"It's not rocket science, kid. We had to extract Cory before the SR ended up killing him; Alex happened to be with him. But that's a story for another day."

I knew that Cory would be shredded, the SR drilling him concerning my whereabouts, but I hadn't thought they would resort to murder. They hadn't killed my dad, but after seeing my brother murdered in cold blood, I now knew that anything was possible with them.

I shook my head in wonder, looking down at them. They didn't have a clue about the massacre that was going on in the Backlands. *Lucky for them*, I mused. Where was Zan?

"I've no doubt they will fill you in when they come to," Mickey remarked after a moment. "In the meantime, let me show you to a shower and get you some food." I just peered at him through tired eyes.

"You've been so . . . kind," I faltered. I couldn't take it anymore. My life, as I knew it, was changed forever. Feeling like a whimpering baby, I leaned against the doorway and put my head in my hands, letting my tears flow freely.

Chapter 15

"Let your hopes, not your hurts, shape your future."
—Robert H. Schuller

Mickey put his hand on my shoulder and squeezed, letting me get it all out. I still felt embarrassed, looking like a blubbering fool, despite all that I had been through that day. Mickey didn't seem to care. He still never brings up that personal breakdown of mine, even today. Awesome guy.

He led me to a room that had a private bath with a shower and he opened a cupboard showing me spare clothes. "This is my room . . . my jeans should fit you." He eyeballed me, sizing me up. He sniffed a towel he had grabbed off an iron towel bar on the wall and threw it at me. "This should be clean." He smiled at me wanly as he left, sliding the door shut. I looked around and saw the same poster with the strange symbol as the one on the wall in the kitchen. I sat down on the bunk, wiping my nose with the back of my hand. Gross. I took a couple of deep breaths to clear my head and started undressing.

The hot water felt amazing after my hellish ordeal today, and I let the shower run for a long time. I stupidly pretended that the water was washing away the palpable throbbing pain located in the deep recesses of my chest. I fantasized I was waking up in my bunk back at my dwelling, with Josiah jumping up and down on my bed. I prayed that my family was okay. I shoved the thoughts from my mind and turned off the water.

When I returned to the kitchen, Mickey had placed some sort of stew on the table for me, but who was complaining? I wolfed it down, realizing I was hungrier than I thought. I shot a glance at the room where Cory and Alex were dead to the world. I motioned to Mickey as a way to ask for seconds, and he waved for me to help myself.

"They still out?" I nodded toward my friends. I wanted to ask them questions. "Thanks for the food, the shower, everything . . . ." My voice trailed off as I sat back down again. I stabbed a piece of carrot with my fork, distracted with my thoughts.

"No problem," he answered through a mouthful of stew. "Remember, you slept for eight hours after we removed your chip," he reminded me with a kind look. "They'll wake up when they're ready to."

"What's that poster on your wall mean?" I gestured over my shoulder with my fork, wanting to talk about something else. "There's one in the phone booth also." I referred to the cell my buddies and I had crashed in. "Yer not SR posers wanting tats too, are you?

"No, it's the symbol for the ADF, but it has a completely different meaning than the SR's tags." I waited for him to continue.

"Which is what?" I pushed him.

He lifted his shirt to show the identical symbol Robbie had, but tattooed on his right pec:

"So you *do* have tattoos."

I raised my eyebrows as he told me that only he, Luc, and Robbie have the symbol as a reminder of what they stand for and what they are fighting for.

"Okay," I offered, hoping I sounded nonjudgmental. "Hey, to each his own."

"I sense some criticism coming." Mickey went back to eating.

"Nah, I'm just no follower."

"Or are you?" Mickey's question had hooks, and my eyes caught his, letting him know I had heard him.

Luc came back at that point and got his own stew. He plopped down at the table and said, "After this, we need to show him the full enchilada, have him meet the others . . . ten minutes is up."

"Others?" I questioned, my brows furrowed. "The Krav Maga gurus?"

Luc just snorted, causing me to turn to him with sharpened eyes.

"Oh, excuse me, I'm sorry. You getting a little sunburned up there on your high horse?" I was in no mood to take any more of his BS. Luc stopped eating and met my fuming stare.

"Son, you have absolutely no iota of a clue what the ADF does, so I wouldn't turn up my self-righteous nose just yet."

I launched to my feet, lunging to take a swing at him when Mickey stopped me.

"Hey, hey, hey! We're all on the same side!" Mickey said firmly, restraining me.

"And Luc, zip it," he ordered. Luc looked like he was hedging his bets, but then he ceded and put down his eating utensil, folding his hands in front of him.

"The war is out there!" Mickey yelled, pointing to the wall. "We have a lot to accomplish and very little time in which to do it." He wiped his forehead with the back of his hand. "I am sure the SR would love that we are bickering over . . . I don't know, you tell me!" He spread his hands wide. "Goro, round two," Mickey motioned for me to follow him again.

This time when Mickey showed me around, I kept quiet. Mickey led me to the same room in which I had seen the dudes doing Krav Maga, although it was empty now. I looked around at the weights, boxing bags, foam dummies, and a rock-climbing wall near the periphery of the room.

"This is where we train. We call it the schoolhouse," Mickey explained with a tired voice. "All ADF become experts in SAR, tactical and survival training, bushcraft, marksmanship, DT, land warfare, and yes, Krav Maga."

"SAR? DT?" I was confused.

"Search and rescue; demolition tactics," he said in a patient voice. "I don't expect you to remember everything I'm telling you; there's no pop quiz . . . not yet, anyway."

"Mickey, that kind of training takes months! The Backlands are being destroyed *now*," I protested. "People are dying as we're sitting around eating stew!"

"Sacrifices have been and will be made for the overall greater good." Mickey said this like it was as simple as taking out the trash without your mom asking. He scratched his eyebrow with the back of his thumbnail. "You have to pick your battles."

"Battles?" I was not believing my ears. "I'm in the Twilight Zone." I sighed and gazed fruitlessly toward the ceiling.

Mickey ignored me. "Son, the lives of the many outweigh the lives of the few."

"That's from *Star Trek*," I snapped, referencing yet another centuries-old show from the Hall of Digital Archives that Stephanie happened to love.

"I didn't know." Mickey tilted his head but then motioned for me to move on.

I shook my head. "So we're just going to let the Backlands crash and burn? That's a lot of lives! And what 'greater good'?" I didn't budge, not waiting before I continued. "I have no idea if my friend Zan or our families are okay!" I couldn't believe what I was hearing! "I gotta do something," I resolved, making a move to leave once again.

Mickey stopped me cold with a hand on my arm.

"Kid, you *cannot* fight Davio head on. He doesn't work that way. You know that. You have to attack him through the back door. The man is evil through and through. His strategies are subversive . . . the use of deception, tricks, the list goes on." Mickey's voice took on a different tone, not fear, but a tone of desperation almost. "There is a battle going on, and time is of the essence."

"Exactly!" I just stared at him when he looked like he wasn't going to say anything more. I broke away and shook my head in disgust. If I hadn't felt so grateful for everything he had done for me in this short time, I would've decked him then and there. I kicked the wall instead.

"I am not minimizing your pain, not at all," he told me. "I understand more than you care to know," he finished, with a tinge of sadness in his voice. "But the SR runs on a completely different mindset."

"Ya think?" I was being sarcastic, but didn't care. "Of course they do; they're brainwashed." I stabbed my temple with my forefinger. I collapsed on a random bench near the wall, deep in thought. I didn't have anywhere to go, I admitted to myself. It was leave and die, or stay and fight.

"Okay," I relented after a long silence, "what else do I need to know?" I really didn't have any choice in the matter. I needed to go along with the ADF and hope that I could contact my family and Zan on the down low—if they were still alive.

Chapter 16

"The more you sweat in training, the less you bleed in combat."
—Norman Schwarzkopf

The next morning when I awakened, I forgot where I was. I had predicted that that might happen, and sure enough, I woke up swinging. Alex and Cory were both coherent at that point, and they held me down. Everything from yesterday came rushing back at me, and I felt nauseated.

"Hey! Relax, man," Alex mumbled.

I noticed I was back in the ten-by-ten-foot cell, and a bunkbed had been squeezed in, if that was even possible. I had slept right through the furniture moving. I struggled under Alex and Cory's weight until they let me up. I glanced at them, rubbing my arms where I had been held down.

"You get your tickets to the show yet?" I asked both of them with a frown.

"Yeah . . . it's a real circus." Cory breathed out hard. "I'm worried as hell about my grandma." He was sitting on the foot of my bed, and he didn't look so good. He had been battered around by the SR something fierce, but he still had a spark in his eyes, thank God.

"Do you guys have any idea where Zan might be?" I asked, avoiding asking Cory what happened to his face. I could only imagine.

They didn't answer. Cory looked down at the incision on his right wrist while Alex averted his eyes.

"Well?" I insisted, suspicious that they knew, but were either unwilling or unable to answer.

"Goro . . . Zan went and joined the SR," Alex finally revealed to the dead air around us.

"What?" I freaked. The chitchat I'd had with Alex at the pub, which seemed like a lifetime ago, immediately leapt to my mind, and I scowled at him.

"Hey, I never said boo," he was fast to tell me, knowing full well what I was thinking. "I guess his mom told your mom when she comlinked Sylvia when you went AWOL." He gestured with his hands for emphasis.

"Holy hell," I breathed under my breath. "We *have* to do something!" I gritted my teeth, rubbing my eyes. I could feel a headache coming on. *Zan! What the hell were you thinking? Always having to prove yourself.* I shook my head in irritation. I was about to grill Alex and Cory on how they had ended up at the compound when I heard someone walking into the kitchen.

Luc stuck his head in our closet of a cell. "Training starts in five, ladies, and you better eat something first."

Alex and Cory just looked at each other, eyebrows raised in a question.

"Our kidnapper's a real chipper guy." Cory hitched his thumb in Luc's direction, waiting until his footsteps had receded out of the kitchen. I became worried for him and Alex, but right now, it was sink or swim, and we had to just deal with it.

"Yep," I quipped. "Let's go." Alex and Cory shuffled after me.

We grabbed a couple slices of bread with peanut butter, and a couple of bananas from the kitchen. We then all three walked to the large cement "schoolhouse" room, me still wearing Mickey's clothes that I had slept in. My eyes bugged out when I saw about thirty-five people gathered around Luc, men and women. I observed that a lot of the guys had longer hair than regulation allowed, and most had a look about them that suggested they'd been here a long time.

Everyone paid absolutely no heed to the three of us standing around in the back, speed eating our peanut butter sandwiches and fruit. Cory and Alex looked a little unsettled, but I was itching to thrash something or someone, hard. I was trying, with no luck, to put all thoughts of what had happened to Josiah out of my mind as I stuffed the last bite of banana in my mouth.

"Wallflowers." Luc waved us forward. "This is Goro, Alex, and Cory—new indocs." Luc pointed to each of us in turn. *Yeah, against our will*, I thought.

"Indocs?" Cory asked no one in particular.

"Indoctrinates," whispered a short guy next to him. Cory just scowled at him, confused as all get out.

Everyone gave us the once over, and a few guys nodded at us, but no one shook hands or introduced themselves. One attractive Hispanic girl with long brown hair eyed me inquisitively, but when I caught her sizing me up, I threw her a look that said *don't*, shaking my head. She sniffed and turned away. I'm usually a pretty nice guy, but things were different now.

"Okay, spread out," Luc ordered. Everyone immediately fanned out throughout the massive room. "Push-ups—go!"

"Aw, come on!" Cory started, but Alex elbowed him in the stomach. "Ooof—ass wipe!"

"Just do it!" I spat out. I fell to the floor and started doing push-ups, watching others as they clapped each time they came up. The women were doing the same thing, and not "girl" push-ups on their knees either. We switched to diamond push-ups while Luc counted from the front. "I don't hear anyone," he shouted out as everyone started chanting in rhythm.

After about fifty, I got winded. Luc found his way over to me and knelt down.

"Move it, sweet pea," he commanded. I gave him a look of sheer daggers but kept going. Cory had stopped and was flat on his back, but Alex kept up with me. After a hundred or so, Luc stopped us and had us do a hundred crunches and a hundred burpees. I disliked burpees just about as much as I disliked Luc right now. As if that wasn't enough, he had everyone run laps, and he timed us to boot.

"The goal is a four-minute mile," he instructed me the first time I passed by him.

"What the hell?" I heard Cory behind me gasp. "Is he for real?"

"C'mon, pussies!" Luc yelled after us. "This is only Indoctrination!"

Alex, Cory, and I came in last, as we had just jumped onto this hamster wheel of hell. I rested my hands on my hips, panting and craving a drink of cold water.

"Congratulations! Twelve point four minutes, the slowest time in history," Luc said to me loudly enough so that everyone two rooms over could hear. A couple of the guys who had finished running earlier smirked in our direction, but the dark-haired girl who had checked me out earlier had mercy on me and gestured to a silver container on a table near the wall.

"Water is over there," she said, extending her hand for a shake. "I'm Genesis."

After a second, I relented and shook her hand, embarrassed that I was sweating like a pig.

I nodded, not really listening, and headed over to the water. She watched me go. I hated that I was being so brutal, but I was not in the mood for pleasantries. Cory followed me. He looked like crap. His face was still bruised, and I could tell he was having a tough time breathing.

"Dude, I can't do this." Cory complained behind me, still breathing hard. "I need to bail." I grabbed a silver cup and turned on the water spigot. "I never enlisted in any corps posse." He said the last word with disdain. "My grandmother is probably having a coronary . . ."

I cut him off, looking down at my cup. "My brother is dead." Silence followed.

"You're kidding." He looked at me all tentative, not sure of how to react.

"Do I look like I'm kidding?" I turned to him, my eyes fierce with anger. "An SR mercenary picked him off in the middle of the street in the Backlands like it was target practice." Each word was infused with hatred for the SR.

"Goro . . . man, I'm sorry." His face went pale. "I don't know what to say. When? How? No, never mind . . . ." He waved his hand back and forth to say forget it.

"Stay, please," I asked him, bending over and placing my hands on the table in front of me. "Truth is, I need you and Alex. You two are my best friends. If you leave, who knows what will happen. At least here, we have a chance to do something, to fight." I couldn't look at him.

He nodded his head, still eyeing me warily. "All right. I'll do what I can, bro."

"You girlfriends done over there?" Luc shot in our direction. The rest of the group had clustered around him with one knee down and one knee up, their arms resting on their bent knee. I wandered over to where Alex had followed suit, and saw that Cory was still standing by the water canister. Everyone was quiet and watching while Cory stayed put and looked at me. He finally walked over and knelt next to me. I threw him a grateful glance.

"Wow . . . I'm a thousand years old now." Luc shot an annoyed look at Cory and me, starting again.

"My name is Luc, and I am your instructor for land warfare," he dictated as if we had forgotten and were still in first denomination. "Some of the most important topics I will teach you are search and mercenary removal, gathering intel, handling POWs, and covert infiltration. When launching a full-scale rebellion against the SR, paying attention to details means the difference between basic survival or being dumped in a random ditch. But then, we do not allow ourselves to be taken prisoner in the first place." I got the distinct impression that he had resisted the SR before.

"On the schedule today is training in recovery techniques, which we will cover later, but right now I will pair you up and give you instructions. Remember, attention to detail is everything, people." He started partnering us, and as I suspected, Alex, Cory, and I were coupled with people we didn't know from Adam. I ended up with the Genesis chick, and I didn't know if Luc was testing me or if he was just amusing himself for kicks.

"But first, a quick contact combat review on punches. Some of you are not punching through the target; you keep dropping your hands. One of you go grab focus mitts, and the other start throwing straight punches, three on the right, three on the left. Then right/left combos. I will circle the room and correct your fighting stance if needed." *Good God*, I thought. *I don't want to hurt this girl.*

She returned with mitts and used her teeth to tighten the wrist straps. I looked at her 5' 4" frame and began throwing punches, keeping it lighter than usual.

"Um, are you playing patty cake or something?" She asked this with a rude smirk. I dropped my hands.

"I don't want to thrash you," I replied to what I thought was rather obvious.

"Don't worry about me." She sniffed. "Let's go!" She waved me forward with the mitts.

I punched her right mitt as hard as I could by way of answering. She took a step back, shaking her hand from the impact, but simply said, "Yes, that's more like it."

I then pounded away, forgetting that I was punching a girl of about 110 pounds.

"Switch!" Luc yelled over the din. She took off the mitts and threw them at my head. I caught them fast before they hit my open eyeballs, and I squinted at her through dripping sweat.

"Okay, let's see what you got." I was impressed she survived my beating.

Her wrapped wrists started flying, and I had to give credit where credit was due. She was strong for a girl. She didn't let up either, not for a minute. The palms of my hands smarted a little when Luc called a cease-fire. I looked her over while tossing the mitts to the side. She was cute in a pixie-sweet, girl-next-door kind of way. I wanted to ask her how she ended up in this dungeon when Luc started in on us again.

"Get in groups of six and let's head to the rec field." We were going outside? I marveled at how we could manage this covertly when everyone started jogging out of the room with Luc in the lead. I searched for Alex and Cory, and caught a quick glimpse of Cory looking downright haggard. Alex looked okay but tired, but I wasn't expecting him to look like he was having fun at an amusement park or anything. Maybe I could ask Mickey to have Luc cut Cory loose for a bit. *Where the hell was Mickey?* I thought, disgruntled.

As we rounded a corner down one of the corridors, I saw several doors that looked like they led to classrooms. Call me a monkey's uncle if I didn't see an additional thirty people or so in each classroom we passed! Various instructors were engaged in lectures in front of control panel screens, going over God knows what. I caught a quick shot of Mickey through one door, pointing at a 3D holographic image in front of him, but I couldn't see what. How many men and women were living here? We jogged past what looked like an open mess hall, and there were folks in there as well, eating breakfast or heck, lunch by now.

We jogged out through the last door into the great outdoors, and I glanced up at the hazy horizon, seeing some sort of black screen covering a medium sized courtyard. It allowed light in, and I could see the sky, but I assumed it provided camouflage so that the SR's satellites couldn't look down and see in. Cool. My eyes swept all around, taking in the broken structures, crumbling buildings, abandoned helicrafts, and other obstacles, creating the perfect landscape for urban warfare training.

Luc ordered everyone to take a knee near the opening of a dilapidated bridge.

"The first drill we're going to cover is called Snatch and Grab," he barked. "Now, this training normally takes about two months, but today we are going to just go over logistics and do a slow-mo run-through. I'm aware that the new indocs are probably lost somewhat, but hang tight." He perused the throng with his sharp eyes for Alex, Cory, and me. I caught Cory's poker stare across the courtyard. I hoped that my reassuring nod would embolden him to soldier on. *Stay with me, buddy,* I prayed to myself. Except that all of a sudden, I saw him bend over and puke his banana peanut butter breakfast all over the ground.

Aw, hell. I sprinted over to Cory and Alex, not caring if I was breaking a rule. I approached the two of them, trying to look cheerful.

Cory was still bent over, wiping his mouth, and I slapped him on the back. Alex just looked at me through lowered eyelids. Good, I could hear Luc carrying on with his orders in the background.

"How you doin', Cory? You look like you've been run over by a freight train," I joked.

"Yeah, I feel like it too." His eyes were bloodshot and watering like crazy. "Gimme a minute." He shook his head to punctuate the truth behind his request. He straightened and started ambling over to a low crumbling wall to cop a squat when I heard Luc cease his commands to the group.

"Am I boring you three stooges?" he shouted at us. All heads whipped in our direction.

"We need a moment," I declared boldly, not giving a damn what his response would be.

Luc's steady eyes bored into mine, looking like he wanted to despleen me right then and there. A short pause followed, and I heard him say something indistinct to the group, who fanned out into the landscape in groups of six. *Here we go*, I thought, as I saw him making his way over to us in my peripheral vision.

I braced myself for the expected verbal assault, but to my utter surprise, he softened his tone. "Okay, you men can take the rest of the day. What do you need?" He asked Cory.

"Um, I need a medic," Cory replied in an irritated tone. Luc put a thumb under Cory's chin, lifting his face and patted his other thumb around Cory's bruised right eye, scrutinizing his condition. Cory winced at being touched, while Alex and I just looked on. "You guys can keep . . . training . . . ." he finished, sounding hammered.

"Don't be a dumbass," I said to him, leaving no room for argument.

"José!" Luc hollered toward one of the trainees. A tall, stocky guy came running over looking seriously ripped. "Escort these indocs to the hospital ward."

"Yes, sir!" He waved for us to follow him. I shot a glance toward Luc, not sure if this was a trick or a ruse, but he had already moved on.

When we were all back in the corridors, he turned to me and held out his hand for me to shake. "José," he said, and shook my hand in a vice grip.

"I'm Goro." I returned his firm handshake. "Alex and Cory." I motioned to my friends in turn. He nodded his head but said nothing more. I felt a twinge of failure, like I was bowing out or something, but I wasn't about to leave my friends.

José stopped outside a doorway and indicated that this was it. "Good luck," were his parting words, and he took off back the way we had come. And then it hit me: I suddenly felt depressed as hell. I just wanted to find some hole in the ground and crawl in it, curling up in the fetal position. *Pull yourself together*, I told myself.

We wandered into the room as a group, and a gray-haired man with a beard approached us. "Take a seat over here." He guided Cory with gentle hands. Instead of sitting on the gurney, Cory full on laid down with his hands on his head. "What happened, may I ask?" the man inquired, laying Cory's hands by his sides. He scrutinized his wounds. "Too much sparring?"

"SR brutality," I answered, my body stiffening. "Wha' d'ya think?"

He just nodded, pursing his lips. "You're going to be fine, young man. I've seen worse, I'm afraid." He walked over to a cabinet and pulled out a metal instrument.

"You men new?" he casually asked as he walked back over and raised Cory's shirt sleeve to administer the medicine. "I haven't seen you around," he mentioned as if he regularly walked the corridors. As the doctor pressed the head of the metal instrument against Cory's upper arm, Cory didn't even bother asking what he was giving him.

"New indocs." Alex rolled his eyes, putting air quotes around the word indocs.

"Welcome," the doctor attempted in a light manner, but it came out strained instead. He pulled Cory's sleeve back down. "This will take the edge off and begin the healing process, and you need to lay low for a couple of days, lots of liquids, soup, that sort of thing." He smiled. "No heavy exercise." Cory did not protest and looked like he was relaxing into a sweet daze. "You can crash here, by all means," he said to Cory, who looked like he was out. He pointed to some chairs nearby, indicating we could join him if we chose.

With nothing better to do, I grabbed two and set them down next to Cory. Alex and I dropped into the chairs.

"Goro," Alex said, "those dudes out there are really built. They look like professionals, for cryin' out loud—they're huge!" He was talking low. "How long are we going to do this? I mean, technically, we are being held against our will."

"You wanna go back?" I asked him while staring at Cory, not at all pleased with his whining. "Be my guest." He just looked at me, surprised.

"Well, my life is no picnic—you'd agree," he glanced at me, and I nodded, "and I wanna be a badass and blow up the SR, yes, but I didn't in my wildest dreams think your revolution plans would happen, like, *now*." He picked at something on his finger, looking distraught. "I thought you were just talking out of your ass and I'm starved, man! I haven't even had lunch yet . . . ."

"Alex!" I lifted my hand, palm out, stopping him. "My five-year-old brother was murdered right in front of my eyes yesterday in cold blood." I sharpened each word as I glared at him head on. "Either you're with me, or you can get the hell out." My eyes flashed.

"What?" he said, panic stricken, watching my reaction, his eyes wide. He looked away, shaking his head in unbelief, and glanced back at me, tearing up. "No . . . ."

"Yes." I punctuated the word, nodding at him emphatically.

He lowered his head and wiped his forehead with the palm of his hand. "I don't know what to say, Goro." We sat, each in his own world.

He was the first to break the silence between us.

"Damn."

"Yep, that's about right," I said. "Look, man, just do this with me. I need you." I flicked a piece of dirt off the leg of Mickey's jeans. I hated that I sounded downright needy, and I was pretty much begging him, but it was no time to be concerned with my pride.

"This is you and me . . . ." I gestured between us with my thumb and pinky. "Cory, Zan, our families, all the good people who aren't SR . . . Josiah," I finished in an anguished voice. He looked over at me when he heard my voice faltering. He held out his fist and, after a second, I reciprocated.

"I'm with you, man," he bumped my fist, his eyes telling me he was serious. I exhaled, grateful he had concurred. We needed to pull every string, pull out every stop, and call in every single favor if we were going to survive this siege on the Sovereign Regime.

Chapter 17

"Hell is empty, and all the devils are here."

—William Shakespeare

The atmosphere was cold. A dark-robed man halted in front of the tall, double oak doors. Without warning, the elaborately carved wooden doors opened inward. He took a tentative step inside.

"Come," said a deep menacing voice from within.

He walked forward until he reached the center circle of the chamber, where he stood under the single candlelit chandelier.

"There are stirrings . . . ." he was cautious, his eyes on the floor, ". . . within the Alliance."

"And what of them," the voice continued in shadow.

"They speak of insurrection."

"Eliminate them."

"The metropolis is vast, my lord."

"Silence!" the voice demanded. "Spare me your platitudes."

"Caution is advised, Dav—" the man blurted, but stopped short, afraid.

"What did you call me?" the voice growled, barely audible.

"Forgive me! I . . . ." The man's voice quavered.

A hand extended from the depths of the dark toward the center of the chamber, and the man arched his back, making violent incoherent noises in a strangled voice. He fell backward, cracking his skull on the marble floor, his body spasming in searing pain, and then he went still.

Two men emerged and dragged the cadaverous man by his robe out of the chamber.

"Ash Sheitan," the voice commanded in an icy tone, after the men had departed.

A second tall man stepped forward, his bald head shorn smooth and pallid, glinting in the feeble light.

"Yes, my lord," the man said to the black void facing him.

"Unearth this congregation and eradicate them," the voice decreed with derisive authority.

"Yes, my lord," the man complied again, bowing low. He turned and strode silently out through the chamber's entrance.

Chapter 18

"Know thyself, know thy enemy. A thousand battles, a thousand victories . . . ."

—Sun Tzu

A couple of hours later Alex and I found our way back to the outdoor arena, leaving Cory to his nap. When we stepped outside, we found the area vacated.

"Where is everyone?" Alex said. I spun around to head back inside with him following close on my heels, and we walked swiftly down the corridor.

"Where's the fire?" Alex joked.

I don't know why I was in a hurry. I didn't really have anywhere to go, but I still pressed forward, peering into empty classrooms as I rushed. The mess hall was devoid of people and quiet as well.

"I don't know," I pondered. I was curious now, heading to the large inner training room. Silence greeted us as we stepped into the room.

"Good grief," I muttered in a huff. "Over a hundred people have to be here somewhere." Alex glanced at me. I led us to the kitchen and our cell, but it was empty.

We returned to the training room, looking all around.

"Are they sleeping or something? Okay . . . what's down there?" Alex pointed to another corridor off to the back of the room that I hadn't seen before. We walked over and I poked my head into the darkened hall.

"I can't see a damn thing," I mumbled, feeling the inside walls for a scanner to turn on the lights, forgetting that I no longer had a chip. I was about to turn around when I heard shouting coming from far down the corridor.

"Wait," I said, and stopped to listen again. "Stop breathing in my ear, Alex."

My interest piqued, and I started down the hall, instinctively putting my hands out in front of me in the dark. Alex followed, with us both moving as fast as we could under the circumstances. There was a faint light emanating from the end of the corridor showing a flight of steps going down into the depths of the earth. The shouting had stopped.

I crept down the stairs, Alex close on my heels as we descended a spiral stone stairway. At the bottom, though, the light went dark again. I extended my hands in front of me and inched forward down yet another hallway. My outstretched hands eventually brushed against a door at the end of the corridor. It was pitch black, but I could hear commotion on the other side. I banged on the door with my fist.

"Hey!" I yelled, feeling like an idiot. Alex hovered next to me, letting me do all the shouting. The door whooshed open and Mickey stuck his head out, blinding us both with a light source he was wearing around his head.

"Goro! Alex! What are you guys doing, banging on the door?" He asked this in complete surprise, as if I was a pizza delivery guy who'd just discovered his secret lair. Alex and I just stood there covering our eyes.

"Mickey, what the hell are you wearing?" I shouted. "Will you tone that thing down? Move that light outta our faces!" He moved the light beam to the side of his head and waved us inside. "We were looking for signs of life," I explained, as Alex and I entered the room. "The compound is empty." I saw spots and closed my eyes for a few seconds.

"Nah, we're here running ops," he answered, as if I had lost my marbles and it was no big deal. "No one's jumped ship yet." He laughed.

Alex and I just stared at him. I felt like I was on the outside of a not-too-funny inside joke, and everyone was laughing because the punch line was me. I could hear shouting in the distance and the sound of people running back and forth. It was still dark, but little rays of light shone through here and there, despite the tall cement wall blocking our view from the chaos.

"We are carrying out the evasive tactical drill I've been going over the last few days," Mickey dictated in a calm voice.

"What is this?" I gestured around me.

"This," Mickey waved a finger around over his head, "is an exact replica of one of the floor plans of Davio's lair in the Dominion. We call it the Labyrinth or Lab, for short. It's not quite to scale, but it works."

"Judas Priest . . . ." Alex breathed, impressed as all get out. He whistled low. "How did you manage to get the schematics?"

"We have our tricks," Mickey replied with confidence. "We use the Lab to practice advancing on the enemy, running a plethora of ops and exercises, over and over again, so that when we *do* end up storming the castle, so to speak, we will know every angle possible to ensure the most successful outcome." He sounded like he was in his element, back in a classroom going over tactical training maneuvers. Alex and I just looked at him.

"Sweet!" Alex exclaimed. "Wish I'd come to Disneyland sooner!" Alex referenced an ancient amusement park that we had learned about years ago in the Hall of History, but that had long since vanished. He had gotten an A on that report, I recalled.

"Mickey," I started, "We are behind the corner, here," I complained, "having just arrived in the last few days, and Cory is laid up in the medic's ward."

"Psssh, nonsense, you will catch up with us in no time," Mickey reassured us as if we'd be martial arts experts by tomorrow. "Look, go up in observation room three and watch us in action to get a feel for what's in store for you guys." He slapped me heartily on the shoulder and ushered us down one side of the wall to another spiral staircase that led up into the darkness. He pointed upward and then left us.

Alex and I started up the stairs, with me feeling like I was late for the opera and was making a rude entrance. When we reached the top, we walked down a long open catwalk into a low-lit room. A massive picture window was set into the wall at an angle facing downward. I saw Luc standing in front of the window wearing an earpiece and some sort of metal glasses that I suspected allowed him to see in the dark. He was focused on the action below. He lifted the glasses and glanced behind his shoulder at us, then went right back to barking orders.

"Tiffnie!" he yelled. "Watch your six! And you're not covering Michael!" He put a finger on his earpiece. "Son of a . . . !"

I walked closer to the window and gazed down. What I saw made me gasp. I waved Alex over to join me. It sure was a labyrinth of many buildings stretching as far as the eye could see. The room below extended in each direction for at least a mile; I couldn't make out either end at all. I observed a patchwork of open rooms and halls with no ceilings. A large courtyard in one section had a circular fountain in the center, with water spouting out of the marble vase perched on the shoulder of the woman depicted in the statue. Every room was lit by minimal candlelight except for a few near the courtyard; some candles were hanging in chandeliers, and some candles were on what looked like tables. There was very little furniture, however.

I saw numerous black drones flying over the array of hallways, targeting the stealth teams below with red lasers. I saw someone raise her rifle and take aim, shooting down one of the drones. The red lasers powered off as the drone landed somewhere behind a wall.

"Holy crap!" Alex said under his breath, amazed. "This is sick!"

"What have I told you about stalking, Kevin? Six inches at a time!" Luc ordered. "How many times do I have to remind you?" It was all Greek to me, but I had to admit I was itching to dive into training headfirst and learn as much as I could and as fast as possible.

What caught my eyes next was the darker section of two or three rooms near the courtyard that were not lit at all. I could just barely make out what looked like a large curtain or drapery that hung near one corner of the darkened area. The largest chandelier I had seen yet was hanging above the larger of the rooms, but it wasn't lit.

"What's that?" I blurted out in Luc's direction, forgetting for a moment that he was busy commandeering the troops below. He didn't answer me right away.

"Davio's inner chamber," he replied out of the corner of his mouth. "No one has ever been inside, so we don't have the layout for that area." He then pointed to another room way off to the side. "And that is the main control room of the Dominion." He stopped and yelled again, causing Alex to clap his hands over his ears. "Joel! Do *not* take that kill shot! You are out of range!" He threw up his hands and started pacing in front of the window, cursing under his breath. I backed up, pulling Alex with me to give the raging bull some room.

The mention of my father's name gave me pause; it was not a common name. I was suddenly overcome by a massive wave of anxiety for my family. Josiah's memorial service had probably been held by now.

Get a grip, my inner voice yelled. I stiffened my resolve and decided to focus on what I could do *now* to help them.

Alex smacked my arm and murmured, "Whoa . . . ." breaking me out of my trance. He pointed to a guy wielding what looked like an AT-4 on his shoulder.

"That's not real, is it?" I asked Luc, not caring if I was interrupting him at this point.

"Of course it's real; we bury the casualties out in the rec yard," he said to my stunned face. He watched my reaction and then gave up. Humor wasn't his strongest suit. "No, son, this is a sophisticated form of laser tag. Parts of their suits glow red when they're hit, depending on where . . . you know how it goes." I nodded, looking again at that blackened area of Davio's chamber, making a mental note of where everything was positioned.

I had never been inside Davio's territory, let alone ever been near the Dominion. I knew where it was located, but I never had a reason to go there. It was like Fort Knox and so heavily guarded that it was downright stupid for anyone to attempt to breach its walls unless someone was down on his luck and wanted to embark on a suicide mission. The three feet thick iron and steel fortress walls surrounding the Dominion were impenetrable and impossible to breach. There was one main gate, which was manned twenty-four hours a day, seven days a week, three hundred sixty-five days a year, and I don't know if anyone was sure of any other smaller exits or entrances located anywhere else in the walls.

It amazed me that someone had collected the blueprints and had taken the time to construct an entire replica of the place. It was a giant maze! The only logical deduction was that someone who *had* been SR at one time had defected or been converted to the ADF, and they had provided this intel in return. *That would be a great campfire story*, I thought fascinated.

"I am so in!" Alex exclaimed, all excited. "Where do I sign?" He was downright giddy.

"Okay, guys, wrap it up!" Luc shouted. He pulled his earpiece out. "I can't watch anymore." He sighed, starting for the walkway. Alex and I followed him like drooling robots down the stairs and into a large side room that had plenty of light. I was fascinated with this whole new development we had just been made privy to. Alex and I blinked our eyes to adjust to the sudden brightness. Pretty soon, sweaty young men and women started filing into the room, unlatching their vests and hanging them on the magnetic wall. The room became crowded with twenty-five or so people, and one guy approached Luc, glanced at us and said, "My rifle trigger is jamming, boss."

"Why'd you pull us out early?" asked a girl with bright red hair. He shot her a look that said "don't ask" and inspected the rifle that had been handed to him. Mickey appeared just then and said, "All right, everyone, go eat. You two come with me." He indicated that Alex and I should follow him.

"That wasn't everyone," I posed the question to Mickey as we jogged behind him. "It looked like I saw around a hundred or so people earlier today."

"You're right, there are five observation rooms spread out in various positions throughout the course, and just Luc's crew is debriefing in that particular room," Mickey explained.

"So, there are, like, teams or something?" Alex asked.

"Something like that," Mickey responded, bringing us through the schoolhouse and past the quiet classrooms. "I never did get to complete your tour. No matter, you'll see everything soon enough." He led us into the mess hall. "Eat," he gestured toward the trays and chow line that was forming fast.

Alex and I joined the line of people after grabbing trays. We went through the motions, putting our trays up on the counter to be served.

I glanced at the food that was plopped onto our plates. *Not bad*, I thought, *considering*. It looked like spaghetti and bread rolls, with salad and corn. We grabbed a table that was empty and sat down, devouring our meals. I had forgotten somehow that human beings still need to eat at least three meals a day. I was famished. I wasn't quite sure what time it was, but it felt like late afternoon. It could have been the middle of the night for all I knew.

Several guys and a couple of girls joined us at the table. I recognized José and Genesis, as well as the red-haired girl from earlier.

"Michael," one guy with a buzz cut announced while stabbing his chest with his thumb. "This is Jeff and Tanya," he pointed at each with the same thumb.

"Tiffnie," the red-haired girl said, holding out her hand for a civilized handshake.

"Hi," I said to everyone. "Alex and Goro," I said, indicating who was who.

"Unusual name," the Michael dude said, looking at me.

"Unusual guy," Alex shot right back at him.

"Thanks. My dad gave it to me for my birthday," I quipped. A few people chuckled at my attempt at humor. "How long have you been here?" I asked no one in particular, biting down on a dinner roll, changing the subject.

"Four months for Jeff, Scott, and me," Tiffnie answered first. "Three and change for Michael, José, and Tanya . . . and?" She looked at Genesis for an answer.

"Six months," Genesis finished for her, buttering her corn on the cob.

"The veteran of the crew," Alex mused. "I better watch myself." He smirked.

"How did you, um . . . enroll?" I inquired, trying not to sound too interested.

Genesis glanced up at me. "What, you didn't enroll?" She sounded like she was mocking me. I wasn't sure what to make of it, but Alex jumped in.

"Ha! Luc showed up on my doorstep and told me this yahoo needed my help." He gestured to me with his elbow. "I asked him, 'What now?' Little did I know that I was in for the roller coaster ride of my life."

"That's you, moron, always up for adventure." I raised my eyebrows at him. "And you?" I directed at Genesis.

She looked down at her food and mumbled, "Nothing exciting, believe me."

Tiffnie glanced over at her and a look crossed her face that I couldn't decipher. *Hmmm, stay tuned for later*, I noted.

"What's after this?" Alex asked, raring to go, throwing his napkin down on his tray.

"Dude, aren't you wiped?" I muttered to him under my breath.

"Someone's a little too eager-beaverish," Tiffnie quipped, not hearing me. "We have rec time, or you can just relax or hit the hay." She swallowed the last of her milk. "We sometimes have to get up at four-thirty." She sat back in her chair, shoving her hands in the pockets of her black hoodie.

"Oh, hell to the NO . . . !" Alex protested, shaking his head. We all looked at him. He jumped up, ready to bolt. "Let's rock and roll!" We all stared. No one moved.

"Whatever." He turned to leave.

"Whoa, whoa, whoa . . . I know you weren't raised in a barn," said an older ADF man who had been patrolling the mess hall with a frown, gesturing to the tray Alex had left sitting on the table.

"My bad." Alex saluted the guy and dutifully picked up his tray, taking it over to the conveyor belt where dirty dishes were deposited.

"Good meeting y'all," I threw out as I followed Alex.

“Dude, let’s hit that rec yard again and run!” Alex started, but I cut him off.

“Why are you pumped up all of a sudden? Look, you can go play with your friends in the sandbox, but I am gonna check on Cory.” I turned in the direction of the hospital ward.

“Hold up.” Alex put a hand on my arm, stopping me. “You’re not his keeper, Goro. Who made you the dad?”

I shrugged free and kept moving. “Come or go, your choice,” I remarked in a monotone voice.

“Wow . . . okay . . . such a naysayer,” I heard him mutter. I listened to his footsteps walking away from me and felt a pang of remorse, but kept walking. I felt bad, but didn’t want to deal with anymore whining. If my best friend started in on me, I was afraid I would snap, along with my last thread of sanity.

Chapter 19

"Take the first step in faith. You don't have to see the whole staircase; just take the first step."

—Martin Luther King, Jr.

When I got to the hospital ward, Cory was not where I'd last seen him. He had either left or been moved to another location. A woman looked up when I entered, giving me a curious once over. I didn't see the gray-haired doctor anywhere.

"Where's Cory?" I asked the medical assistant sitting at a control panel.

"Who?" She just shrugged. "Check the dorms."

I dismissed the question with a shake of my head.

"Never mind," I muttered, and headed back to the mess hall, having no idea where the dorms were, finally deciding to look for

Genesis and her peeps again. When I approached the table we had been sitting at, only Genesis was there, sitting with her chin propped on her folded hands. She threw me a bored glance as I sat down across from her.

"You in a foul mood?" I ventured, crossing my arms in front of me. "What's up?" I attempted to sound concerned without wanting to pry.

"Ah, it's nothing." she waved her hand to diminish the importance of whatever she was mulling over. She sat there for a minute, picking at one of her nails, and I just watched her.

"M'kay." I got up. "Can you direct me to the barn where the herd sleeps?"

"I'll take you there, how's that?" She offered, chuckling at my attempt to lighten her up.

"Even better." I threw her a thin smile as she stood up. I studied her body from behind as she led me to yet another side corridor, her hands in her back pockets. *Not bad*, I thought.

When we got to an open archway, I saw about fifty bunk beds lined up on each side of the room. *Great—barracks*, I thought, sighing. The last thing I wanted was to have a massive sleepover with a hundred people I didn't know. Maybe I could sweet talk Mickey into letting me have that shoebox of a cell off the kitchen, which didn't look so bad after all, I mused. I scanned the room for Cory, my eyes landing on him about midway down the room. He was spread eagle on a lower bunk. Genesis and I walked over to him, and I bent down to examine his face. He looked a heck of a lot better. I debated whether to rouse him or just let him sleep.

"Dare I ask what happened to him?" Genesis inquired.

"The SR beat the hell out of him during their interrogation concerning me, I'm guessing," I said quietly.

"You?"

"Long story," I replied, not wanting to get into it. "It's personal."

"Yeah, everything is personal, m'kay?" She couldn't suppress the strained tone of irritation in her voice. She looked directly into my eyes then turned and left. I let her go without a word, sitting down on the bunk next to Cory.

Just then Alex walked in, bee-lining over to me. "Dude," he began, looking like he wanted to launch into a sermon.

"Look, Alex . . . ." I was in no mood for this.

"No, you look," he said abruptly. "You may reek with an overconfident sense of self-worth and have a damaged touch of self-absorption, but it doesn't give you license to treat your friends like cow manure."

"What?" I almost laughed in his face. "I don't reek of anything." My tone was dead serious.

"You think this is a game?" he asked me, his face flushed.

"No, Alex! What the hell is lodged in *your* ass?" I was getting heated now. He paced a few steps then turned back to me. "Stop acting like a clown!" I yelled. Alex paused, looking at me intently.

"You and me, right?" He mimicked pointing back and forth between us like I had done earlier. He was silent for a second, letting me get the message.

"You're like my brother, Goro. I'd take a laser hit for you—you know that," he reminded me. God, he was so emo. I apologized and slapped him on the leg, mostly to get this awkward moment over with.

"This our new digs?" He looked around at the neat beds and footlockers. One great thing about Alex was he never held a grudge. When it was over, it was over. "Think you could bounce a quarter off this?" He chuckled, pressing up and down with his fists on the bunk Cory was lying on.

Tiffnie stuck her head into the room. "Some of us are playing Signs if you want to join us." She left with a parting glance.

Alex rolled his eyes at me. "I'm gonna take a wild guess here and say she thinks yer smokin' hot."

"Stop." I shoved him with my bicep.

"Ooh, that's getting meaty," he joked in a high singsong girl's voice, squeezing my upper arm. I grabbed his neck in a headlock.

"Dumbass," I muttered. "We should prolly mingle," I agreed, not making any moves to get up.

"The sooner we befriend peeps, the better."

We followed the laughter to one of the classrooms and saw Genesis, Michael, Tiffnie, Jeff, Tanya, José, and a couple other dudes all sitting in chairs arranged in a circle.

"Hey guys, this is Kevin and Scott." Tiffnie introduced the two additional guys to us that I recognized from the schoolhouse earlier this morning. They just nodded at us. "Take a seat. The way you play this game is everyone picks a visual sign that is unique to them. For example, my sign is thumbs up," she stuck her thumb out like she wanted to hitch a ride. "Genesis's sign is . . . ." She looked to Genesis to flash her sign, which looked like a gun she made with her thumb and forefinger on her right hand.

"Understand?" Genesis asked.

"Pick a sign," Michael said to me in a bored tone.

"I got it, thanks," I said to him, too tired to be polite. I flashed a hang-loose sign at the group, consisting of only my thumb and my pinky facing out, with my inner three fingers folded down. Tiffnie nodded her head. I could tell she was someone who made things happen. I'd never have to worry about her not taking the lead in organizing . . . whatever, if I was ever grouped with her in the future.

Alex circled his thumb and forefinger in an A-OK sign for everyone to see. "I guess I'll do this one."

"You guys all show your signs again so we know who's who," Tiffnie ordered.

"Are you sure we should be throwing up gang signs?" Alex laughed at his own dumb joke. I rolled my eyes a little. Leave it to Alex to goof around no matter what the circumstances.

Jeff was the only one who bothered to answer. "Man, that's so twenty-first century." He put his thumbs together in a shadow bird, flapping his other eight fingers as wings. Kevin put his hands on top of one another, fingers facing forward, and he rotated his thumbs on either side.

"Turtle," he clarified for Alex and me.

"Cute," Alex quipped. Scott rubbed his nose with his index finger, Michael ran his hand through what was left of his crew cut, and Tanya stuck her pinky in her ear, wiggling it around like she was scratching an itch.

"José?" Tiffnie asked the last person in the group. He flexed his bicep for us. *Of course the biggest dude here has to show us little people how cut he is*, I ridiculed inwardly. "Good, let's start!" Tiffnie announced in a lilted voice.

"Hang on, what's the objective of this miming game?" Alex stopped her, pretending to mime a wall with his hands.

"Oh yes, directions," she continued, with me feeling like a moron. "One person sits in the middle of the circle. When their back is turned, I throw someone else's sign to a person; say I throw Michael's sign to him, running my hand through my hair. Then he throws his sign, running his hand through his micro hair, and he follows with someone else's sign right after, like Genesis's gun and so on and so forth. The person in the middle has to guess who the very last person was who threw a sign. So it's like, the person is spinning in the center, trying to catch someone in the act. If they guess correctly who the last person was to throw a sign, that person has to be in the middle of the circle next. It's harder than it seems."

I was lost, but didn't wanna seem dumb, so I just nodded my head and hoped I would catch on as the game progressed.

"Can we just do a practice run?" Alex asked, with me breathing a sigh of relief. *Thanks, homie.*

"Sure!" Tiffnie chirped.

It ended up being more fun than I thought, and it took my mind off everything that I didn't want to think about. Alex, bless his heart, ended up in the middle of the circle so many times I felt sorry for him. The guy sucked at the game. I was pretty quick at nailing the person who had gone last, so I didn't spend much time in the middle, thank goodness. I wasn't about to be concerned with impressing some girls. It was just the whole male competition ego thing that so often plagues us guys.

Genesis and I exchanged looks every now and then, with me trying to smooth things over between us with my eyes. I could be rude sometimes because I expected everyone to get with my program. They were either on my side, or they weren't. I don't know if that could be classified as cockiness or confidence, but Alex's earlier lecture resonated in my head, and I decided to be more gracious with people. God knows enough instructors at the Hall of Academics told me to have more grace.

The game ended up going about an hour, but soon people were getting tired, so everyone broke up and headed back to the dorms. I followed the crowd like a zombie, forgetting that I didn't have a bunk with my name on it yet. I stopped short when we entered the dormitory. I didn't see Cory anywhere; he had disappeared again.

"Oh . . . we don't know where we're sleeping," I said to no one in particular.

"Uh, yeah," Alex agreed, nodding his head. "Being newbies and all," he stated the obvious. The rest of the group had made their way to their bunks and were getting ready to call it a night, not really hearing us. I chose that moment to motion for Alex to leave with me.

"Come on," I mouthed at him. Like a dutiful little puppy, he followed me back the way we had come.

"Where are we going?" He asked me a little louder when we were out of earshot. "You're always such a rebel," he added. I didn't answer, but kept striding forward. "Dude, slow down! I'm bush-whacked." Alex complained.

"Yeah, you are whack. Who wanted to run laps earlier?" He merely sighed behind me.

I moved back through quiet corridors to the kitchen area, hoping to find Mickey or Robbie. Sure enough, I saw Mickey sitting alone at the large wooden table. I plopped down next to him with Alex following suit. He looked up from his hand panel, eyebrows raised.

"Yezzz?" he asked with a grin. Such a positive guy.

"Game on," I announced to the air. "I'm in. I'll train as fast as I can and learn everything possible in order to take down the SR—whatever you need me to do."

"Me too. Well, me and a hundred other folks," Alex chimed in. "Playuh, play on!"

"Great. You are telling me something I already know because . . . ." Mickey paused for me to fill in the blanks. He sounded like Luc.

"I know I haven't been exactly the most agreeable person the last two days, and my attitude has been crappy." This was my version of saying I was sorry. I glanced over at Alex who was busy nodding his head, concurring with me. He saw the irked look in my eyes and stopped bobbing his head.

Mickey put down his control panel and leaned back in his chair. "Son," he said after a beat, "this is it." He spread his arms wide, taking in the whole kitchen. In a serious, sober tone, he added, "If there was ever a time to take up arms and fight for the good of mankind, it's now. We live in the wickedest, most venomous, perverted, and downright crappy time in the history of the world." He shook his head as if he was about to have a meltdown. "There aren't even words to describe . . . ."

I sat horrified for a minute, thinking he was going to burst into tears, but he just looked into my eyes again and smiled a thin smile. I nodded, letting his words sink in solid.

"Hear, hear." Alex pumped his fist in the air half-heartedly, breaking the silence. Guess the ambience was too moody for him. Mickey gave a short laugh and wiped his closed eyelids with the palms of his hands. He looked drained, showing his age.

"Okay, you know what I need." Mickey said it more as a fact than a question. I saw him lower his eyes to my chest once again.

He wants my grandfather Howard's chip. I sighed, reluctant to give it up. I reached under my shirt and grabbed the chip. I paused a moment then lifted the chain over my head, handing it to Mickey in a solemn gesture, my eyes never leaving it.

He took it, smiling at me with relief, it seemed. I watched like a forlorn puppy as he put the chain around his own neck, holding up the dangling chip in his fingers.

"Don't lose it," I whispered to the air around us.

"Trust me," he returned in a strong voice.

"What's on it?" Alex blurted out the question of the day, asking what he and I were both wondering. We all stared at the chip as if the balance of life itself was encased within the micro plastic.

"You don't know this, but your grandpappy and I were friends once upon a time. You might recognize my name . . . Mark Mitchell Bradley," he said to me, dropping the chip on his chest.

Wait, what? "You're Mitchell?" I asked flabbergasted, stunned into a stupor. He nodded his head.

"Mickey's a nickname I got saddled with years ago." He dismissed it with his hand.

I just stared at him wide-eyed like he was a god. I couldn't believe my luck! I had listened to my grandpa talk for hours about his and Mitchell's antics and missions in days gone by. And now he was sitting next to me, in the flesh.

"Now don't go having me bronzed or anything when I finally kick the bucket," he joked.

"All that time at the Hall of Academics?" I questioned, curious as all get out.

"Eh," he threw out, "I was busy keeping my nose down and cleaning toilets," he said as if it was his dream job of all time.

"And let's not forget selling passcodes to twitter-pated teenage girls," I reminded him pointedly. Mickey snorted under his breath.

"Oh yeah, I forgot about that side gig," he mused, gazing at the ceiling, taking himself back to those times. "I'm sure I assisted many a youth in retrieving the necessary data in establishing happy young love." He cleared his throat and changed the subject. "Okay, you guys tired?"

I cringed as we both shook our heads no, even though we were wiped out. He got up and gestured for us to follow him. Alex and I trailed behind Mickey, so tired I could barely pick up each foot and place one in front of the other, but once again, curiosity had won.

Chapter 20

"Never give up, for that is just the place and time that the tide will turn."

—Harriet Beecher Stowe

When we reached the corridor of classrooms, he took a hard left down a short hallway. He stopped at a doorway, pressed his left forefinger onto a fingerprint scanner, and looked up into a camera mounted on the wall. The door whooshed open. It was blazing hot inside, and I felt uncomfortable in the heat that enveloped us.

I looked around the room and saw about ten men sitting at multiple control panel workstations. I also saw Luc leaning over one of the control panel screens, pointing at something while talking to the panel operator. Mickey walked over to Luc and whispered something to him that Alex and I couldn't hear.

Luc glanced over at Alex and me with an unreadable expression on his face. He looked back at Mickey and nodded his head. I was still shell-shocked from the news of him being my grandpa's buddy.

Mickey came over and told us this was the "brain" of the compound, where encryption programs were run on hacked intel, and where weapons and Nitesite glasses were printed on high-speed 3D printers; it was pretty much the main hub that kept the entire compound fully operational. I picked up a pair of the glasses that I recognized Luc had been wearing earlier. I spaced out a little during Mickey's lecture on computers because I had not been born with a technological bone in my body. I finally stopped him with a raised hand when I was about to fall asleep.

"This is Alex's deal; I suck at technology." I slapped Alex on the shoulder. "He's your man."

I tried to bow out and hang back on the sidelines, but I saw Mickey take off my grandfather's chip and hand it to Luc. I watched Luc give it to a man sitting at one of the panels. I walked over to the man's station, intrigued. Mickey, Alex, Luc, and I then crowded around the man. He took the chip off the chain and pressed it against a small port in one of the control panels. I saw the control port seize each end of the chip. Its perforated steel cover was split down the middle and pulled back on each side by mini metal arms, revealing the inner microscopic matrix of the chip itself.

"Egads!" Alex muttered to himself. "I never knew that's what they looked like inside."

We all stood mesmerized while the man's fingers flew over the touch board in front of him.

"Initiating extraction program now, sir," he informed Mickey, tapping a blue square of light in the corner of his control panel.

"Wonderful," Mickey breathed, his eyes glued to the screen. "Run replication as well." We watched as trillions of symbols and numbers flashed in horizontal lines across the screen. I started to feel dizzy, so I looked away. I noticed that everyone in the room had stopped whatever they were doing and were all staring at the screen with a look of intense concentration on their faces. Was I seeing *hope* in their eyes?

"Did anyone interface with him?" Mickey inquired.

The man did a quick search. "Looks like one person did, but it's truncated."

"And encrypted?" Mickey tried again.

"Yeah, but it just stops on each axis . . . weird . . . ."

"Let me see. He could've shadowed it behind the ADF's main thread and . . . ." Mickey leaned in closer.

"That's not possible," Luc interrupted.

"How is that not possible? Anything is possible with this chip. Howard could've mimicked the main thread as a decoy, unless . . . ."

"Unless what?" I asked. I was getting pissed at Mickey and Luc with all their techno-jargon. I hated not knowing what was going on. "No one's listening to me," I muttered to the humid air, frustrated.

In that moment, the seated man leapt out of his seat, startling us. The strange code streaming across the screen had shot out of the computer screen, taking the form of 3D moving pictures hovering over his workstation. Everyone gasped, circling tight around the images in the center. I squeezed into the ring, enraptured by the video erupting from my grandpa's chip. And then I saw my grandfather, in the flesh, materialize before us. I couldn't tell where he was standing. In a field? In his old dwelling? My eyes welled up with tears.

"Mitchell, my old friend . . . ." My grandfather was speaking as if he were still alive! "If you are seeing this, I am gone, but I have not failed. What you seek is located in the tome we studied years ago, within the category we so often quarreled about." He chuckled over some past familiar memory. "Take it and do with it what needs to be done, and in all things, remember this: *know thy enemy*." He was so serious it spooked me. "Know his general as well as his specific attack methods. Study his armor, his weapons, his doorways . . . ." My grandfather spoke with authority. He paused and softened. "Godspeed . . . I will see you again one day, my friend." I wiped one eye, trying to look like I was rubbing my eyelid. The image of my grandfather faded from our sight, and several rapid 3D images took over.

"Tome?" Alex asked no one in particular. "What the heck is that?"

The 3D images were dark and punctuated from time to time with candlelight. I recognized the large drapery from the rooms I had observed earlier in observation room three. Suddenly, we saw the image of a hand pulling back a dark velvet curtain to reveal a larger inside room. Was that my grandfather's hand?

"Is this what I think it is?" Robbie asked, whistling. "Davio's inner sanctum?"

"Yes . . . but the trick is to find what I hope Howard left there," Mickey replied, focusing on the images, and then his hands got to work. He grasped images within the moving pictures, moved a table aside, lifted what looked like a tall throne, and inspected the overhead chandelier.

"Which is . . . .what?" Alex asked, entranced, his eyes flitting from Mickey to Luc.

"Wait!" Mickey yelled at the computer operator. "Go back!" He had the man shuffle in reverse to one of the previous 3D images. Mickey's eyes brightened with excitement as he zeroed in on an old black book lying open on a large table. He picked up the book, turning the pages yellowed with age as he sifted through the text, which didn't look familiar at all.

"There it is . . . ." Mickey beamed with excitement as he lifted a line of numbers hidden behind the script in one of the paragraphs. He pinched the line of numbers with his thumb and forefinger and tossed it onto another blank grid for clearer viewing. We all turned and inspected the numbers. There were a total of ten numbers, and I didn't have the foggiest idea what they meant. Alex looked over at me, confused. I had a feeling no one else knew what this row of numbers meant either, except for Mickey and Luc.

"Oh . . . a tome is a book." Alex nodded, snickering at his delayed realization.

Mickey and Luc both stared at each other, the light of realization flooding their eyes at the same moment. The room was so quiet you could hear the sweat dripping off my forehead onto the tiled floor.

"Incredible," Luc breathed. "But it's only half the equation, you know that," he directed at Mickey.

"What equation?" I tried again, throwing up my hands in irritation. Mickey turned at last and answered my exasperation.

"You know how each living person has a twenty-digit code that is at the SR's disposal, correct?"

"Yeah?"

"Well, it just so happens that your grandfather discovered and located Davio's twenty-digit code that could possibly . . . just maybe corrupt the SR's mainframe database." Mickey tossed this out to me as if it was common knowledge. "We now have the second half, courtesy of Howard's chip."

"Where's the first half?" I scoffed.

"We already pulled it from your chip," Mickey replied, looking me straight in the eyes.

"Wait, what? My chip?" The hits just kept on coming.

"Your grandfather input the first half in your identity chip when you were born." Mickey answered me like it was no biggie. How come I never knew this? No wonder they wanted me in the ADF: to extract my grandfather's and my info.

"Wow." I took a minute to absorb this new intel. "Um . . . okay, but the whole thing doesn't seem feasible." I was still trying to wrap my mind around all this info being flicked at me.

The men stopped and stared at me as if I had just belched in public. "How's that?" Luc flung his critical eyes my way. Figures.

"Don't you think Davio or his goons would have thought of that already? Seems too cut and dried and . . . obvious." I wasn't buying it—not for a second. "Davio doesn't even *have* an implanted chip. He's the only one who is exempt; everyone knows that."

"You've been here, what . . . three days now? And you have the end all, be all answers?" I had no trouble picking up on Luc's sarcasm. I rolled my eyes.

"With all due respect, sir, I am not implying that I know what's up. It just doesn't jive with how the SR operates. They are way too intelligent for random loopholes." I hoped I sounded a tad contrite . . . just enough to keep Luc from being angry with me. I didn't need him as an enemy.

"Doesn't seem like you're implying at all," Luc countered, his eyes snapping. "You sound pretty explicit to me, kid."

Mickey cut Luc off before he started in again.

"Remember what I said, Goro. This is not a front and center battle with Davio. You just heard your grandpappy."

"Yeah, hah!" I scoffed. "It all looked like Morse code to me." I knew I was being just plain mean at the moment, making fun of everything, but I was so tired I couldn't halt the verbal diarrhea erupting from my mouth.

"Get out your umbrellas folks, he's raining on the parade," Alex muttered out of the side of his mouth.

"Excuse me?" Luc cocked his head at me, not bothering to hide the rude edge in his voice.

"What armor?" I exclaimed. "What the hell doorways is my grandfather referring to?" I couldn't stop. "There is only *one* door into

Davio's *lair*." I spat out that last word. "The SR will see us coming from frickin' miles away, not to mention spearing and filleting us on a spit, whether we're stalking six inches at a time or ten!" I was shouting now, my tone oozing with scorn.

"Oh, man . . . ." I heard Alex say this under his breath toward one of the guys standing near us. "When he gets started . . . ." Alex mimicked a missile whistling toward the ground with his hand, ending with a loud explosion upon impact.

"Are you mocking your late grandfather?" Luc asked me, sounding like he was mid-boil and ready to blow. He had squared off with me now—and to my surprise, no one intervened, not even Mickey.

I faced off with Luc, chin to chin, not backing down for a minute. "You wanna go a few rounds, old man?" I baited him, my eyes flashing with intensity. "You may have a black belt in Krav, but what I wanna know is if your fists can keep up with your middle-aged mouth."

"Why, you insignificant little prick," Luc shot back at me, low and fierce, our noses almost touching.

"Goro." Alex put a hand on my arm, but I shrugged it off. "Stop!" he whispered in urgency. Everyone was silent, watching the two of us with bated breath.

"Your grandfather would have been so ashamed," Luc finished with a sneer, tilting his head to accentuate his words.

Something snapped in me. I raised my fist to strike when Mickey and about three other guys held me back. "You don't know anything about me or my grandfather!" I shouted, my voice breaking.

At that point, I was spent. The weight of everything I had endured came crashing down on me, and I turned on my heel and ran out of the room, feeling like a coward, with Alex close behind. I ran all the way to the compound door and fumbled to get the key in the lock with shaking fingers when Alex stopped me.

"Goro, you coward! Don't leave!" He gripped my wrist. "It's not safe, idiot. What, you always gonna run away?"

I didn't listen. I yanked open the door and stepped outside when Alex planted all his weight into the ground and gripped my wrist like an iron vice. He leaned back and would not let me go. I struggled with him, but dammit, he was so determined that I couldn't budge him. After breathing heavily and wrestling for a few seconds, I finally gave up and slumped to the floor, hanging my head. I felt so weak, and I despised myself. Alex shoved my legs out of the way, shut the door again, locked it, and ripped the key out of the lock. He threw it at my feet and sat down next to me, breathing hard.

"Damn," I exclaimed when I had caught my breath. "You're *strong*, you turd."

Alex just nodded.

I don't know what I would have done or where I would have ended up if Alex hadn't stopped me, and I'd never admit it, but to this day, I am grateful he did.

Chapter 21

"An open foe may prove a curse, but a pretended friend is worse."
—John Gay

Zan huddled in a tight ball on his cot. His body ached and his left eye twitched from the procedure they had performed on him the day before. He shivered in uncontrollable fear and anxiety, willing his left eye to open, his frantic pupil grasping whatever slim sliver of light emanated through the cracks in the walls. It was so cold in here, there might as well have been Arctic tundra growing in the corners of his cell. He pushed his one eye open further. A dim green glow hovered somewhere near the recesses in the ceiling, and he could just make out the iron mesh in front of his cot. This place looked more like a penitentiary prison than soldier barracks. Feeling weary, he sighed even though it hurt to do so.

Welcome to the lifestyles of the twisted and insane, he mused. He was still alive at least.

What he couldn't figure out was why he was quarantined from the rest of the men here. He punched his thin mattress hard. Why was he always "damn the torpedoes, full speed ahead!" when he had some cockeyed plan? He was sick and tired of being treated like a sewer rodent. He just wanted to make something of his life. Show them he was capable of doing this. Help his family get out of the Backlands somehow. He thought this was his ticket. He wasn't stupid, by any means, but he knew he could be reckless, making rash decisions when unwarranted. This had to top his list of regrets. He thought of his family, what his mother must be thinking, what his sisters were doing at that moment. He thought of Goro and Alex, knowing exactly what Goro would say if he knew about his defection to the SR. He grimaced in pain, wondering where in the heck his friends were, but he didn't dare to hope that they'd ever come for him. No, he got himself into this trauma, and he would have to figure some way of getting out while he was still fairly human . . . .

Chapter 22

"The tyrant is a child of pride who drinks from his sickening cup recklessness and vanity until from his high crest headlong he plummets to the dust of hope."

—Sophocles

Ash Sheitan stood before the darkened ledge surveying the vast quiet city below him. The task Davio had appointed him was achievable, but would take time. He suspected that the Alliance Defense Force was located in one of three places: the Hall of Sepulcher, in what was left of the Backlands, or in an underground location he knew about but had not yet sent mercenaries to breach.

He would appease his lord with two invasions, but he would leave the final location's raid to his timing and *his alone*. His army had penetrated and searched many dwellings, Halls, and vacated malls, and had not yet found them. He knew his lord was getting impatient with this itch of a mosquito bite, and he wanted the ADF dismantled far more than Davio did, but he would order that siege on his own malicious terms.

The sacred Hall of Sepulcher was an educated guess, as it would be rather ingenious to hold the mutiny headquarters in a mausoleum among the deceased, intending misdirection. The Backlands had been all but razed with few survivors left, but that area could provide enough cover for even a rogue military organization. His final choice was an abandoned water treatment plant centered in the intermediate area of the ancient and now defunct Los Angeles, not far from their Hall of Academics. He did not presume their operation would be above ground, and he knew with every fiber of his existence that the ADF was indeed in this location, but he was saving it for last, for one reason only. *Let them play their games*, he thought with a wicked smile. He wanted the Alliance to have plenty of time to devise their puny schemes so that when he did crush them, the fight would be strong and it would be undeniably indisputable as to who was truly sovereign.

Chapter 23

"It's not the size of the dog in the fight; it's the size of the fight in the dog."

—Mark Twain

Loud explosions jarred me out of my slumber, and I fell out of bed like I was on fire. I bolted blindly through the kitchen in my boxers toward the deafening sound. But I stopped short when I saw Josiah standing at the end of the schoolhouse. An SR mercenary was yanking his head back with a knife at his throat. What?

"Goro!" Josiah screamed in pain when he saw me. I ran toward him in slow motion . . . my feet churning through what felt like molasses, my eyes darting around, searching for other SR threats in the vicinity. I stretched my right hand out to him when the SR goon, smiling, decided to let him go. After hesitating for just a second, Josiah took off for me.

He was running toward me when he transformed right before my eyes. Instead of my little brother coming to me, a tall, ominous, black-robed man that I had never seen before was running toward me.

It horrified me so much that I ground to a stop; with one look at his face, I spun on my bare heels and high-tailed it out of there. Even though I couldn't hear his footsteps pounding after me, I could feel the man gaining on me. When I felt his foul breath on the back of my neck, I put on a burst of speed and kicked it into fifth gear. When I had rounded the corner to the exit corridor of the compound, I saw that the heavy iron door at the end was standing wide open. I pulled out all the stops in a final wind sprint and flew through the open door to freedom. Only I didn't end up under the bridge in the city, where I expected. Instead, I found myself skidding to a stop in a large darkened circular room save for one lit pillar candelabra sitting on some kind of altar to the side. I whipped around wildly, searching for the tall guy, but all I saw was a massive set of oak double doors closing behind me. A slight sound made me turn forward again. I recognized the heavy velvet curtain hanging in front of me, which was being pulled back by someone's hand. Just then, my grandfather walked out from behind it. My eyes were wide with amazement.

"Goro," Howard murmured, "I'd like you to meet Davio . . . ." He was spreading his right hand toward the curtain when my eyes bugged out at the SR symbol lasered on the inside of his forearm in red. Was that blood? Oh God, no! A man veiled in shadow emerged from the darkness behind the curtain.

I sat up coughing and shuddering from the nightmare to find Mickey sitting on the end of my bed.

"You okay, son?" Mickey put a hand on my shoulder. I nodded, more shaken than I wanted to admit. I shook my head hard for a second.

"Here." He held up what looked like another identity chip.

"Are you kidding?" I asked after a stunned pause. "This the fake chip?"

"You're gonna need it for the next op." He flipped it in the air and caught it again, placed it into a small holder on a wristband, and tossed the whole thing to me. "See you in the schoolhouse." He left me to get dressed.

When Alex, Cory, and I convened with everyone again in the schoolhouse, Robbie ordered us to take a knee. *Luc must be taking a day off,* I thought. Maybe he was exhausted from our sparring yesterday, or maybe he was just avoiding me. I was indifferent to the whole thing anyway, having pushed it out of my mind. That is what is awesome about being a guy; we can compartmentalize things, and we don't have to take them down off the shelf until we want to. I don't know how girls do it, ruminating over everything, when everything in their head touches like food on a plate. I hate it when my food mixes.

Cory and Alex kneeled next to me on the padded flooring. I saw that Cory was looking like himself again, thank God. What I didn't know was how his dance of death with the SR affected him internally. I made a mental note to find out the honest details later from my friends. I would try to be more civil today, I thought.

"Today is packed, guys, so we can't afford to lag it," Robbie informed us, jumping in place. How did he have this much energy this early? He gestured to the itinerary on the schedule panel next to him. "Today I want to go over unarmed close quarter combat, some free climbing, and round everything out with some SERE basics," he said as if he was shooting the breeze about his favorite sport. "We need to revisit some of the disastrous op that occurred yesterday, which should not be a surprise to any of you." He smiled at us, but his eyes were stern. "After BC of course."

"SERE?" Cory asked me out of the corner of his mouth. "I know BC is basic conditioning, but what is . . . ?"

"SERE is survival, evasion, resistance, and escape," whispered Tiffnie, who was standing nearby.

"Guys, take it outside if you are going to have side convos," Robbie barked in Cory's direction. Cory jerked to attention next to me, shaking his head "no." Tiffnie didn't seem to care. I couldn't believe he'd even heard us. *Guy must have the radar of a bat*, I mused.

Robbie had us spread out doing jumping jacks, which reminded me of earlier days at the Hall of Academics. Following that we ran timed laps as usual, and my time was getting better, but still no four-minute mile. Then more rides on the callisthenic roller coaster.

"You know what I've noticed?" Alex mentioned as we continued with jump squats.

"No, Alex, fill me in," I huffed in a monotone voice, breathing heavily between squats.

"There are no female instructors in this zoo," he pointed out, pleased with himself.

"So?" I said, exhaling in a rush of exertion.

"Well, don't these dudes ever get lonely?"

"Dude just has the urge to merge at the moment," Cory addressed Alex with raised eyebrows. We all dropped into diamond push-ups at Robbie's command.

"Shut up, fool," Alex joked.

I could tell my boys had given it some serious thought. I shook my head while we were doing the hellish bear crawls that I couldn't stand. "I think they have more pertinent matters on their mind, idiot. Romance takes a back seat." So much for being nice.

"Maybe there are some women who teach, but we just haven't met them yet, hmmm?" Cory ventured.

I stared at both of my friends, frowning. "Are your brains on empty? Did you two forget to refill your heads with air this morning? That all you been pondering lately?" I laughed at my wittiness, taking a quick swipe at my face with the bottom of my T-shirt. I gave up and took it off.

Alex crinkled his eyes in mock disapproval at me and continued doing reverse tricep lifts off Cory's knees. "Ha ha, nerd."

"Lighten up, man. You can't tell me you haven't noticed that Genesis bae." Cory nodded in her direction.

"Yeah, bruh, you better get in before you get friend-zoned," Alex informed me.

I didn't answer, but instead rolled up my T-shirt into a tight tube and snapped Alex on the leg.

"Ahh!" he yelped. "Jackass!" He wrenched my shirt out of my hands and whipped it over his head, the shirt landing on some girl's butt who was bear-crawling her way across the schoolhouse. She scowled at us as I retrieved my shirt, smiling at her sheepishly, and I wrapped it around my head like a turban. I grinned to my friends as we launched into a series of one-handed push-ups. Despite Alex's shameless comment about Genesis, I was secretly hoping I could pair up with her or just "happen" to be in her general vicinity during an op or something.

Robbie then had us practice front kicks, knees, and 360 blocking, and we finished with a recap of escaping front, side, and rear chokeholds. Speed was one aspect of Krav that I knew I was lacking. José was wicked fast and always ripped out of my holds, no matter how hard I held on. He always made me feel legit, though, saying it was more of an explosive action than speed. I knew I would need to keep on hoofing it into the schoolhouse every day to improve my explosive reaction time.

Robbie instructed us to climb the rock wall. Free climbing was a little harder than I thought; it wasn't just rock climbing, which I mistakenly thought it was. We had safety ropes, yes, but there was no assistance for us on ascent. I had to employ serious upper body strength to reach some of the higher holds. Alex and Cory championed through, keeping up with me, and I was damn happy to have my two closest friends with me during this unrelenting drama.

When we rappelled down the wall for the last time, Robbie let us take ten, and I wandered over to where Genesis was standing at the water container.

"Hey," she said, handing me a cup.

"Thanks, bae." I filled my cup with water and downed it in one gulp. "Better day today?"

"Why do you ask that?" She looked at me quizzically. I couldn't tell if she was flirting with me or if she just plain wanted to know.

"Oh, ya know, you were contemplating life, liberty, and the pursuit of happiness in the mess hall yesterday is all." I gave her a look.

"Wow, you're presumptuous." She cocked her head at me and refilled her cup from the water canister. "I'm good." She gave me the once over, staring at my sweaty shirtless chest. Okay, she was flirting in a teasing sort of way. I got the feeling that she was not about to elaborate, so I dropped it.

"I'm more than presumptuous; I'm an enigma, baby. You'll never figure me out." I winked at her surprised expression and walked back over to my friends.

When we headed to the classrooms after chow time, I saw Genesis glance at me then look away as soon as I caught her eye and smiled. *Gotcha*, I thought. *It's all good; sweetheart, you can look*. When we all sat down, Mickey got right to it.

"Always have your SERE and blowout kits at the ready, keeping your medical kit in the same right pocket so that your team members don't have to waste time trying to find the damn thing. Your blowout kit needs to have double pain patches and double seamless sutures in case you have to assist a buddy and then have to patch yourself up if you get a laser hit as well."

After Mickey finished with his final SERE tips, Robbie launched into reprimanding those involved in the op that Luc had cut short the day before. I thought it might be rude to sit there and listen to Robbie rip into the mission trainees, but no, he insisted on taking those of us who hadn't participated on the same tour. I didn't know what half the terms were that he was throwing around like confetti, and I was curious as to learn when I would get invited to the flyer party.

It was fascinating stuff, to be honest. It made throwing darts in Zan's backyard look like playing some ancient game of pickup sticks with our thumbs up our butts. I used to think I was King Crap whenever I beat Zan with bullseyes. That now seemed like a lifetime ago.

"You guys *know* this stuff." Robbie gestured to the control panel behind him. He was fluent in sarcasm today. I saw yesterday's op notes and diagrams splashed across the screen. I saw the schematics of the dominion laid out, but when Robbie touched a panel, the whole thing took on a 3D life of its own. He twisted and flipped the sophisticated holographic floor plan to point out various errors in positioning, strategies, and premature movements so there would be no mistaking the areas where the mission had gone sideways. What *not* to do 101, I thought with an inner chuckle.

"Was this appropriate violence of action?" He paused the instant replay and hooked his thumb over his shoulder toward the two opposing team members engaged in combat in the hologram. "Were you playing smack tag or something?" He was sounding like Luc.

He went on to direct our attention to the holes in the mission and demonstrated how it could all be tightened up. "Kevin—yes, I am calling you out on this one—you failed to camo the stems of your Nitesite glasses, and light was blinking off them like a Christmas tree. Tiffnie, you failed to stack your opponents; your six was wide open for assault. Joel, well, you know you were out of range for that last laser shot; the angle was impossible even though there's no weather obstacles in the indoor maze, but in the real environment there could be dust, wind, whatever, to contend with. Enough said."

"Don't hesitate in manhandling everyone and anyone," he went on. "I don't care if she's your luscious crush, if she is coming at you with a weapon, deflect it, and elbow strike her ass. If you hold back, trying to be the nice guy, you are going to get burned. Because I can guarantee you she is not going to play." A few laughs rippled throughout the crowd and the atmosphere lightened, though everyone sobered again when he said, "In reality, any op that has zero loss of life is an amazing op, but the chances of that happening are . . . well, they are non-existent. The powers that are sovereign over our world will execute you on sight." He bowed his head slightly, his words hovering over us, resonating with us.

I sneaked a peak at Genesis. This was getting depressing, and I needed a momentary distraction. Her hair was up with loose curls framing her face in sweet ringlets, her locks still wet with sweat from the intense exertion we had been subjected to thirty minutes earlier. She had that women's intuitive feeling of someone watching her, and she turned in my direction, catching my eye. I smiled a little, feeling foolish. She surprised me when she smiled back, a look of . . . was that slight adoration in her eyes? She had given me a "look." Nah, I shook off the uncertainty, already having decided that ship had docked. What was wrong with me? I of all people should have learned by now that anything was a go at this rate, however I loved that electrical staticky heightened awareness of one another—the flirtation of possibility, that new love was in the air. When I glanced back at her again, she had moved on.

I tried to empty my mind of all things Genesis. I found that spending about four hours a day in physical conditioning with three hours of classes in the afternoon helped me stay busy. I preferred the intense action; I could shut off my brain and let my body go through the motions. The classes were interesting and knowledgeable, but I often found myself getting antsy and wanting to run an op already.

I was growing accustomed to the idiosyncrasies of our instructors. Some instructors were hyper and made us condition like maniacs

(Robbie), and some were just steady and thorough (Luc). After BC every damn morning, we ran all sorts of drill exercises before curriculum classes except for Sundays. Mickey insisted on letting our tight, contracted muscles and our minds have a rest, thank God.

Everyone else pretty much pulled their weight. I was impressed with Cory and Alex, I had to admit. A lot of the guys and some of the girls, too, were in better shape than me and my threesome swag pack, I unfortunately recognized, but I was hoping we three could be up to speed sooner rather than later.

Every night I fell into bed exhausted, unable to think of anything at all—I was so thrashed. It was the first time in my life I could say that stupid cliché of falling asleep before my head hit the pillow. As the weeks progressed, I could see a definite toned line to my body that wasn't there before. My buddies were becoming stronger as well. If it had been any other time in my life, I would have been thrilled, wanting to showcase my physique in a shameless plug to snag some potential girlfriend candidates. In the reality of my situation, however, I just shrugged at my reflection in dorm room mirrors and didn't really give it a second thought. If we launched an all-out siege on the almighty SR, I'd be ready.

Chapter 24

"Great minds are to make others great. Their superiority is to be used, not to break the multitude to intellectual vassalage, not to establish over them a spiritual tyranny, but to rouse them from lethargy, and to aid them to judge for themselves."

—William Ellery Channing

The next day, Luc woke me up at the crack of ass with some sort of air horn. I shot out of bed like I had been dunked in ice cold water. WTF!? It's a rude awakening every morning when you've joined the "military," but I had to get used to it. Cory and Alex were back in the dorms. Mickey had relented to my request of not sleeping in the barn with the rest of the cattle, and he let me sleep in the shoebox off the kitchen again. I quickly dressed and joined my friends on the way to the mess hall. Alex and Cory nodded at me, their eyes at half-mast.

"Let's head to the op room, folks," Luc announced above the din of chattering people one morning after BC. Yes. I wanted to scream, hoorah! I was already feeling the impending anticipation of the mission. My buddies Cory and Alex fist bumped me on our way out of the schoolhouse. "I think you guys are ready to take another whack at the piñata. But let's collect all the candy this time, k?" We all laughed.

"'Bout time," Alex lamented. "I've been running drills in my dreams."

"Tru dat," Cory seconded. "I've heard you yelling 'Execute!' in your sleep too many times, man."

We all made our way to the hallway at the end of the schoolhouse, the same hall that Alex and I had ventured into before, with me banging on the door and yelling like a banshee. Déjà vu, I thought. I couldn't help being psyched, though, for my first op as a participant rather than a casual observer, as was the case last time.

Once inside the basement, Luc had us split into the three teams we had created in class earlier in the week, with each team heading to separate laser equipment rooms. He had pre-split Alex, Cory, and me in class so that we were each in a different group, and I had been butt-flustered about that. Why? Were we being stalked by ADF admin or something? Not that it mattered, but it was disconcerting to think the three of us could be targeted on purpose. Was being tight with my friends considered a weakness? Was this a "buck up and deal with it" type of training tactic? This thought nagged at me like a tick burrowing into my bare flesh.

I chose a laser shield vest off the wall and tightened the clasps around my chest and waist, deciding to let it go for the time being. It wouldn't serve me well to ruminate on assumptions while I was running an op drill. I touched the test button on the circular target on the front of my vest and saw that it lit up red. My earpiece and Nitesite glasses I kept in my vest pockets for now, as well as the chip Mickey had given me yesterday. Luc opened up the weapons vault in our gear room, and I grabbed a laser rifle and a knife. I liked knives for some reason. Something about gripping a weapon and using my arms and hands in a combination of close fighting was what pumped my nads the most. The black match grade laser rifles were identical to the real McCoy, except they were benign, just for show. I was glad I would be getting to use an exact replica, though, so I could memorize the feel of the trigger and familiarize myself with the weight in my hands. We also had this very cool crossbow looking type of weapon that could launch laser arrows that exploded upon impact. Besides ammo, they served other purposes as well. You could aim at any wall and these babies could jettison rappelling rope, securing it to any surface with steel rods.

Robbie made his entrance just then, along with Mickey. They would be leading the other two teams, and I speculated it would be from high in the bird's nest observation rooms. My team was stuck with Luc, the abominator. Who knew what surprises our ADF instructors had peppered throughout the Dominion maze. Any new conjured obstacles or mock enemies would determine the team's direction of movement when clearing a room or saturating the hallways. Remote controlled drones would no doubt be flying low, ready to replicate enemy fire from all directions.

Luc and Mickey had chosen random ADF members from other classes to act as SR and had instructed them to give us hell. Anyone of us could expect to be chosen to play the other side in our meticulously planned ops at any given time, and we were to be as vicious as possible, simulating the real thing. This was the only way to fully prepare ourselves for encountering anything from physical brutality to cunning mind games. If a mock SR mercenary came at me with a heel strike or a hammer fist from behind a blind corner, I would not hold back. That's why in training, we actually practiced real chokeholds to know what it feels like to really be choked out, and to learn the proper countermeasure in a "no holds barred" situation.

Davio's "lair" in the Dominion had a complex floor plan consisting of everything from stacked rooms to the large center chamber in which his inner circle allegedly congregated. I appreciated the time and dedication it took to prepare an op. I couldn't care less what impression I made on the team in this first drill; I *was* interested in challenging myself to push the boundaries of my capabilities. I needed to rebuild my ego after the Luc altercation from a month ago. I was still smarting from the crack about my grandfather. Why did the dude always insist on pushing my buttons? I had this morbid thought that we would actually end up becoming close. Ugh.

My team assembled outside our designated gear room for final instructions. There were seven of us, an odd number, but Robbie liked uneven teams—one leader, six back-ups. I quickly ran through the drill in my mind before we took our positions. Protect my head, strike first above the collarbone, and keep moving in the event that I was disarmed. If this were the real deal, of course, I would take three shots center mass, and it would be game over, but some of these guys (and girls) were good with disarmament tactics. All was quiet for a second, and then there was the sign to engage.

Adrenaline kicked in and I cleared my mind of all distractions. José took the lead and initiated the predetermined tactical plan we had pored over the last week in class. He used the first of the hand signals we had created for our team, using his weaker hand so as to keep his dominate hand on his weapon. I was glad we were advancing through the first hallway in a tight tactical column rather than single file because the fire range was wider even though it was a narrow hall, and besides, single file was so blah. Upon reaching the larger corridors, we could break out into a Y formation, and it would make flanking our designated operator easier. We had to watch out in hallways because they could quickly become "fatal tunnels."

A shooter could fire random shots down these long corridors and hit any target at will. We'd perused our op plans ad infinitum, so I thought we were okay.

I could feel my pulse popping out a rhythm beneath my temples. Luc's mantra of "attention to details" pumped through my brain at a low voltage. All five senses were running in the red-line, ready to discern the slightest tremor of anything abnormal. I followed my team in a tight line, three deep in formation. I glanced behind me periodically. My whole body moved like a well-oiled machine. I knew to keep silent for as long as possible, because as soon as I heard laser fire or shouting or whatnot, all hell would break loose.

Rifle raised, I approached the end of the corridor behind my team. It was so quiet; all I could hear was my own breathing. My nerves were on edge, waiting for my team to move to the sound of violence. Nitesite glasses were on and camouflaged after Robbie's last debriefing comment at Kevin's expense. Visuals in this labyrinth were really challenging due to the lighting that Davio and his cronies seemed to be accustomed to. I knew from past intel classes that any bright, blinding light was detrimental to Davio and his crew, so I had included larger stylus flares and laser flash bangs in my SERE kit when prepping my gear today. I wasn't going to run into him today in this simulated op—not a chance, but it was always good to prepare for that possibility. I looked forward to the day when I would square off with the dude, but then I wasn't looking forward to it either, ya feel me? Pummeling his face into oblivion was the fuel that kept my eyes on the prize.

José and Genesis pied the end of the corridor for better vision in clearing the double blind corners, and José, Kevin, and Joel went left at the T while Genesis, Michael, Tiffnie, and I headed right. *So far, no threats. Okay, still silence. So far, so good. No chatter from Luc through my earpiece yet. Maybe this will be cake*, I thought. Tiffnie, now leading my group, cleared the next alleyway then suddenly motioned a hard stop.

We halted, with me bringing up the rear. I couldn't see jack, what with sweat dripping into my eyes, not to mention being the caboose in this locomotive. Why hadn't I worn my sweatband? I cursed inwardly as I let go of my laser rifle with my left hand to wipe the slick perspiration from my forehead. That's all the time it took.

Two guys jumped me, knocking the wind out of my lungs. In the nanosecond that occurred, I could see Tiffnie in slow motion swinging her head in my direction, her mouth forming an O, though I couldn't hear anything above the rushing of blood in my ears. Michael and Genesis had leapt forward at exactly the same time, coming to my aid, but everyone was too late. The taller guy had placed me in a headlock from behind before I could even determine whether I was flat on the ground or being yanked up by my hair. Oh,crap. I was getting ready to tap out, using the signal to let the dude know that I had had enough, when Genesis sent a strong front kick to the guy's groin, but he jumped back in an explosive counter move, jarring my neck in the process. I saw stars. The guy squeezed tighter, and knowing full well that I hadn't turned my head defensively when his arm had slid across my neck, I knew it was only seconds before I would black out. I had no escape hole. Michael was facing me and screaming something incoherent, right about the time that I lost all consciousness.

When I came to, I was lying on my back on the floor of the corridor where I had been attacked, except Luc was standing over me and talking in indistinct whispers to someone behind me. My head felt like it was filled with sand. I just closed my eyes and took deep breaths to curb the nausea. Luc bent down and grabbed my left hand in a grip, pulling me to my feet whether I wanted to get up or not. A tidal wave of dizziness swept over me, causing me to stumble toward the wall.

"Whoa, pardner." Luc steadied me with his hands on my shoulders. I blinked a few times, letting my vision clear, when Mickey came into my line of sight. I put a hand on my neck, rubbing circulation back into my jugulars with my fingertips. Mickey gave me the most empathetic look I had ever seen, making me feel like a jerk, and I could instantly tell I was going to have a mother of a headache sooner rather than later . . . .

Luc sighed and bit his lip, heading down the hallway for the light.

"Hey, man, I didn't die!" I yelled after him. Why did I care what Luc thought? I was more aggravated with myself for caring whether or not he approved of me than I was with failing the mission ten seconds into the op. Dammit! I hammer-fisted the wall, bowing my head. I had royally screwed my first op. I was maddest at myself for not turning my head as soon as I felt my adversary's arm slide across my neck.

"Goro . . . ." Mickey tried the obvious gentle approach, probably because he knew I might take a swing at anyone at this point. My demeanor sure put off that vibe.

"I was ambushed!" I yelled at maximum volume. He let me calm down, raising his hands palms out while nodding at me. I couldn't stand the sympathy in his eyes.

"You're mortal, son. It could happen to any one of us." He pointed to the rappelling ropes dangling against the opposite wall. Of course. Place a threat ahead of us in our path while sending other SR members to double back and rappel down, pigeonholing our team. I was pissed. I had glanced behind me enough times, covering the rear, but I had completely missed the stealthy dudes dropping down behind me because I was so focused on Tiffnie's signals. I closed my eyes, feeling vulnerable in this moment, and I wanted to beat the crap out of someone and *now*.

"I wanna go again." I was insistent, pointing my forefinger at the floor. Even as I said it, I knew it was useless; neither Mickey nor Luc would allow another go-round after that epic fail.

Mickey shook his head no. "Rest is the order of the day now."

"Yeah, well, if I get choked out in the Dominion, there won't be any water breaks," I sneered.

"True, but it would be a moot point, because you'd be dead, son. Davio does not retain prisoners unless it serves some purpose for him, which is rare. He doesn't need anything, trust me."

"He needs power," I objected, jogging along on the verbal tangential path Mickey had started down. "He needs to subdue every human being in order to subjugate them to his sick plan of being god of the world, or whatever. He's a coward, for all I care." I paused, speaking with steady anger. "I swear, as you are my witness, that I will destroy that man, once and for all, no matter the cost." I ended my rant with force and determination. I knew I would face him one day. I felt in my gut that it was a given. I planned to take him down by my own hand.

Mickey looked at me with something in his eyes I had not seen before. I don't know; was it belief? Hope? Faith? Did everybody know something about me that I didn't?

"Okay . . . ." he finally said in a "calm down" tone of voice. He kept looking at me with that look, and it was making me uncomfortable. I turned, my emotions spent, and decided rest would be a good thing after all.

When I got back to our gear room, everyone on the team was averting their eyes. I felt like a fool. I felt like a victim of wrecking myself. If only I had checked myself! I only supposed Alex and Cory were still with their teams running their own successful ops, I thought with envy. I needed to step up my game; this was ridiculous. I was better than this. I shoved my rifle back in the rack in anger, not caring who noticed.

I felt someone's presence over my left shoulder, but didn't turn. "Look," I said to whoever was standing behind me, "I could use some people-free time right now." I ripped my vest off and slammed it onto the wall.

"Regardless of what happened out there today, you are amazing, Goro." Genesis spoke with true kindness in her voice. My shoulders eased a tiny bit. Hmmm. This was unexpected. Despite the hellish embarrassing ordeal I had just stumbled through, I couldn't say that I didn't like hearing what she was saying to me. I finally turned to face her, my eyes narrowed in suspicion. Her gentle expression didn't change at all.

"There's something very unique about you . . . you're all talk, and think you're all that, no doubt, but people are drawn to you." She looked into my eyes. "I can't put my finger on it, and I don't think you're about to be typecast. Deep down I think you are just as uncertain and insecure as the rest of us. You just have a better way of masking it."

Her banter was putting me on edge because she was hitting too close to the target. I was intrigued by her yet irritated at the same time.

"More," I said with a grin, referring to her steady stream of compliments. I peeled off my fingerless gloves and exited the gear room. She didn't follow me right away; either she was lost in her thoughts or letting me be. I kinda wish she had joined me, not behind me, or in front of me, but by my side like a friend.

I lumbered back to where the showers were located and hoped Alex and Cory were around so we could make fun of everything that happened in our ops. It would make me feel better and would take my mind off the fact that I was frustrated all the time.

Chapter 25

"For the poison was in the wound, you see, and the wound wouldn't heal."

—Vladimir Nabokov

I found myself dwelling on Josiah's death at the most inopportune times, and I was developing a desire to take a side trip to the Hall of Sepulchers to pay my respects to my little brother. I wasn't sure how Mickey or my buddies would respond to such an outing, considering what happened with Alex the last time I tried to fly the coop, or in this case the compound, so I didn't mention anything until I figured out what I wanted to do. By nature, I am a super private person, not fully trusting anyone. Alex, the sensitive one in our trio, has given me crap before about not trusting people close to me, and he has a point, but I just struggle with telling someone close to me *everything* that's going on with me.

I'd be the first to admit I am a thick-skinned natural leader who challenges authority all the time, but I am extremely loyal to my friends and family. I've always had a strong sense of justice, wanting to pummel anyone who is treating someone unjustly, and I am quick to jump to their defense. I don't know if that arises out of my Russian blood from my mother's side or the Arab in me from my father's side, but I know it is a volatile combo nonetheless. I tend to be a regular bone-headed guy who thinks he is right all the time; I'm often non-committal, wanting to survey all my options, indecisive most days, and arrogant as all get out, much to my mother's chagrin. I did, however, excel in Debate when I was at the Hall of Academics, bringing home As all the time, so she couldn't complain too much.

My mother, sister, and I are all close, due to the three of us being fluent in wittiness, keeping things real. I was pretty close to my dad as well, but in a different way. He was the strong thoughtful type who never hesitated to tell me how proud he was of me, but he also wouldn't hesitate to thunk me on the head if I was too cocky. I am fortunate to have had his wisdom guiding me throughout my years.

Thinking about my family gave me pause. I was sitting in one of the classrooms with Alex and Cory, listening to Mickey talk about the extensive underground tunnel system that connected the ADF compound with the Dominion.

"One of the reasons we made this old sewer sanitation building our headquarters is because it provides access to the ancient tunnel system." Mickey gestured to the tunnel schematics on the panel behind him.

"Wouldn't the SR know about this?" Genesis piped up from the back. My thoughts exactly.

"Not sure, but according to our outside sources, they do not know about it. If they did, they are choosing not to bother with it. They are more focused on what is going on above ground."

I thought about Josiah again as I heard Mickey change subjects and drone on about the structure of command in the Sovereign Regime. I knew a lot of this stuff already, but some of it I needed to hear. Some of the info was definitely new to me, such as the fact that Davio has power, yes, but it is a limited power. Limited how, Mickey didn't explain. As it stands in the world right now, he has *absolute* power. Dude is a brutal and barbaric man, if he is even human. I know that he uses extreme aggression, and he revels in initiating death and destruction, but what I didn't know was that he ultimately can't control the outcome of his own decisions, as much as he thinks he can.

I didn't know that he doesn't like being called Davio, but some other lame name like Apollyon or Abaddon or something dumb. I knew Ash Sheitan was his second in command, the one who was content to take a backseat by forcing all attention onto Davio, but I didn't know that Sheitan was apparently more evil than Davio. Also news to me was that Sheitan was set to take over someday, or was next in line, or whatever. Probably made sense; I read something like that in the Hall of History, where once upon a time the former USA nation's vice president would step up if the president was unable to perform his duties. But that was different; those former presidents weren't mass murdering entire populations.

Ugh, such oppressive talk. I also knew that Luc would be reprimanding my team for what happened in the op yesterday, as if I needed to be reminded of my failure. *That's it,* I thought. *I need to see Josiah.* I made up my mind to slip out sometime tonight, undetected. I would need to raid the mystery cabinet for the fake chips that I never got to implement in the last op. I had had to give Mickey back the wristband chip when we had de-geared post-op. The only thing is, I would need to be careful scanning doors at the Hall of Sepulchers when visiting Josiah, because it could pop up as unscannable or whatever. I'd plan out a strategy later, say I needed to jog laps in the semi fresh air outdoors if I happened to be questioned. I had been resting my chin in my hand, and realized I was going to conk out if I didn't get up and move, so I raised my hand as if I was in third denomination and waited for Mickey to call on me. He stopped lecturing and looked at me, and I just jerked my thumb toward the door, with him nodding that he understood. Perfect, because I felt stupid anyway.

Lucky for me, everyone was running simulated ops on their hand panels, and they were so concentrated on beating their last time quotas that no one could afford to look up or see who was leaving class, so I slipped out undetected. *Hey, now is the perfect time to bail out to see Josiah*, I thought. Everyone would be thus engaged for quite some time. I made my way through the schoolhouse to the hallway containing the door to the brain of our compound. It was now or never. I knocked on the door and looked up into the camera, feeling dumb. I had no clearance for this room.

It was a few seconds before the door slid open, with some operator's head sticking out.

"Yeah?" Mr. No Name asked me, looking pissed at being disturbed from whatever he was doing in there. "Isn't everyone in class?"

I was tempted to lawyer him with a sarcastic comeback, but I reminded myself that honey is sweeter than vinegar.

"Mickey needs a chip for a lesson he is illustrating, man. Thanks." I said this in a bored tone, scratching my head in an attempt to look as casual as possible.

No Name eyeballed me critically. "He never said anything about needing one today."

"Yeah, he said you might say that, being at the last minute and all; you can comlink him if you want to." I prayed this folly would work.

He looked like he was going to argue again, but he finally turned with a grunt.

"Stay here."

He came back in a moment with a wristband and a chip. "Tell Mickey that next time I'm gonna comlink him, even if I am interrupting his teaching." He plunked them into my hand with a bit more force than needed as a way to drive his point home.

"Will do." I threw him a grateful grin, turning with a small smirk. I couldn't believe it worked.

I jogged toward the compound's exit. Nobody was around, as everyone was in class or training or whatnot, so I was able to go quietly. It was dusk out, the sun having slipped low on the horizon, so darkness would not yet be available to cover my tracks. Oh well. The train had left the station, so to speak, and there was no going back now. I put my wristband on.

I kept to the shadows as best I could, pulling Alex's antiquated Dodgers baseball cap down on my head that I had managed to hock from him. I couldn't recall when the Hall of Sepulchers shut down for the night, so I moved as fast as I could in the general direction where it was located.

It took longer than I thought, but I didn't see any SR wagons out yet, which was kind of weird. But, hey, I wasn't gonna whine. When I came in sight of the Hall, I saw that there wasn't any type of cover near the door, so I would need to wait across the street until it got a little darker. I waited in a grove of trees until I could slink over to the doorway under the cover of night.

I caught sight of someone familiar sidling up to the front door of the Hall. I saw brown hair tucked inside a hoodie, and when she turned slightly to see if anyone was watching her, I saw that it was Genesis. What was she doing here? I was astounded at her brazen act during twilight. I recalled she had been in class with us; she'd snuck out also? For some reason, that struck me as cool. *Hmm, another kindred-spirited rebel.* I waited about twenty minutes until it was completely dark, and then I walked up the steps as if I had every right to be there, and let myself into the building.

It was somewhat dark inside, the surrounding area punctuated only by a few electric lanterns. I didn't see Genesis anywhere. The last time I was here was to visit my grandfather, and the things that I had said to Luc yesterday reverberated in my head like the loud exterior curfew alarm we were still subjected to every night. *I'll make amends for my hotheaded remarks later*, I reassured myself, so that I could stop feeling like such a prick.

I walked over to the directory panel in the foyer, tapping the console to bring it to life. It lit up under my fingers. The Hall of Sepulchers was an older building than most, and was one of the few buildings in which you didn't have to scan your wrist to be admitted. Yahoo for me, because the fewer unscannable messages that popped up on screens, the better. I searched quickly through the thousands of names for Josiah's, and found it halfway down the "J" column. I shook my head in sorrow, feeling like I was living in some alternate universe, with him sequestered in here. He was located in section M, space 267. I headed for one of the eight portal lifts and stepped into the only one open. I said "M" aloud, and the portal lift hummed to life. So far, so good.

The floors in the Hall of Sepulchers started with A ascending all the way up to Z, so I only had to go midway. When the doors whooshed open and revealed a massive circular hall, open and spacious with a soaring cathedral ceiling, I stepped onto a small platform that had another console panel on it. I first glanced over the railing at some of the lower levels and then at some of the higher levels. I saw that there was no one around. Good. I knew there were cameras and microphones located sporadically, but I hoped and prayed no one was watching me. I kept my cap pulled down low as I located space 267 and scanned it with my wristband, my heart beating fast. The platform moved silently to the right, passing the caskets numbered in the hundreds, then on to the two hundreds, until it gradually stopped in front of M267. I scanned the small gate on the platform in front of me, which obediently slid back to allow me to stand closer to the casket.

I stepped to the edge of the platform, my heart catching in my throat. Tears sprang to my eyes. I was staring into Josiah's face, his small body suspended in clear liquid encased in a thick glass tank. His eyes were closed, his brown bangs combed to the side on his forehead. He was wearing a long white tunic and little white slipper shoes. The epitaph my parents had secured above the casket read, "From the lips of children and infants you have ordained praise. Rest in peace, my son." He looked so serene, with his arms outstretched toward me, just like he had reached out for me when he had seen me coming for him in the Backlands. I immediately put my hand inside one of the rubber gloves extending into the tank and grasped his cold hand in mine, a tear slipping down my cheek.

"Josiah . . . ." I whispered, lowering my forehead to rest on the cool glass. "Forgive me . . . I will avenge your death, little bro. I promise you." I stood there for a long time, not having the courage to look up again into his youthful face, as I was afraid I would completely unravel for sure. I kissed the glass and moved back onto the platform. The gate slid shut, and I scanned the panel to return to the portal lift. I couldn't resist looking back again at Josiah as the platform moved sideways toward the lift. He looked like an angel. *Yes, that's exactly what you are . . . rest in peace, brother.*

When I stepped into the lift, I was jolted out of my moment when I saw Genesis standing in the corner. There were eight lifts, and she just happened to be in the same one I had summoned. During my minute with Josiah, I had forgotten I had seen her slinking in here. She was so shocked to see me entering the portal lift that she looked at me like I was a purple-headed alien. *Not the only escapee tonight*, I mused, and nodded to her.

"What are you doing here?" She demanded, after she had recovered from her surprise, stuttering over her words and sounding . . . what? Embarrassed? Nervous? I couldn't tell.

"I could ask you the same thing, sweetheart," I returned, shoving my hands in my pockets, meeting her gaze head on.

"I . . . um . . . I was . . . it's not your biz," she retorted, looking miffed, like she had just been caught stealing the proverbial cookie from the cookie jar.

"Ditto," I shot back, but I looked down at her with a quizzical rather than a rude look. I was super curious as to why she was here. "You okay?" I tried again, thinking, *what the hell—if you can't beat 'em, join 'em.* We landed in the foyer and she bolted out of the lift, heading for the front door. I instinctively reached out and touched her arm to stop her. "Hey," I said, all gentle. She turned to face me.

"Wow, he actually does have a compassionate bone in his body," she mock-marveled, blinking up at me. I let go, dropping my arm to my side. For once, I didn't use a witty comeback, and she looked down at the floor for a moment.

"I came to see my five-year-old brother," I offered without thinking, surprised at my own forthrightness, and she looked up into my face.

She seemed startled for a split second, either at my very personal disclosure, or at the fact that we might have something in common. I wasn't really sure which. "I'm . . . I'm so sorry," she said, hesitant in her response, her voice quiet, uncertain. I guess she expected she was supposed to reciprocate, because she opened her mouth to speak but closed it in surprise, and her eyes widened at the sound of footsteps on the other side of the front door coming up the stairs, and fast.

Everything stopped, and we both whirled in the opposite direction, sprinting toward the portal lifts. I was frantically scanning the lift doors closed when the front doors of the Hall blew open. I blurted out "H," the first letter to come to my mind, and the lift sprang to life, taking us upward. We stood stock still, waiting for it to hit the H level. I realized I had been holding my breath when the doors whipped open and I let out a rush of air. We both jumped off the lift.

"Wait!" I grabbed her. "We are both off the grid; the SR can't track either one of us. It could just be some old lady coming to see her dead husband or something."

Genesis arched one eyebrow in skepticism. "An old lady pounding up the stairs at this time of night?" She was right. She hesitated for only a second before taking off at warp speed.

"This way," she ordered, with me following; but hey, there was no time to bicker. We passed hundreds of glass caskets of people long since gone. It was eerie seeing the faces flash past of strangers young and old. Genesis seemed to know where she was headed, so I fell back and let her take the lead. She was moving like a stealth cat with me close on her heels when we heard one of the portal lifts spring into action, being summoned from below.

Awesome, I thought, when we reached the end with nowhere else to turn. Genesis seemed unconcerned. She stopped in front of a door panel in one corner of the wall, pulling what looked like antique, tarnished fingernail clippers out of her front jeans pocket. She opened them, sticking the small nail file end into the slim crevice between the door and the wall. I heard a small popping sound, and the door panel opened a few inches.

"How'd you know this was here?" I whisper shouted. She didn't answer me but swung the panel open to reveal an iron ladder bolted to the inside wall extending upward as well as downward out of sight.

"C'mon." She gestured for me to follow. She stepped inside, putting her feet on one of the lower rungs, grabbing a higher rung. "It's all downhill from here," she reassured me as if we had been biking uphill for an hour and we now got to coast down the other side. She descended into darkness. I stuck my head inside, watching her.

"It's pitch black in there!" I protested, not budging an inch.

"Whatever, then stay, moron!" She shot up at me. I couldn't see her face anymore. I heard portal lift doors opening somewhere in the distance.

"Pssshh . . . ." I started, but then said "screw it" and climbed in after her.

"Don't forget to shut the panel after you're in!"

"Great . . . so I can be even more blind," I said to myself. I descended in absolute darkness, listening to her move below me so I was careful not to step on her head or her hands.

We climbed for a while, with my uneasiness dissipating at a slow clip. I wasn't sure who was busting into the Hall of Sepulchers at this time of night, but Genesis was right, it was better not to take any chances.

I heard a thunk, and it sounded like she had reached the bottom, so I slowed down and tapped around for the floor with the toe of my boot. My foot found solid ground, so I stepped off the ladder, my hands groping around out in front of me.

"Here, stay close to me." She grabbed my hand, causing a burst of electricity to shoot up my spine. *Hubba hubba*, I thought, despite our situation. She dragged me down what I assumed was a cement hallway in a basement or cellar in the bowels of the Hall.

"This is nuts . . . ." I blurted out, feeling like a blindfolded little kid who had been forced to play pin the tail on the donkey. "Could we have it darker in here? Cuz I don't think it's quite dark enough." I couldn't resist being facetious in the moment.

"Sshh!" She squeezed my hand with her own. Her hand felt warm.

"Where are we going?" I asked in a more serious tone, stumbling over my own two feet.

"In circles . . . back to where we started in the foyer." She paused, waiting for me to protest. "No, dummy, we are headed out. There is a hatch leading outside at the end of this hall."

"Oh . . . okay." I felt bemused, as if it made perfect sense, no problem. "How did you know all this would be here?" I knew it was really not the time for chitchat, but I was curious as all get out.

"Here it is," she said by way of an answer. "Damn, it's locked. Step back a bit."

Fine, don't answer me. I did as I was told, waiting in the darkness. I heard a fast movement and a loud bang that made me jump out of my skin. She kicked it again, whatever it was, and I heard what sounded like wood splintering. I guess the building was old enough to have wooden hatches. We then saw a faint shaft of light protruding through the narrow broken slit.

She pressed her face close to the opening in the hatch. I heard her suck in her breath.

"What?" I blew through gritted teeth. I was so tired of being incognito. She grabbed my shoulder and pulled me closer to the opening so I could see for myself. What I saw made my heart sink, the warm familiar flush of fear flooding my face. *Oh, man . . . .* I saw a horde of SR mercenaries, rifles raised, advancing on the Hall of Sepulchers. It was impossible to tell how many of them there were. I looked up at the ceiling for a moment, thinking hard.

"What the hell do they want?" asked Genesis.

"I don't know . . . ." I whispered, knowing she was just asking a rhetorical question. "But hold up, something tells me that they are not here for us; they don't know we're here," I finished with more strength.

"But, it doesn't make any sense! Why advance on dead people?"

"When does anything the SR does make any sense?" I threw out, frustrated. "I think we learned enough in class about the heffa to discern that the dude is two quarters short of a dollar." I was referring to the ancient monetary system last used in the twenty-first century. "God knows what he is stirring up. What we need to do now, though, is figure out how to exit this building. Do we sit tight and wait awhile, or do we make a run for it hoping they will just saunter around the corner and keep heading down the street? I personally don't want to be in here when they decide to search this dirty dungeon."

I then shut up and resolved to pry some of the wood away from the splintered opening.

Genesis assisted me, but it was making too much noise with the two of us working, so I made her sit down out of the way, ignoring her sulking. I didn't stick any appendages out of the opening yet. I merely watched. Most of the soldiers had moved around to what I assumed was the front of the Hall. It was hard to have a true sense of direction in the dark confines of the basement. I waited a good five or more minutes before I attempted to punch the rest of the wooden hatch outward. It was gonna be loud, but I threw all my weight into my leg as I kicked open the hatch. Cool. I was curious, though, as to why they hadn't surrounded the building in standard formation. I crouched low, listening for any possible straggling SR goons who might decide to come see what was up. I couldn't discern any movement, so I helped Genesis to her feet and cautiously put one foot outside.

We extricated ourselves from the basement in such slow motion that it was painful, but it was the only way we could get through the opening without being detected. Once we were both out, she took my hand again, and we tiptoe-dashed toward the little park across the street so we could observe the SR parade.

"Think they brought enough back-up?" Genesis quipped from our hiding spot behind some trees as we watched the mass exodus of soldiers emerging from the Hall emptyhanded. I snorted then stopped myself. "Wait, they didn't find whatever they were looking for," we both said the last few words at the same time. We looked at each other, and we both turned to go when I put out a hand to halt her.

"Oh, man," she breathed, seeing what I was seeing.

Chapter 26

"This principle is old, but true as fate. Kings may love treason, but the traitor hate."

—Thomas Dekker

Ahead of us were two SR soldiers coming our way through the park, recognizable by the outline of their rifles in the dim light. *Wonderful*, I mused, *a fabulous ending to a fabulous day*. I stood stock-still; it was so dark now that I was pretty sure they hadn't made us yet. Genesis, however, grabbed me by the arm and pulled me behind the trees out of their line of sight. We both flattened ourselves against a tree. I peeked out and saw one of the soldiers jogging to the left, with the second stooge headed right for us, which was odd, because the SR never work solo. They always stalk in twos and threes. I had a crazy wild thought that if we ended up being backed into a corner, so to speak, maybe I could take this one on alone.

I made a move to step out and face the soldier head on, but Genesis yanked on my arm.

"What are you doing? Did you have a brain fart?" Genesis's breathing was hard and ragged.

To be honest, I was fed up with running. I didn't give a rat's ass anymore. Maybe if we both froze, he would just sail on past without detecting us. He was getting closer, and he seemed hell bent on reaching his target. He still hadn't seen us, and I could hear him responding to an invisible order he'd heard through his earpiece. Wait. I recognized that voice!

When he got within an arm's length of Genesis and me, I reached out and put a hand on his chest to stop him. He jumped, smacking my arm away and lifting his rifle in one swift movement, pointing it at my head. I could tell I had given him the shock of his life. Genesis squeezed my other arm so hard I thought my circulation had been cut off. I heard her suck in her breath in surprise. She probably thought I had gone off the deep end.

"Stand down," he said sternly.

"Zan."

He didn't respond right away. Time seemed to slow down.

"Back off," he repeated with an aggressive tone that I had never heard him use before.

"It's me," I offered in what I hoped was a calm voice. "Goro." I said the familiar name hoping he would snap out of it. He still didn't speak. This was my chance. I motioned to him to put down his rifle.

"Don't . . . move," he barked viciously. I stared at him, feeling helpless. Maybe I had made a grave error in thinking I could have a casual convo with my old buddy. I had no idea how far down the SR's rabbit hole he had ventured. I didn't know what sort of brainwashing techniques they had attempted on him in the short time I had not seen him. We faced off for what seemed like an eternity, his finger on the trigger, and I felt like he was going to blow the whistle like the Rolf dude in one of Josiah's favorite old flicks, *The Sound of Music*. I got mad. Enough dancing around the maypole.

"Zan! Knock it off, man! It's Goro!" My hand shot up in the split second advantage I had created, and I deflected his rifle to the right, blocking it while grabbing it with both hands and rowing it out of his grip like I was rowing a boat, a move I had learned in Krav. There was no time for crying over allegiances as I pointed the rifle right between his eyes. He jumped back, and I could see the whites of his eyes in the light of the streetlamps as he looked around wildly. "Is this how you want Nana Mares to see you, or your mom? What the hell are you doing?" I wanted to slap the hell out of him, but I kept him in my sights.

He lunged for his rifle, but I countered and caught the back of his leg with my foot, sending him flat on his back. I could tell it had knocked the wind out of him. I handed the rifle to Genesis and knelt on either side of his chest as I pinned his hands together above his head against the ground. He struggled briefly, but he was losing it. Once he saw there was no longer any fight, he relaxed under my weight and set his mouth in a grim line, his eyes shooting hateful daggers at me. I felt awful; I loathed having to do this, but I needed to reach him somehow.

"You're family, Zan. Your sisters are like my nieces. Morgan and Meagan would be freaked out to see you right now." I paused, watching for any sign of recognition in his eyes. "Tell me you know who I am!" I said through clenched teeth, gripping his wrists harder. I nodded toward the bracelet I still wore that Josiah had made for me, not realizing he wouldn't be able to see it in the dark. "Remember this? My little brother gave me this on my last birthday. You helped him pound out the brass to make it. Listen to me!" I was getting desperate.

He bucked and rolled over in a flash, knocking me off him and freeing himself from my grip. He didn't even glance at my bracelet as we launched to our feet in a fighting stance.

"Zan! Do you really want to be a part of this unholy legion of government?" I gestured toward the Hall of Sepulchers. "What are you trying to prove?" I could feel the hot blood pulsing through my veins. All the venomous words that I wanted to preach to him that I had rehearsed over in over in my mind came rushing out.

"Goro, we need to go." Genesis spoke up, at a loss as to what to do with me, the wild card. She glanced nervously around at our surroundings, while aiming Zan's rifle at him.

I'd had it. I faked a straight punch and then sent a hard left hook to his chin. Zan failed to defend my hook, and it knocked him to the ground again. Genesis covered her mouth with her hand. He stayed bent over on his knees, holding his head in his hands. I watched him rock back and forth, wondering why he wasn't retaliating, with me standing over him and closing and opening my fists at my sides. He sat back on his heels, running his hands over his shorn head, and when he glanced in the direction of my bracelet, I could see his face crumple in sorrow. His shoulders heaved, and he again covered his face with his hands. I put a calming hand on his shoulder. I let out the breath I had been holding and grabbed his arm.

"Zan, buddy, what are you doin'?" I asked him gently, helping him to his feet. "You know it's me. Stop this insanity, please . . . understand?"

"I know," he answered in a feeble voice, looking down at the ground. "I . . . ." He sniffed, brushing away a tear with the palm of his hand and wiping it on his pants leg. "I don't know what I'm doing anymore." His words were barely audible. He placed his hands on his hips and shook his head at the ground.

"C'mon." I gestured for us to leave. "Let's get out of here."

Something shifted in Zan just then. "Wait, I can't just go with you, Goro." He held out a hand emphasizing his point, shaking it back and forth slightly. "It's not that straightforward." He sounded older, more mature than I remembered.

I squinted my eyes at him and exhaled loudly. "Oh really? I'll be damned if I am going to let you waltz back over to the jungle," I said, referring to the SR, hoping I sounded like there would be no argument about it, because I really didn't have the stamina to deal with this. "Do you know where your family is?"

"Don't read me the riot act, Goro. I know they're concerned, but I have to do what I. . ."

I cut him off sharply. "They may not even be alive!" I yelled, shaking my head in disgust.

"Sshhh!" Genesis whispered loudly. "Let's go!" She tugged on my arm, tossing Zan's rifle as far away from us as she could.

I tried a different tack. "Why did the SR storm the Hall of Sepulchers?" I asked him in a sneering tone. "Huh?"

He didn't answer me right away, staring me down. "We're looking for the ADF." He lifted his defiant chin toward me as if the SR was still his new crew.

That gave me pause. My heart skipped a beat. Zan pressed his finger on his earpiece. "Yes, sir," he addressed the unknown speaker, looking at me one last time with deadened eyes. He moved over to where his rifle had fallen and picked it up. "I'm gonna let you civilians go this time, but don't think for a second that I will be merciful should we meet again," he directed to me in a voice I had never heard him use before. It's like a switch had been flipped and he was a different person altogether.

"Oh, is that so?" I was furious again. "You chicken shit!" I moved to rush him, but Genesis grabbed my arms and pulled with all her strength. Girl was strong.

Zan took off toward the Hall of Sepulchers, and I stumbled alongside Genesis in the opposite direction, lost in my thoughts. Luckily, she didn't say anything, and I was grateful for the silence. I'd been blindsided by the interaction I had just had with my friend, or ex-friend. I wasn't sure which he was anymore, I realized with a deep sense of loss. Learning about the SR's search for the Alliance's whereabouts was troublesome, no doubt. I wondered if Mickey or Luc knew about that. Surely, they weren't so naïve as to pretend that the SR would just let us do our thing without trying to find our location.

I allowed Genesis to drag me back to the compound through the shadows, her watchful eyes peeled for any followers. I was too dazed to help her keep a lookout.

When we reached the door under the bridge, she made us stand in the shadows for a bit in order to make absolutely sure we had not been tailed. I hung my head, not speaking or moving. I needed a minute to process what had happened to my buddy Zan. Several minutes passed before she dug in her pocket for the key and opened the door, with me slamming it closed behind us.

I had no sooner taken a step down the corridor when I felt strong hands grab me by the collar of my jacket and slam me against the wall.

"Who said you could take unauthorized field trips without parental consent?" Luc snarled in my face. "Are you demented?" He let go after shoving me back into the wall again for good measure. He grabbed my right arm, ripped the wristband off, and tossed it on the floor.

"You're not my parent," I stated the obvious. "I had something I had to do." I met his gaze; I was not about to back down.

"Oh, okay . . . you had something you had to do. I'm sorry, I forgot who I was talking to!" Damn, he was temperamental. "The twerp who doesn't listen to a damn thing anyone says, and who flips the bird to authority, thinks he knows better." His eyes bored into mine. "You are a part of us now!" He was pacing back and forth in front of me, oblivious to Genesis. She made a move to leave all quiet like, but he stopped her with a look. "He drag you into his bogus clandestine plan?"

"We didn't know that either one of us were going to the same place," Genesis answered in a meek voice. "I'm really sorry."

I switched gears in an attempt to cool him off. "Luc," I said in a calmer tone, "the SR is actively searching for our location; who knows how soon they could end up busting down our door." I watched his eyes for any signs of light bulbs going on. "It could be a matter of days," I continued.

He sighed at the floor, ceasing his pacing, and crossed his arms in front of his chest. "I am aware of that." He looked up, meeting me head on, not a hint of regret in his eyes.

WTF? When was the so-called leadership of this compound going to alert us to this crucial information? "Wonderful," I spat out, ticked off. "You mind telling me when you were going to fill us in on that info? Don't you think that particular piece of news might be important for everyone to know about? Or am I the only one playing hide and seek in the dark?" I shifted my weight from one foot to the other. "We can't be an allied force if you are busy playing Santa Claus and keeping all the presents secret." I threw sarcastic air quotes around the words allied force. Genesis raised her eyebrows, listening to me spouting off.

"Certain intel is on a need-to-know basis," Luc told me point-blank, not the least bit sorry. "But then your little outing may have made the SR's job that much easier," he remarked, pointing at my face. He made sure to accentuate his next words so that I understood I would not be dodging this one. "Where did you go?" The only sound for the next seconds was crickets.

"The Hall of Sepulchers," Genesis answered for me. Luc and I both whipped to her, forgetting she was still there. "Goro went to see his little brother, and I went to see my . . . ." She trailed off, not wanting to finish her sentence. "He was paying his last respects, Luc."

Luc was quiet for a moment, choosing not to prod her for any more details. He turned to me again and declared, "Mickey wants to see you." He grabbed the wristband from the floor where he had hurled it and took off down the corridor leaving Genesis and me in the wake of his moody outburst.

"You never did tell me who you were visiting tonight," I punch-smacked her on the arm with my fist, trying to distract myself from dwelling on my encounter with Luc. I waited for her to answer, but she just left abruptly without a word. Dumbfounded, I watched her disappear. I wasn't used to people ignoring me. "Fine!" I yelled to her retreating back. "Be that way!" Wow, I sounded like a three-year-old throwing a tantrum. Yikes. I needed a reprieve . . . from life.

I sauntered back to the kitchen, dutifully looking for Mickey. He was sitting at the far end of the table eating dinner. I sat down at the opposite end and braced myself for whatever lecture was sure to come, but he just looked up at me with his fork mid-air in his hand.

"Son, I need you to do something for me." He continued poking around in his food with his fork, taking a swig from his glass with his other hand.

"Yeah," I shrugged, tilting my head to look back at him. I wasn't really in the mood for a long-winded speech, but if there was anyone at the compound for whom I would return a favor, it was Mickey.

He paused, putting down his fork and swallowing his last bite. Dude would definitely have been nominated for an academy award once upon a time, for his skills in building suspense. He folded his hands together above his plate, stroking his lower lip with his thumbs.

"I need you to mentally prepare yourself for the fact that we may lose this battle . . . ." He trailed off watching me intently.

I searched his face for some punch line. "I refuse to think that way, Mickey. Choose your battles, yes, but win the war," I said, reminding him of his earlier pep talks to me. "I'm willing to die."

"I applaud you, but it's not a question of bravery or the sacrificial laying down of one's life for the cause. Besides, I'm who Davio wants anyway, his public enemy number one." Mickey pointed his index fingers toward the table for emphasis. "I'm sorry about your brother, Goro," he added as an afterthought.

The guy had a sixth sense for knowing why I had left the compound, possibly even discerning where I had gone. His instincts were right on.

"Okay . . . ."

Mickey talked right over me without stopping for a breath.

"It's a matter of the sheer evil we are up against. It's the crappy, in-your-face truth. Even though we are force multipliers, we only have about a hundred and fifty ADF soldiers, where the SR has around a hundred *thousand*. We have our tricks, but the odds are still insane."

"I'm really fed up with everyone's defeatist attitudes around here! You of all people, Mickey . . . ." I leaned forward in my chair. "I don't even understand it all myself yet, but that doesn't mean I am going to fall over and surrender."

"That's not what I am saying, Goro."

"So what are you saying then?" I was bold in challenging him. "I'm gonna take a stab at humility here and say that I need you to be resolute . . . you know, all that 'if you don't stand for something, you'll fall for anything' mumbo jumbo." I rolled my eyes, frustrated. *Don't throw in the towel yet, man*, I thought with a pang of trepidation. "You don't strike me as someone who pleases in the moment, only to let people down in the end."

Mickey nodded his head, moving past my cheesy clichés. "We are conditioning and refining skills for open combat in preparation for an imminent attack on the SR." He drew a square on the table absentmindedly with his fingers, and I couldn't help but notice that he suddenly sounded old and haggard, and it was wigging me out a little. "But that is just the soldiers. Davio and his preeminent inner circle will be a balls-to-the-wall encounter. That is the mission in which we will most likely die."

"So all that talk about knowing thy enemy was just horseshit? I see. Okay." I stood, ready to exit the kitchen before I really blew a gasket. "I don't care if Davio is the devil himself; I will sever that prick's head from his body, tactically or no," I firmly resolved. It felt good to finally state that out loud. "And don't give me that 'you can't fight Davio head on' rhetoric again. I am not afraid to cap his ass, right before I get offed."

Mickey just looked at me and pursed his lips, nodding his head again. Whether he was just humoring me or tired of mentoring me, I couldn't tell.

"You think capping his ass would actually bring him down?" He raised his eyebrows, challenging me to answer him. We sat there in silence for a moment.

"Go get yourself something to eat." He pointed his fork toward the mess hall. I didn't think the mess hall would be open for business still, but I did as I was told. I pondered what he had just asked me, and it got me started down a whole tangential line of thought about Davio that I didn't care to visit. God help me if Davio and his stooges were indestructible.

Chapter 27

"The battle against terrorism is not only a military fight, but primarily a battle of information."

—Ahmed Chalabi

When I walked into the mess hall, I saw Alex, Cory, and Genesis seated at one of the tables talking, heads bent close together. No one else was around. They looked up all tentatively when I got closer. I felt like I had just walked in on a hushed conversation that had just halted, with me being the key topic.

"Well, well, well . . . if it isn't the rebel with a hellacious cause making an appearance after all," Alex drawled sardonically. I knew Alex well enough to pick up on his annoyance.

"Genesis filled us in on your little picnic in the park," Cory reiterated. "What makes you think you can just split like that?" He frowned, ticked off at me; he wasn't playing.

"Don't preach, Cory." I straddled the bench next to him. "Not in the mood."

"Don't care," Alex added, jabbing a finger at me. "I don't give a damn, Goro, what your holier than thou missions are. Don't *ever* take off again and leave us scratching our cracks while you're off pissing at the powers that be. Luc—point, on that one." He jabbed his finger at an imaginary point in the air.

Good grief, I thought. I gave Alex a hard look. He stared right back at me, daring me to go on. The mention of Luc's name got me agitated again, and I moved to get up and vacate the premises when Alex yanked me back down. "Alex, shut the f–."

"Guys! Cut it out." Genesis spoke over me, putting out a hand to steady Alex. "God, you're like a bunch of toddlers that suck at sharing." I don't know if it was because she was a girl or if she just had a nurturing, calming demeanor, but we thawed out a bit. "I think we have bigger pots to piss in right now. The SR is going to end up storming the compound—that's definitive, but the question is when?"

"Bring it!" I spread my hands wide. "Let's go." Nobody paid me any attention.

Cory leaned his elbows on the table in front of him. "I would hazard a guess that it will be sooner rather than later. Let's just treat that as a reality show that could film any day now. Sleep with one eye open, man." He was always so pragmatic, and it bugged me to no end.

Alex spoke up. "I, for one, think we should huddle with the others and have some sort of strategy in place for when a raid occurs. I don't wanna be caught busting a nut if the SR . . ."

"That's inappro-pro, man," Cory cut him off, flicking him on the bicep with his thumb and middle finger.

"Yeah, how do I get out of this convo?" Genesis made a face.

"Ow, back off, prick!" Alex flicked him back, letting his middle finger linger on his chest, flipping him off.

"Hey! I don't want any random visual images in my head." Genesis held up a hand, rolling her eyes.

"Would you guys shut up!" I said fiercely. "I wanna know why the omission of info. I don't know about you, but I feel like a lab rat that never gets the cheese at the end of the maze."

"Mickey and Luc know what they are doing," Genesis defended the leadership. "They prolly don't want to freak people out. They have their reasons." She met my gaze without flinching, as if she was challenging me to say otherwise. I just looked away, too tired to embark on a verbal tango.

Changing tack, I said, "Alex, you and Cory are tech nerds. Is it possible for you to hack into ADF's mainframe?"

"And why would we do that, may I ask?" Cory looked over at me sharply. "We're the good guys, traitor."

I ignored his traitor jab. "I just want to have a look see and, well, see if Luc is holding any other cards under the table."

"Goro, no," Genesis protested, like I knew she would. "Bad idea."

"Shocker," I quipped, oozing sarcasm. "Says the one who snuck out *before* me on her own mission." I gave her a knowing look.

"Uh, yeah . . . I have to hitch a ride with Genesis on this one, Goro." Alex hesitated. Wow. I was disappointed, to say the least.

"Alex?" I turned to face him in an exaggerated move, leaning back to inspect him. "Are you wimping out too?"

"It's totally unethical, man," he said after a second, avoiding my eyes.

"Of course . . . ." I stood to leave. "Dumb question. What was I thinking?" What a bunch of pussies! I was so frustrated I wanted to scream. I left the mess hall in a stormy silence.

"Goro?" Cory called after me.

"Just let him go . . . ." Genesis sighed, picking at a dried, crusty speck of food on the tabletop.

I wandered back to my cell off the kitchen feeling damned defeated. I was living in another lifetime; my friends, my family, this compound . . . everything felt like an alternate reality. I was gonna implode if one more thing ended up tipping the scale against me.

I sat down on the edge of my bunk and stared at the poster on the wall with the unique symbol that Mickey had tattooed on his chest. What did it mean? I was pondering what it stood for when I heard someone coming into the kitchen. I looked up and saw Genesis standing in my doorway, hands in her hoodie pockets. *Damn, she is cute*, I thought, even though I was still irritated with her for defending the ADF's leadership.

We just looked at each other for a few seconds, and when I looked away, she meandered over and sat down next to me on the bunk. I was caught off guard because her vibe had gone all gentle. Not to mention the fact that I was struggling lately with containing my feels, and if I went all emo on her, I would be mortified. She reached out and tapped my knee with her fist, breaking the ice. It was cool, just having someone come after me to check in on me, and her of all people, though I would never say that out loud. I'd caught other guys sneaking peeks at her royal hotness besides yours truly.

"Um . . ." she started, all shy like.

"It's all good," I surrendered, leaning back on my arms on the bunk.

"You don't even know what I was going to say."

"You don't have to tell me who you were visiting when you were out and about tonight. You don't have to tell me why you're here to begin with . . . ." I waved my hand in the air as if to say whatever, letting her off the hook of answering any question I had ever asked her.

"Oh, okay," she said matter-of-factly, getting up to leave.

"But you can if you want to," I added, not wanting her to go. I was famous for being one part not caring, two parts come back here. I tugged lightly on the hem of her hoodie. She sat down again and smiled, revealing that she had been yanking my chain.

"What I was gonna say was that I'm really sorry about your little brother, Goro. We've all suffered casualties. But you are strong; I have faith in you—you'll weather this storm and rise up out of the ashes a diamond."

"Flattery will get you ev-," I joked with a straight face.

"Nowhere!" She cut me off, but she was smiling. She looked deeper into my eyes, a certain chemistry flashing between us.

"I was gonna say everything, but whatevs. Peeps might say I was being suss . . ."

"Suspect?" She threw her head back and laughed a welcoming music to my ears.

There was an innocent sweetness about her, comfortable and steady. She was so beautiful. *Ah, what the hell,* I thought. I sat up and touched her face with my hand, running my thumb over her lips. She unexpectedly leaned in, intertwining her fingers with my hair, and kissed me without hesitation. It wasn't just a peck, either; girl went for the gold. *So much for innocence,* I mused, but hey, it was all good! A warm glow filled my whole body.

When we came up for air, she pushed me back against the bunk and stood, shoving her hands in her pockets again.

"I better get to bed," she said, and headed for the doorway.

I shook my head, trying to clear my brain, and jabbed my bunk with my index finger.

"Here's good, chica," I replied, momentarily forgetting the fact that my cell had no door. Wait, what was I saying!

"No bueno, habibi. We need to keep our eyes on the prize. Besides, I'm a good girl." She tilted her head to the side and winked at me. Didn't seem like it a minute ago, but then I didn't really know the nuts and bolts of this woman.

I chuckled, scratching my head. "I was kidding. It's okay. Good for you." I saluted her. "Carry on."

I flopped back down on my bunk, letting her depart, thinking about the term of endearment that she had used—the same one my bro Josiah and I had often said to each other. I recalled something he had said to me when I last had a girlfriend. He ran up to me in our front yard after she left one day, and grabbed the front of my T-shirt in his fists, ordering into my face, "No hanky panky, Goro!" I laughed so hard I cried; he was always older than his years and saying the darnedest things. I sighed, pain filling my insides (in more ways than one). Sometimes fate had *no* mercy. I yanked my jeans off a little too hard and climbed under the covers with a renewed desire to perform open-heart surgery on Davio, minus the anesthesia.

Chapter 28

"Oaths arise because men are so often liars."

—A. M. Hunter

In the light of the single chandelier, Ash Sheitan stood facing the young soldier on his knees in front of him. The man's head was bowed and his hands were bound behind his back.

Zan's worst nightmare was coming true. He had been spotted talking to Goro and Genesis, and someone had ratted him out.

"Are you certain?" Sheitan was icy, stroking his chin with his thumb and forefinger.

"Yes, I am positive it was him," Zan answered, barely above a whisper. "He was talking to someone . . . a girl," he added, his body involuntarily shaking from fear. "I saw them from a distance, though."

"But he was allowed to leave." Sheitan steepled his fingertips, his eyes flashing.

Zan's eyes shot up in panic at the 6'6" figure towering over him.

"I . . . I didn't . . . I wasn't sure of . . . what procedures . . . ."

Sheitan cut his feeble excuse short. "Are you confused as to where your allegiance lies?"

Zan cowered, shaking his head in a definite no.

Sheitan paced back and forth in front of the young soldier, pausing to stare long and hard into his eyes. "Don't be nervous; you are safe." Sheitan's eyes looked kindly upon Zan, and he smiled a warm smile down at him.

Zan relaxed a little, sitting back on the heels of his feet. His hands were going numb from being tied so tight, and he could feel his microchip pressing against a ligament in his right wrist.

Sheitan flicked his eyes to a dark corner of the chamber, and two guards dressed in black came forward. One of the guards leaned down to scan the young man's steel shackles, freeing his hands, and then stood behind him; the other guard formed a third point in the triangle now surrounding the young captive.

"Stand to your feet," Sheitan ordered.

Zan stood, and he grabbed his wrists and massaged the blood into circulation once again.

Zan's eyes flitted between the three men. Anything could happen next. It was dead quiet in the room. His shallow breathing reverberated in his eardrums.

His breath quickened as Sheitan reached out a finger and tapped his chest. "I am not to be feared . . . you are protected in this dominion." Sheitan broke into a wide smile, turning away in soft laughter.

In an instant, Sheitan spun and his hand shot out, gripping Zan by his throat and lifting him off his feet as the two guards watched, unmoving. Zan thrashed his legs and grabbed Sheitan's death grip with his hands. His fingers frantically clawed at the vice around his neck. Sheitan's cold eyes bored into him, his laughter dying away.

"I am not interested in your babbling human incompetence; do you understand?"

Zan struggled to force incoherent words from his throat.

"When you see him again . . . and you will, you will detain him, and you will have him escorted directly to me." Sheitan's last words were dripping with murderous rage.

Zan's face was turning a deep shade of crimson. He made one last desperate jerk of his body to free himself when Sheitan let go. He crashed to the marble floor hard, gasping loudly for oxygen, his vision blurring then refocusing. His hands flew to his neck, and he tried to control them, but they were shaking violently. He looked up like a deer staring into oncoming headlights; all traces of strength and bravery had vanished from his eyes.

Sheitan looked down at him, shaking his head and clicking his tongue. He glanced at his guards, who took that as their cue to grab the young man by his arms.

"Remind him who he serves," a voice punctuated the air from the deep recesses of the room. Sheitan looked over his shoulder beyond the velvet curtain.

"Yes, my lord," he answered with a slight bow of his head.

"No!" Zan choked out in terror as he was dragged from the chamber into the darkened night.

Chapter 29

"When it comes to civilian deaths, violent hostilities play no favorites."

—John Conyers

Running . . . stumbling . . . I threw my hands down to break my fall . . . my palms scraping against the jagged gravel, the familiar sting of blood soaking the knees of my jeans. I raised my eyes heavenward, feeling the sharp rifle muzzle grinding into my back. This was it. *God, meet me on the other side*, I resigned. I felt the searing hot rifle laser electrocute my entire nervous system a split second before I blacked out . . .

I jolted up in bed, gasping for breath, the painful nightmare lingering in my mind. These crappy dreams were becoming more frequent. I slowed my breathing and looked around my cell, running my hands through my now longer, curly dark hair. My sheets had gotten tangled up in my thrashing during the night. *Damn, that was a bad one*, I thought morosely of the nightmare I was suffering on replay every night.

I pulled myself from the knotted sheets, swinging my legs over the side of my bunk. I thought about my parents and my sister, wondering if they were stirring awake at this very moment wherever they happened to be holed up. My father's wounds would have healed by now. Was the SR still targeting my family? Had my sister been trying to find me? I could picture Stephanie tapping in my passcode, over and over again, with the same error message popping up. The thought of anyone so much as touching a hair on my sister's head set off a wave of anxiety that rippled through my body. *Keep busy*, I tell myself, deciding I might as well get up. Ugh, I hated the way bad dreams lingered throughout the rest of the day. They added an unfortunate layer of foreboding, like an unwanted blast of humidity that smacks you in the face on a hot day.

The last few days I had felt stressed as hell. I don't know if it was a premonition that things were about to come to a head, or if it was just me acting dumb. As I dressed in my black ops gear for the day's drill, I tried to put my finger on it, but it was like a weird inner ear itch that plagued me from time to time, impossible to reach with a relieving scratch.

We all had been practicing a butt-ton of drills, and I was feeling confident that Alex, Cory, and I were fairly comparable with the rest of the ADF in terms of training and battle readiness. I boasted a nice little six-pack, and Alex could now outlast me in endurance during ops. Don't think I've ever been more fit in my life. I wasn't sure if I would ever end up face to face with Davio, and I privately hoped to GOD I would not, but I would at least die knowing I would be sporting a nicely ripped bod in the Hall of Sepulchers. I made a mental note to let Alex know that should I perish, my first parting wish was to be displayed shirtless in my watery tomb. It sounds morbid, but it'd be nice for my family to gaze upon yours truly as a svelte Adonis rather than a flabby pooched lightweight. Let Genesis drool over what might have been. She had been acting all sketchy and weird since our little romantic encounter, which bugged me. I knew she was attracted to me, and I felt the same. Sigh . . . we could've been something, but she be playing.

I thought about my little run-in with Zan and wiped it out of my mind like a dirty window that was obscuring my view of how things really looked in the world. No sugar coating the truth: Zan had gone over to the dark side. I was very adept at shoving all nonessential issues into the recessed corners of my mind, only to take that box down from the attic shelf to dig around in it later if needed.

While we were all slaving away at drills, our main contact with the outside world was with a dude named Decker. He sent us bits and pieces of news regarding the SR, in an encrypted format of course. He was the ethereal eyes and ears of the ADF on the outside, scouting and performing reconnaissance for us. Where and how he got his intel no one really knew. Rumor has it that his work assignment is pool and fountain maintenance man for the Dominion. Prolly true, because I am not sure how lucrative the swimming pool world is on the outside. Water is a precious commodity. All I know is that whenever Mickey and Luc gathered for a whispered huddle, something was up on the buzz line. Shortly after that, announcements were made to the rest of us as to what information had been acquired. I was surprised at what was shared with us and what wasn't. I was still butt hurt about being kept in the dark by Mickey and Luc regarding the whole SR's constant search for our location.

When I entered the mess hall for this morning's breakfast, my eyes scanned the crowds for my squad. I caught sight of them settled in a little group at a table next to the far back wall, and I moved in that direction after I had gotten chow. People were acting weird, throwing shifty glances at me. I shrugged it off as I headed for my friends. They all stared at me making me feel like a dork, considering the op that went south yesterday.

"I suppose you've heard," Kevin threw out to me tentatively as I sat down between Cory and Alex.

"What?" I was acting indifferent, even though I was curious as all get out.

"You're the hot ticket right now, dude." Michael pointed his piece of toast at me in a not so pleasant way, which was perplexing.

"Shut up, fool!" Alex was quick to rise to my defense before I could speak. My insides froze up in an instantaneous knot. I knew some of them privately thought I got special treatment from the leadership. But seriously? Were they still holding my op faux pas against me? Trying to hide my alarm, I turned to address him.

"Can I help you with something, Michael?" I looked straight at him.

"Wow . . . ." Michael scoffed at my blatant tone.

"Quit giving him grief," Cory jumped in. I snuck a peak at Genesis and saw that she was looking at me with such concerned compassion that it unnerved me.

Everyone else was quietly assessing the palpable tension between Michael and me.

"What grief should I be worrying about?" I shoved scrambled eggs dripping in Tapatio into my mouth.

"The SR is actively on your ass." *Thanks, Cory, for breaking it to me gently*, I snarked inwardly.

"I already know that. Old news," I said with a full mouth, grabbing the orange juice pitcher and pouring myself a tall glass.

"No, Goro, you don't understand," Alex said in a quiet voice. Nobody else spoke. They had all paused in their eating and were watching me intently. I became aware that it was deathly quiet at our table, and come to think of it, it was pretty quiet throughout the mess hall. I glanced over my shoulder at the rest of the room and found a lot of people staring at me.

"What?" I finally said in exasperation to Alex. I spoke through gritted teeth.

All eyes at my table were on me, watching my reaction for the moment when Alex chose to spill the beans. Even Cory was spooked. I had an awful feeling in the pit of my stomach.

I watched Alex open his mouth to enlighten me when everything paused as if time had stopped. Everyone turned to look just over my shoulder. I twisted around on the bench and saw Luc and Mickey walking in my direction, their eyes honed in on me. Their faces wore grim expressions. My mind raced. *Oh God*, I thought. *My family? No!*

I didn't take my eyes off Mickey's as he approached me.

"Son, you need to come with me." He placed an urgent hand under my bicep in an attempt to get me to come with him. I shrugged him off, looking from him to Luc to Alex and back to Mickey. I swallowed hard and got up to follow him and Luc. Walking out of the mess hall with all eyes on us was eerily uncomfortable, to say the least. It felt like I was marching to my death, and I was pissed off at being in the dark again about what was happening to me.

"Wanna tell me what's up?" I tried to hide my alarm.

Luc and Mickey flanked me as if I was some sort of flight risk. We continued walking in silence with a million questions bursting open in my head. The only thing even slightly reassuring about this unexpected turn of events was Mickey's hand on my shoulder, as if he was bearing some unknown burden I was about to be handed.

We turned down the hallway and headed to the brain room of the compound. Luc fingerprinted the panel, looking up into the camera, and the door whooshed open. I was ushered toward a chair in front of a panel screen. The ambience in the room was chilling, despite the heat radiating from the equipment.

"You'll wanna sit for this," Mickey said and gestured to the chair. Luc hadn't said a single word during the whole walk of shame, and maybe he was counting that as a mark of wisdom on his part. I wasn't sure.

I glanced around at everyone watching me, taking in the apprehensive looks on their faces, and then reluctantly sat down facing the screen, my heart pounding against my ribcage. I felt like I was going to hurl from the unwanted suspense. Oh man, I didn't want to see what was about to unfold in front of me. I had no choice, however. Luc nodded at the operator standing nearby, and a grainy image popped up on the panel.

I saw a young man on his knees, dressed in black, with his hands behind his back. He was wearing a black hood over his head and was facing the videographer. A hand shot out and yanked the hood off the man's bowed head. He lifted his face, and then I knew.

"No!" I yelled. I involuntarily popped up, but Mickey tightened his grip on my shoulder, keeping me rooted in my seat.

Zan's face was almost unrecognizable. He looked into the camera. "Goro, please . . ." he forcefully spit out through a raspy throat. "Meet with Davio, or they will execute me . . . ." His voice faltered. His face was split in several places with dried blood caked in his hair. "Come to the Dominion. You won't be harmed."

Just then, an arm behind him off camera swung a sword out swiftly and sliced Zan's head from his body in one move. I shut my eyes to the resulting carnage.

"Those bastards!"

I screamed, and jumped up from my chair, gripping the sides of the panel, Mickey's hand still holding on to my shoulder. Someone shut off the video. I choked and retched, throwing off Mickey's hand. I ran to the corner of the room and vomited into the wastebasket, my eyes watering uncontrollably. Oh, my God.

I glanced down at my shaking hands. I wiped my mouth with the edge of my T-shirt and stood unsteadily to my feet, my eyes closing again as I regained a sense of balance. I would never forget that image of Zan, beheaded, for as long as I lived; it was permanently burned into my conscientiousness.

He never saw it coming. My friend was gone.

"Please tell me no one else has seen this." My voice sounded unsteady in the stillness of the room. "Or that anyone else knew about this information before I did."

"No one else has." Mickey spoke in such a calm, confident manner that I was grateful he was the only one talking. I didn't trust myself or the reaction I might have if anyone other than him spoke to me. "The rumor was leaked in here about the SR being after you, which is unfortunate, but the rest of the ADF doesn't know the specifics. The details were vague; we only received this message this morning," he finished in a quiet tone.

My face crumpled only for a moment before I found an inner resolve, and turned to the rest of the men.

"What does he want?" I forced through clenched teeth, my anger rising in an alarming pulse. "With me?" I finished, seeing red through my bloodshot eyes. I addressed Mickey alone.

Mickey looked down at the floor for a moment before responding, as if he were calculating the damage of the words he chose.

"He knows about your grandfather's chip. He knows what is at stake."

I closed my eyes tight, putting my fists over them, wishing with every fiber of my being that this was all a horrific nightmare.

"Of course he does," I whispered, shaking my head. "You have the chip's intel," I continued, forcing my eyes open, putting my hands on my hips. "You *have* it!" I gestured with my right arm toward Mickey, emphasizing that the whole issue was out of my hands.

"Yes, but . . . ."

"Don't say it!" I yelled, cutting him off. "I don't want to hear or see any more of his bullshit magic show! I'm done!" I sliced the air with my hands.

I stormed off toward the door, forging an unstoppable path through the group of men. And fortunately, no one made a move to block me.

"Dammit!" Luc exclaimed. "If that little piss ant takes matters into his own hands, he could end up crapping on everything we have worked on!"

"Oh ye of little faith," Mickey said, leveling his eyes at Luc. Everyone else was quiet, waiting.

"You gonna just let him go rogue?" Luc's voice reverberated in the heated room.

"He's not going anywhere. It doesn't really matter at this point; it's time to stop the bloodshed." Mickey looked around the room at everyone in turn, his calm demeanor settling on Luc once again. "He's going to need backup."

"So, game on?" Robbie asked what everyone was thinking. Mickey nodded. "Copy that." Robbie put his hands on his hips, considering the next move.

"Rally the troops in the schoolhouse for prep then," Luc said, and he twirled a finger in the air in a sarcastic gesture, his eyes fixed pointedly on Mickey. "The man has spoken."

Mickey waited until everyone had left the room. "I need you to trust me, cousin."

Luc just stared at him. "Doesn't matter if we win or lose; there will be death. You know that. The grass is not greener on the other side, Mickey . . . it's brown on both sides." Mickey chuckled under his breath, nodding. "Buddy, we'll down a cold one once this whole Armageddon is over." A deafening crash exploded over their heads as alarm bells clanged throughout the compound.

Chapter 30

"Heroes are selfless people who perform extraordinary acts. The mark of heroes is not necessarily the result of their action, but what they are willing to do for others and for their chosen cause."

—Susilo Bambang Yudhoyono

I felt the explosion just as I reached my cubicle of a bedroom. *Doesn't sound like Davio is waiting for my response—bastard.* I grabbed my Evac pack and my meager personal belongings, preparing to head to the steel door exit, the evacuation drill we had practiced for months rolling through my mind. When I stepped into the kitchen, ready to leave, I almost bulldozed Genesis in my haste. I wasn't thinking very clearly—I was just damn the torpedoes, full speed ahead.

"Goro!" She shouted above the alarms, gripping my upper arms and looking into my eyes. "What are you doing? Let's go!" She urged me forward.

"Don't." I shrugged her off. "I'm out." I tried to step past her, but she planted herself squarely in my path.

"What!? Are you crazy? We have to follow the Evac plan! You just going to bail on us? Flip off all the hard work you've put in?" Her words were logical, and she delivered them calmly, but I wasn't about to be waylaid. "Can't you hear the compound crashing down all around our ears?"

"Genesis! I'm not jumping ship. Let me go." I roughly pushed by her and left the kitchen. This was no time to stop and ponder the ramifications of my intended actions. Dammit, girlfriend was hot on my heels. I ran past the swirling red lights in the corridors, knowing that the SR probably knew where we were the whole time, but was just biding their time. I broke into a run for the elevator that led to the underground tunnels just as more explosions rocked the compound.

When I reached the elevator door, Genesis looked as if she was preparing to leave right along with me! I stopped, turning to see her watching me with patient, kind eyes, but with determination etched across her face.

"You can't come with me, Genesis," I said, finally acknowledging her presence. She left me, but a few moments later I heard a rush of running feet.

"Goro!"

Alex and Cory were thundering down the hallway toward me. *Thanks, Genesis.*

"Goro, what the hell?" I could see genuine confusion and pain in Cory's eyes. "What are you doing, stupid?" He came up to me, looking directly into my eyes. "What, you planning to take Davio and his crew on alone?!"

I couldn't tell him in one brief sentence what I was feeling right then. I wanted to rip Davio's head from his body so bad. I wanted to face him head on. I wanted to run—not hide, and fight him *now*. Time was of the essence. But I couldn't let Davio and the Dominion fuel my emotions. I couldn't let him get to me. I knew that.

"Over my dead body, dude," Alex was crystal clear in his message to me, coming up next to Cory. "You're not doing this solo. We're a team." Alex gestured towards the three of us, emphasizing his words.

Debris was raining down on us from the carnage happening over our heads. We took off in a pack the way we had come just as another explosion ripped through the corridor, causing us to stumble in our haste.

A rush of exhaustion blew over me, and I had a sudden urge to take a nap. I was so tired of everything. I didn't have the strength to do anything but lead everyone to the weapons vault and hopefully locate Mickey. I was mentally and physically exhausted from always being on yellow alert. The only thing that mattered now was ending this siege of terror in any way possible.

When we reached the weapons vault, Luc looked up as we came rushing in. Michael and some others were already there. I braced myself for Luc's immediate scorn. He just nodded to me as he doled out rifles. I was grateful it was looking like he wasn't going to give me crap about my outburst earlier.

"Look, man, I'm sorry for my comments earlier," Michael yelled over to me. "I was being a prick." I appreciated his sentiments, but this was no time to stop and shake hands.

"Grab what you need," Luc shouted above the din. "We need to get out of here STAT. You know the drill."

The building was being rocked with destruction every few seconds. I saw fear in Genesis's eyes. I could only guess that everyone was thinking the same thing: this was it. Time to put our training to the test. Hopefully, the building didn't collapse on top of our heads in the process! I looked around frantically for Mickey, but he was nowhere to be found. Where was everybody?

Luc signaled for all of us to follow him. For a second time, we ran over to the hallway leading down to the op room. Luc scanned open the door at the bottom of the stairs and we jogged through to the far end of the room, running past the Dominion's floor plan. Pretty soon I would be seeing this in real time I realized, shaking my head at how bizarre this whole scene was.

We reached the end of the room where Luc scanned open the grate of an old freight elevator, and everyone piled in. I glanced at Luc, who seemed calm as a cucumber despite the bombing going on around us.

"Where is everyone else?" I finally asked, not able to keep my mouth shut any longer.

"They are beneath us making their way through the tunnels already."

"And Mickey?" I threw out as an afterthought, thinking he was probably leading the team.

"He's walking the compound, making sure everyone is out."

Go figure. Mickey was always the selfless leader. He would want to make sure everyone had vacated safely.

"We need to wait for him!" I exclaimed. "We can't just leave!" Luc made a motion with his wristband to scan the grate shut. I grabbed his wrist, frantic.

"Goro, this is standard procedure. He knows what he is doing." Luc easily broke my wrist hold. He lifted his wrist again to scan the grate shut.

"Goro, stop!" Alex was frenzied as he pulled me back. "He'll be okay!"

I gritted my teeth and squeezed my eyes shut as Alex let go of me. The grate was closing, and I made a split second decision. A feeling of déjà vu hit me; this was the same situation I had encountered at my father's workplace that day I drove the delivery van. It seemed like a hundred years ago. As if on autopilot, I dove through the grate opening just as it closed behind me.

"Goro!" Alex, Genesis, and Cory screamed after me as I fell into a roll and took off running back toward the schoolhouse. I was damned if I was going to let Mickey be the last man down.

Chapter 31

"Alone you run faster, but together we go farther."
—African Proverb

"Mickey!" I screamed above the siege of bombing coming from the heliplane ambush overhead. I darted into corridors and empty classrooms for any sign of him.

"Mickey!" I ran through the mess hall, shower rooms, dormitory, and still no sign of him. Maybe Mickey was already in the tunnels ahead of us, and we had just missed him.

Another particularly loud bomb went off, crumbling the cement and iron ceiling as I dodged the falling chunks. I ran into the kitchen, getting more worried and anxious with every step. It had been nearly destroyed as I picked my way over the rubble.

"Mickey, where are you?" I ran back out of what was left of the kitchen to the weapons vault in the schoolroom, checking one more time for him. Nothing. I almost gave up in despair, turning to jog back toward the freight elevator, when I heard an animal-like cry coming from down a shorter side corridor I had not checked. Damn, I had forgotten to check his quarters!

I bolted down the hallway and lurched to a stop in the doorway.

"Mickey!" My voice choked in my throat as I saw him on the floor, his legs pinned underneath a heavy oak wardrobe. The poster with the ADF's symbol had ripped off, and I kicked it out of the way as I scrambled over to him. I put all my weight into my legs as I attempted to lift the side of the wardrobe. It didn't budge. Where was that adrenaline rush my body needed that people get in emergencies? I needed superhuman strength to get this thing off him.

Another explosion tore through the building, and I heard rumbling as portions of the building collapsed in other parts of the compound.

"Son, leave me . . . ." Mickey breathed hard with each word. He was wearing his dorky headlamp for the impending journey underground and clutching an old picture frame in one hand.

"Can you move at all?" I ignored his directive and got down on my stomach to get a better view of how his body was situated underneath the furniture.

"I'm wedged in pretty darn good, I'm afraid . . . ." He chuckled, weak with pain. "Go!" He waved toward the door with his free hand.

I wasn't having it. "Hang tight, Mickey." *God, please give me the superhero strength that would have made my little brother proud*, I begged.

I took a deep breath and lifted with all my might. The wardrobe rose slightly, though it was enough to free Mickey.

"Go! Move!" I panted to Mickey. "Now!"

He put the picture frame in his mouth, grabbed the edge of the wardrobe, and pulled himself out slowly, getting one leg out and then the other. When he was free, he took the frame out of his mouth while I gripped him under the arms as I helped him to his feet. He faltered, almost collapsing and taking me down with him.

"Let's get out of here! I will help you walk." I started to put my arm around him, but he declined any assistance.

"Thanks, Goro. I got it."

The real trick would be to sidestep any more explosive destruction on the way there. I was surprised that the SR wasn't attempting to breach the compound on foot as well. I brushed that thought out of my mind and followed a limping Mickey toward the elevator, where he scanned the grate open. Someone had sent the elevator back up for us, and I made a mental note to thank that person later if we survived. Just as we stepped onto the elevator, the ceiling in the op room came crashing down onto the walls of the Dominion's floor plan.

Flashbacks of the Backlands permeated my mind at a relentless clip. Did I have post-traumatic stress? I realized I had been clenching my fists as the elevator descended. I glanced at the picture frame Mickey was holding.

"Who's that?" I motioned to the photo Mickey was holding. He tilted the frame for me to see. I saw a faded black and white photograph of a young girl, her brown hair in ponytails, tied up high in ribbons.

"Is this your granddaughter?" I ventured hesitantly, as he popped the photo out and chucked the wooden frame on the floor of the elevator. Guess he was keepin' it real.

"My daughter Arabella . . . ." Mickey gazed down at the smiling face. "One of the many casualties of this crappy life."

"How? Never mind. Sorry man, that sucks." I glanced at him; he was being unusually pensive. I didn't know how to respond to that.

Stepping off the elevator, Mickey pulled a waterproof map and small penlight out of his Evac pack. There was no one in sight. Whatever…I understood. I still tried them on my earpiece, but got no response.

Mickey and I bent heads, studying the map together.

"The team is advancing in this direction." He pointed to the western region of the elaborate maze of an antiquated underground tunnel system running beneath the city formerly known as Los Angeles.

"We've poured over these blueprints enough in class that I'm sure they could find it blindfolded if needed," I reminded him with confidence. "Let's blow these bastards to kingdom come."

I grinned at him and started off when he stopped me.

"Thanks, son . . . for coming back for me." He reached out his hand for me to shake.

"Yes, sir." I shook his hand firmly.

We took off at a steady clip, heading for the Dominion, still feeling the residual shuddering of explosions overhead. We had followed our route about a quarter of a mile, but when we rounded a corner, Mickey stopped short. I ended up smacking into to the back of him.

We both stared across the expanse of tunnel we needed to take, which was now completely blocked by fallen chunks of rubble and cement. The ceiling had collapsed. My heart stopped as I felt hopelessness wash over me. I thought of the rest of my team, Alex, Cory. I turned to Mickey.

"We need to backtrack and detour," he announced as if it was no big deal.

I pulled my own map out as Mickey pointed to another shorter tunnel path that was tricky, because it was known to be booby-trapped. It led to a basement area underneath a main part of the Dominion compound, and had the potential to be heavily guarded. For those reasons, this route had always been dismissed in training, but it looked like we didn't have a choice now.

"You've gotta be kidding me."

"We don't have any other option," Mickey said soberly. "Let's do it."

Mickey's limp was almost unnoticeable as we cut back to the shorter tunnel entrance. I felt a little bit like a jerk, because I felt like I was rushing him. Time was precious. This was not in the plan. But when does anything ever go according to plan? One thing we always repeated in training was, *whatever will go wrong, will.*

"Luc, Robbie, come in." Mickey tried again, but nothing.

I matched Mickey's slowing pace, fear rising in my chest.

"Dammit!" I sucked in my breath when I saw what he was seeing.

We stared at the patchwork of green laser lights that crisscrossed our intended escape route. The alarm system stretched as far as the eye could see. I had a hunch and took my Nitesite glasses off, and I was right. You couldn't see the thin laser threads without the glasses on. Someone could just go barreling through here with a flashlight and trip the alarm.

"We're screwed." I put my glasses back on, searching for a control panel.

"The SR knew about this shortcut all along," Mickey commented as if it was obvious.

"Well, unless one of us is a contortionist or gymnastic rock star, we aren't getting past this." My attempt at humor fell flat. "Damn! They're always one step ahead. What now?" I rubbed my face with my hands, racking my brain for ideas, anything.

"No worries, mirrors will do." Mickey cracked his knuckles. "Get the pocket signal mirror out of your gear kit. We can use them to diffract the light." He rummaged in the side pocket of his black cargo pants and held up the small mirror.

"Mickey, that only works in fantasy, not real life. Are the edges of our mirrors smooth enough to not break the beams?" I ran my finger over the beveled edge.

"Oh ye' of little faith." Mickey clucked, "If anything, we'll probably end up deflecting a laser into the main outsource and short circuit the whole system."

I walked as close to the network of lights as I dared, scanning the walls for the main control panel.

"It's there." Mickey pointed about midway down to a panel set into the wall that housed the main circuitry.

"Okay, but how exactly are we going to do this?" I was becoming more discouraged by the minute.

"You can cut the whining." Mickey approached the first laser, and I held my breath as he lowered his handheld mirror into the laser light. No bells went off as I breathed normally again, seeing the beam redirect toward the wall of origin.

"But, we're just going to hold the mirror?" I couldn't help it. "How are we going to move through this maze holding up pocket mirrors and rerouting this laser light show?"

"We'll do this slowly, in a chain, snaking our way down until we get to the control panel. Hurdle the lower beams." Mickey turned to me again, as I moved past him to the next beam. "Trust me."

I inserted my mirror at a snail's pace into the second laser beam, throwing the green light back against the wall at an acute angle. I felt like I was doing some weird twister dance as Mickey and I painstakingly made our way down the tunnel, sidestepping the lower lasers.

I was the final laser before the control panel, and as soon as I was in place, he broke his laser contact and limboed over to the panel. Mickey scanned it with his free hand, and it popped open. Thank God for the fake identity chips that he had created.

Mickey tinkered away inside, using various tools from his gear kit to disassemble the panel. It was so quiet my ears were buzzing. About three minutes went by, and I was ready to ask what was up in my generally impatient way when he suddenly ripped a large piece of the panel off, startling the heck out of me. All the lasers shut off at once, and I exhaled with relief, slapping Mickey on the back.

"Let's move," Mickey ordered, and hoofed onward.

"That was genius, man." Gotta give credit where credit is due.

"Thank you, but I doubt that is the end of the exciting booby traps the SR has set up down here," he responded with a sober face. I had thought of that already, but I was done being the Debbie Downer. I was sounding like a broken record with all my complaints.

"Maybe that laser maze was the one deterrent. We could be home free now." I was spit balling and didn't really know, to be honest.

Mickey stopped me so we could look at the map. He held his penlight angled over the maze of tunnels and discerned our distance by some of the points we had passed: a large drainage valve, a fork in our path, and other various pipe configurations.

He cut the light. "Three quarters of a mile down, three to go."

We had just rounded another corner when I glimpsed yet another roadblock.

I sighed, "This nonsense is tiresome." I slowed to a stop, with Mickey halting next to me.

"I'm not sure what the hell this is." Mickey peered closer, walking toward the patchwork of small canisters standing on end. Each one looked like a small silver thermos emitting a soft green glow near the top rim. I took off my Nitesites again, and the glow disappeared, just as I suspected. However, when I put my glasses back on again, I noticed one canister nearest to us whose green glow was flickering on and off intermittently. Was this one burning out? Was this another SR prank? Who knew how long they had been down here.

"Mines?" Mickey snorted incredulously. "This equipment is extinct!"

I knelt down next to the malfunctioning mine and without touching it, got as close as I dared with my penlight. I didn't see any other flashing lights or anything written on the surface, nothing that indicated to me that there was a motion detection system present.

"How are we going to surpass this obstacle course?" My piss-o-meter was off the charts.

The mines were littered throughout the tunnel for the next hundred yards or so. "Setting them up like dominoes above ground is cunning. You want to be the one to skip the first stone across this river of metal?" Mickey looked over at me, not really expecting an answer. "These suckers are laser bombs," Mickey continued in a whisper, as I got closer to the mine. "Any slight tremor will set them off."

"Awesome."

Mickey sighed next to me. "There's not much we can do. They are extremely hard to dismantle, and we can't just tiptoe through the tulips, I'm afraid."

"Seriously?" We hadn't come this far, figuratively as well as literally, just to turn and scamper back to the demolished compound with our tails between our legs. Screw that. I thought hard. I concentrated on bringing to mind any training I had received at the Academy, any research I had done in the past, any conversation I had overhead to help us in this dilemma.

"Wait!" I shouted. My eyes were glistening with excitement at the fact that I might be able to contribute some sort of a tech solution. I remembered my father's hobby of tinkering around on old scanners and whatnot in his shed back home.

"I know what to do. My dad jerry-rigged a lot of his stuff and, well, he didn't know he was specifically teaching at the time, but I paid attention."

"Except each of these landmines contains mercury that can detect the slightest vibration. Mercury poisoning on top of laser explosives is not a pretty sight. I also doubt they will have any anti-handling fuses," Mickey objected.

On a hunch, I checked my wristwatch and timed the glowing of the green canister light as it blinked on and off. I was assuming that "glow off" meant disarmed.

"This mine is at death's door." I gestured toward the sputtering canister. "It's armed to be on for exactly ten seconds and off for thirty seconds."

"Don't get any closer!" Mickey peered at it through his Nitesite glasses. "I'll do it."

I glanced up at him sharply.

"I've got nothing to lose, son," he said, and knelt, slowly reached out his hand, waiting. I didn't press him further as to what he meant by that, deciding to let it go for now. As soon as the green glow sputtered out again, he grabbed the land mine and inspected the top.

I almost lost my lunch. My nerves were wound so taut. I breathed in and out raggedly, watching my timer as Mickey unscrewed the top. He shined his penlight inside, confirming his suspicions.

"This is a mercury- and laser-infused explosive, magnetically sealed and equipped with anti-leveling trip vibration technology. High-end, very difficult to disarm."

"Put it down!" I yelled, giving him a five-second leeway.

He set it down, right side up, minus the cap, which made me nervous as hell. Mickey pulled some tools out of his gear kit.

I consulted my watch. "Okay, now."

Mickey deftly lifted the canister in one hand while lowering one of his tools into the interior of the mine. The suspense was making me want to scream.

"Okay, finished." Mickey set the mine down, screwing the cap back on. My eyes never left my watch as I waited for the thirty-second mark. Three, two, one . . . .

No glow. However, Mickey still stood up slowly and backed away, pulling me backwards with him.

"So they do have anti-diffusion fuses, huh?" I wiped my forehead with the back of my hand. My knees cracked after having rested on my haunches for the last two minutes.

"Negative, they don't—I rerouted two wires on a hunch. Luckily, it worked."

I shook my head in amazement. Talk about a tough old coot; he didn't care if he walked out of these tunnels alive or dead. Something about the fact that he had a martyr's death wish made me profoundly sad.

"We don't have the time or resources to disable the rest, Goro; there are far too many of them to count, and dismantling each one would take a hundred years." He made a wide sweeping motion with his right arm.

I shook my head in the feeble light of Mickey's headlamp, considering our options. "The only way through this is either blowing them all up before we proceed, which is inadvisable due to the possibility of collapsing the tunnel on us, or going over it with our rappelling ropes and doing a soft landing on the other side."

"That's possible. I got excited earlier because my father knows some tricks, and he had a method of minimizing vibration when disassembling tech equipment."

I glanced overhead for a possible grappling point for my rope. There were a couple of pipes running along the top of the tunnel ceiling; I guess the SR wasn't concerned with someone monkeying their way over the top of their playground.

"We have anti-vibration gloves in our gear. We can affix those to the bottom of our boots to give extra padding and absorb the impact." I wasn't totally convinced it would work because the gloves were meant to keep your hands stable when handling vibrating equipment, but it was worth a try.

"One swing across isn't going to cut it. The distance is too long."

"Just track with me. Get out your gloves." I took mine out of a side pocket and loaded my rappelling rope into my crossbow, which had been strapped onto my back. I then took some black adhesive tape and taped my gloves to the bottoms of my boots, cushioning them for impact.

"We're not going to Tarzan across this thing; we'll shimmy across." Didn't matter what circumstances we were in, I had to crack at least one joke in the moment, relieving some of my tension and stress.

I backed up really far so I would have enough room to make the attempt at aiming and attaching the hook without having it crash down into the minefield if I missed. I was hoping to make this in one shot.

Mickey's voice of reason reared its ugly head. "Wait, what is your plan? We can't just go launching steel grappling hooks into the air willy-nilly."

"Trust me," It was my turn to preach. I prayed to God that my idea would work. I loaded my steel peg-ended rappelling rope, coiled and ready to spring, into the crossbow. I aimed the crossbow at a point on the ceiling close enough to one of the pipes but far enough away that it wouldn't puncture a pipe if I missed.

I briefly closed my eyes, reopened them, and tapped the trigger. The rope went hurtling toward the targeted area, and the steel peg pierced the ceiling snugly upon impact. Yes!

"So far so good." I slapped Mickey's shoulder. "Now, watch."

"Not a chance. I'll go first, rookie."

He approached the dangling rope, which was still a good twenty feet from the path of the mine canisters, and grabbed it, pulling himself hand over hand to the top of the tunnel. He grabbed the seven-inch diameter pipe above me and wrapped his hands and toes (barely) around the circumference. He hesitated for a second, hanging there and looking down at me, who was watching him in silence.

"Be careful not to drop anything," Mickey cautioned. "Not even sweat," he added in case I forgot about this possible dilemma.

"Or fall," I added with a snort.

He began the painstaking trek of hanging from the pipe, inch-worming his way upside down. It would be tedious work, but I believed traversing the distance was doable. It was so quiet as he slowly made his way down the pipe; he took a quick break every thirty feet or so to wipe the sweat from his forehead.

When he cleared the minefield, he kept going another twenty feet before he used my rope that he had brought to secure to the pipe. He gripped the rope with his feet, descending hand over hand, touching down lightly on the other side. He stood there for a second, breathing hard and turned to look behind him at the undisturbed mines. I had a sudden urge to shout "Hallelujah!" that it had worked and no one had died. I made a giant gesture with my arm indicating I would follow, while I grabbed the rope.

My mind briefly flashed to my family, doing God knows what, wherever they were. My father would have been damn proud of me just about now.

As soon as I had that thought, the gravity of our situation hit me full force, and I was filled with sobering apprehension. Our compound had been ambushed unexpectedly, no surprise there. We had a limited number of ADF members, around 115 or so compared to the approximately 100,000 soldiers enlisted in the SR assigned to the Dominion. The odds seemed impossible. A suicide mission no matter how you sliced it, and we knew this going in. If (or more like when) I was killed, my life wouldn't have been lost in vain. I tried to clear my pounding head, not wanting to dwell too long on what the future held. The ADF was doing the best they could. Someone had to take on the Sovereign Regime. Might as well be us, and might as well be now.

Chapter 32

"Courage is not the absence of fear, but the triumph over it. The brave man is not he who does not feel afraid, but he who conquers that fear."

—Nelson Mandela

I followed in Mickey's wake, grunting my way across using the same method he had used. At one point, one of my feet slipped, and I hung on for dear life, my leg dangling. I sucked in my breath when I saw I was right smack over the mines. I swung my leg violently back up over the pipe again, sweating like a madman. I'd forgotten my damn sweatband again. It looked so geeky on me, but that wouldn't have mattered now. I didn't want any drops to land on a canister below, God forbid. When I made it to the rope, I took a minute, and slid down, soft landing on my gloved feet.

I copped a squat next to Mickey, and rested my head against the wall, taking a couple of deep breaths.

"Good times, man." I held out my fist for a bump. "Pound it."

Mickey complied, standing up, resolute and ready to press on.

"We have only about a hundred yards to go," Mickey shoved his map back into his front pocket. "Let's roll."

We took off running for the end of the line: the door that would take us into the SR's domain. We made it to the grated elevator under the Dominion with no more surprises. Problem was, it looked liked it hadn't been used in a millennium; the whole thing seemed welded into place and inoperable. The outside grating was coated with rust and dust and draped in cobwebby muck. The glass covering the scan area was cracked, with no lights emanating from the control panel.

Fueled by adrenaline and sheer impatience, Mickey and I threw all our strength into lifting the grate. It didn't budge, so we ended up micro-lasering through some of the rust with a tool from my gear kit, and it worked. The gate inched open.

Piling in, Mickey scanned the interior panel, which miraculously lit up; it still worked. I was hoping the rest of the ADF was busy engaging the SR in attack, and no one would be able to detect that something had been scanned. We steadily rose into the underbelly of the Dominion, grinding to a halt on the other end. Mickey did a quick sweep of the outside room with his headlamp. So far, so good. I went to open the grate, but sure enough, it didn't open either.

"Torch it," Mickey directed. When I had lasered through the steel bars on the grating, I wrenched it open as quietly as I could. I stepped out, seeing that we were in some sort of basement storage room.

"It smells like ass." I wrinkled my nose in disgust.

It was dark and dank, and smelled moldy and wet. I had no sooner taken a step when I heard a fast movement and an arm wrapped around my neck in an attempted hold. This time I was fast, turning my head to the side, plucking the man's hands away and sending a razor sharp elbow into his groin. Grabbing his hair, I spun around and kneed him in the groin.

Mickey had also been accosted, but was grappling with the man on the ground. He yanked the SR soldier to his feet and put him in a guillotine choke and ended up lifting him off his feet, choking him out. My adrenaline shot through the roof, as we cleared the rest of the room for any other stragglers.

I recognized the corner spiral staircase from the Dominion's floor plan that had been bored into us in countless classes. I wondered again where the rest of the ADF was right now and was about to try them again, but Mickey put a finger to his lips and then pointed up the stairwell, indicating that there may be more SR goons just on the other side of the door at the top of the stairs.

I knew the ADF was sticking to the planned op even though they were minus two; I could only hope they were succeeding and unharmed. I led us silently up the staircase. Wait, how did I end up being the point man? Maybe Mickey was letting me take a leadership role for the satisfaction of seeing the student become the teacher. I forged ahead using the hand signals that had become rote over many months of training.

We crept up to the door at the top, rifles raised. It was absolute silence from here on out. My heart was pumping like 160 beats a minute. The black steel door was closed. Of course, why would the SR leave anything standing open? I pulled out my small laser torch and circled a hole in which to insert my mini cam. I watched the attached view panel for any movement. I could only see three cameras in this neck of the woods. It appeared that this corridor was vacant. Probably no one ever came down into the basement anyway. I also assumed the SR legions were no doubt focusing their energy on our team, not realizing Mickey and I were absent.

I lasered a larger hole around the initial small hole, put my fingers through, and pulled. The door slid open a few inches, and I tossed out the cam scramblers, two circular black electromagnetic discs that distorted the images for whoever might be watching on the other end. Our identities may be chipless, but we were still susceptible to surveillance. No invisibility suits over here. Cam scramblers aren't fool proof, but it bought us some time before they came investigating their malfunctioning camera equipment. This lair was immense, and the scrambled camera images would draw the attention of the SR sooner rather than later.

I heard the small pop as the discs made contact with the corridor walls. It would be a while before we were in the heart of the Dominion, and I was a little perplexed as to why I wasn't hearing any battle sounds yet. Maybe they were focused on terrorizing the city? The ADF compound was most certainly a total loss by now, lying in a rubble of ruins. *God bless the world*, I told myself sarcastically before stepping through the doorway.

Chapter 33

"The only thing necessary for the triumph of evil is for good men to do nothing."

—Edmund Burke

Darkness enveloped the cavernous room, save for the one candle atop the altar. A man faced the shadows beyond the curtain.

"The petulant resistance scum have arrived," Ash Sheitan spoke in a scathing tone.

"Wonderful." The voice hidden in shadow was low and strong. "This will be entertaining."

"Step on them now, while they are clenched within our possession," Sheitan insisted.

"Patience, my prophet . . . all in due time."

Sheitan steepled his hands. "How would you wish the young man be delivered?" Sheitan raised his eyes, addressing his master directly.

"No need for provocation." Davio paused. "He will find his way to me."

Chapter 34

"Only those who dare to fail greatly can ever achieve greatly."
—Robert Kennedy

I signaled for Mickey to follow, and we crept through the hallway quietly, alert for possible threats. We silently advanced in stealth mode side by side. I was grateful we had practiced drills in the Dominion's floor plan room, because we knew the hallways and rooms like the backs of our hands.

We approached the end of the first hallway, covering all areas of danger, seeing that the coast was clear. Either the SR was unaware yet as to our presence, or they were biding their time, waiting to pounce. I threw down more cam scramblers as we rounded the corner. As soon as Mickey could get to the control hub, he could work his magic and shut down the entire system, not the least of which was the surveillance system.

We whispered through our earpieces in calling out which doors were closed, clearing each room we passed. Our primary mission was to take out the SR's mainframe and corrupt the entire identity chip system. Getting to the control hub as quickly as possible was paramount. Terminating Davio and his legion of underbosses was necessary, though just icing on the cake.

All of a sudden, the familiar sound of laser fire accompanying a loud commotion in the distance had us advancing down the hallways as quickly as we could. When we reached the noise, we flanked the hallway corners, seeing multiple SR soldiers and about ten of our own ADF engaged in battle. Man, were they a sight for sore eyes; my energy renewed in a rushing second wind as I saw our men returning enemy fire behind their laser shields. They inched forward in a stack, attempting to corner their prey. I saw several SR shot down as relief washed over me; I had identified Alex by the ADF sticker he had slapped on the back of his vest and I recognized Cory's squat build. I couldn't tell who the other few ADF members were though; we all looked the same in our gear.

Luc was leading the pack forward in full assault mode, gaining ground on the SR. He tossed out a laser flash bang, as the last of the SR soldiers retreated rapidly. However, it wouldn't be long before more SR roaches would come crawling out of the woodwork and we would soon be outnumbered.

At that point Mickey and I both rounded the hallway corner and joined the back of the team, rifles raised and at the ready for back-up. I could hear the two remaining SR soldiers yelling for reinforcements through their earpieces, but Luc and Mickey blazed ahead through the smoky haze and shot both men, killing them instantly.

"Let's go!" Luc's orders echoed in my earpiece following the ensuing silence. He signaled to the team to head in the direction of the courtyard, to resume his plan of assaulting bottom-up, however, this was in the exact opposite direction from the control hub. El Hefe was back in charge, I could see. Everyone started to move when I stopped, refusing to budge.

"Hold up," I protested, "we need to get to the control room- and judging from the hours of homework we were all subjected to, it's this way," I hooked a thumb over my shoulder, a bad feeling starting in the pit of my stomach. Luc halted and faced me.

"First order of business is to rendezvous with the rest of the team, continuing the mission of seizing the courtyard and encircling the enemy." Luc countered, speaking to me like I was an idiot. "When separated for any reason, it is the ADF's standard procedure to reconvene in the previously decided appointed location."

"Whoa, whoa, whoa…you're whole idea was to crash the identity chip system from within. The Dominion's mainframe is that way, Rambo." I didn't stop to explain what I had called him.

He took several steps back towards me. I met him halfway.

The last thing anyone wanted was to stand by and watch Luc and I locked in a power struggle showdown.

"First things first, cowboy," Luc pointed out. "The courtyard is our first foothold to acquire; you've been briefed a hundred times." His tone was slow and deliberate. He was just *waiting* for me to object.

"I understand that gaining footholds is critical, however, if and when the team breaks contact -like you did when you left Mickey and I pissing in the compound's cellar- the aforementioned footholds can be utilized for congregating again at a later time, sir." I didn't miss a beat as I thrust my index finger towards the floor in anger.

"Oh, come now, you had your buddy with you; you weren't solo!" Luc's words were dripping with sarcasm.

"Goro, calm down." Someone had pulled off their tactical head gear and I could see it was Genesis. She tried to pull me away from Luc. I stood firm.

"There you go again with your Indian chief syndrome," I taunted in his face.

"Can't we just get through one cozy game of Candy Land, playing nice, without you acting the insubordinate clown, breaking rank... again?" Luc was egging me on and I could feel myself getting ready to snap.

We were nose to nose again, as I felt a hand on my arm.

"I dunno, can't you just be the solid leader we need right now? But I guess being a rebel feels good, old man."

"Stand down," Luc roared.

I made a move to leave, but Luc's quiet sneering words stopped me. "I dare you."

"Do you triple dog dare me, you prehistoric f–"

I pulled back my fist, but Mickey cut me off, pulling my arm down.

"Knock it off." Mickey left no room for argument. "We'll breach the control hub, Goro, cool it! For now, let's regroup with the rest of the team."

I was sullen as I fell into step behind the team as we quickly made our way back the way we had come towards the open courtyard. This was BS.

We reached the doors to the courtyard without any other incidents, which was odd, but as soon as we reached the double doors in stealth, Luc held up a full stop signal. Any and every mission we'd been trained for ceased in that very moment. The scene that lay before us, I hope never to see again in my lifetime.

Shell-shocked, I stared at about twenty of my fallen comrades, hung upside down by their feet from trees and posts, their throats slit. Blood was dripping down their faces, gelatinizing in their hair. I saw Michael, dangling a few feet away from Kevin, his eyes still open.

I whipped around and choked on the vomit threatening to project out of my mouth. I knew we would have to account for some casualties, but this? This was barbaric.

Luc signaled for us to stay exactly where we were hidden in the shadows. I glanced at Mickey; his face was grim. I looked around at the rest of my horrified team. I saw Cory keel over out of the corner of my eye and I knelt to steady him.

"Cory, stay with us, buddy! Don't cave now. Come on!" I was faltering; my pep talk days were severely numbered. My voice caught in my throat. His eyes had glassed over, and I slapped his face lightly to get his attention.

He snapped out of it and straightened up, readying his rifle, looking me in the eyes. "I got it." His eyes were hollow though.

"Where's the rest of our team?" Alex whispered, as Luc pointed off into the distance.

It began to rain, just a drizzle, as I watched the remaining members of our team being herded out of the courtyard into a building, taken as POW's, no doubt. The remaining defeated ADF marched slowly, hands bound behind their backs, while SR soldiers shoved some of them forward, Robbie being one of them.

Just then, Mickey grabbed Alex by the front of his vest. "You have to get to the control hub." He looked really ill.

I hesitated as he shoved something into Alex's hands. "Do it."

It was the chip holding the destruction virus code.

"Go!" He pushed me backward, rasping- I didn't stop to think; I just obeyed.

"Alex," I hitched a thumb over my shoulder indicating he would follow. I placed one hand on Cory's shoulder and the other on Alex. We briefly put our heads together.

"Hoo yah!" The three of us quietly chanted.

"See you on the other side," were my parting words as we left Cory.

Genesis made a move to accompany us, but I stopped her with a firm hand on her arm.

"No, stay with the team. Besides, you know Davio is a one-man deal." My tone made my intentions very clear.

"Behebik, habibi," she whispered into my ear. I relented then, embracing her quickly.

Alex and I took off, me worried about Mickey, Cory and the others. I cleared my mind of all noise and attempted to enter the warrior's mindset, the zone where I focused on one purpose alone. However, the image of the pallor of death on the faces of those I trained with kept slapping me in the face. Grieving would have to wait.

Rifles raised, Alex and I crisscrossed in stealth mode through corridors, tossing cam scramblers down as we went. On about the fifth hallway, while attempting to clear a corner, I saw four SR soldiers marching robotically in our direction. Great, but then I hadn't expected to come out of this unscathed. They hadn't made us yet, so I signaled to Alex, who had seen them about the same time I had. He signaled to me his preference in eliminating this threat, and I concurred. Taking them by surprise was our advantage.

As soon as the first SR had turned the corner that we were crouching behind, I headlocked him, slitting his throat. Nothing short of hatred fueled my fire and propelled me forward.

Three other SR members behind him were so startled that Alex and I were able to get off three rounds together, bringing them down. We left them in a heap and continued forward, undeterred by the realization that we didn't have any more cam scramblers. *Screw the cameras*, I thought. I didn't care anymore. The control hub was within our grasp.

Alex and I reached the door panel to the Dominion's entire mainframe without any further SR entanglements. There were sure to be SR inside, however. Alex flat out pounded on the door, bold as brass. Bet they weren't expecting that; nobody knocked on doors anymore.

He and I flanked the door and waited. It slid open after a few seconds. When the SR dude's head emerged from inside, I round kicked his face and hammer fisted the back of his brainstem as he went down. That brought about four more SR guys shouting and firing continuous lasers through the open doorway. Alex and I dove through the doorway, rolling to the right and to the left. Since we knew the layout of the room, we approached the designated coverage areas from which we could return fire.

I don't know if these particular SR goons had air for brains or what, but they looked totally caught off guard. Didn't they prep for situations like this? I took aim as I let my lasers rip, killing two of the men right between the eyes. Alex neatly knocked off the other two, and we dragged the first dude back into the room, closing the door.

"Alex, you're up," I patted down the nearest SR soldier, grabbing his earpiece. I shoved it into my ear and could hear orders barking non-stop. It sounded like the Sovereign Regime knew the entire time that the ADF would be dropping in on them. Dammit, of course this raid had been expected; it was just a ruse to amuse Davio.

"Listen!" Alex's words pierced the quiet room. "Do you hear that?"

I humored him for a second, straining my other ear for whatever he was referencing.

"Hear what?" I was busy searching the fallen SR men.

"That's just it. Nothing. It's way too frickin' quiet right now."

"Who cares? Do your thing! Of course it's going to be quiet, dumbass, our team has all but been decimated!" I was much too shaken with emotion and wanted to cut the chitchat, get business done, and get the hell out of here.

Alex sat down at one of the stations and tapped commands onto the console at lightning speed. *Gotta love his expertise*, I briefly admired as I stood behind the tech genius.

"Wait!" I yelled. Alex twisted in his seat to look at me, confusion in his eyes.

"Pull up the passcode screen," I ordered him, "Once this thing goes under, I won't be able to do this again."

Alex complied, and I leaned over and tapped in my father's passcode on the off chance that he might not be wearing Alex's metal cuff invention. I hoped to God I would find some information, anything, and I sighed with relief as a list of his last recorded activities popped up. I scanned the top few lines. He was stationary right now in a location unknown to me on the outskirts of the city. At least he was alive, and I now knew the general area where he was hiding out. That would mean the SR would also know where my family was located, dammit, but I was hoping the SR would be distracted and I could get to my family before they could.

"Okay, go." I stepped back again as Alex took the chip from his pocket and inserted it into a small port in front of him.

"Running twenty-digit extraction . . . now." His fingers flew over the touch keyboard in front of him. Alex literally crossed his fingers as I sent up a quick prayer. We both watched the screen before us go black. No 3D images popped up.

"Nothing is happening!" I spat through gritted teeth.

"It might take a minute, bro—damn, no chill!" He screamed. His nerves were just as frayed as mine.

I stood behind Alex for what seemed like an eternity before a small speck of light appeared before us on the screen. It started small and then spiraled outward, catapulting off the screen in a shower of 3D sparkling bytes, causing us both to jump backward out of the way.

"Is it working?" I cried out.

Alex was so focused on the scene before us he didn't answer.

The light spun in a dizzying array of images that gathered steam as they conjoined to form a larger structure until we observed what looked like a 3D control room before us. Alex walked into the 3D room and stood in front of an identical control panel. My eyes bugged out of my head as he tapped some commands into the panel before him. I couldn't believe this was really happening. I saw the three-dimensional room disintegrate, one pixel at a time.

Alex finally looked at me and said, "Go do what you need to do, Goro! Kill that sonofabitch!" He shoved me backward. I spun and took off out the door, knowing that hell may be waiting next.

Chapter 35

"The hardest walk is walking alone, but it can be the strongest."
—Unknown

I stealthily made my way toward Davio's lair, my senses on high alert. My heart was pounding in my chest; my pulse quickened, and the blasted sweat started trickling down my forehead again. I made my way to the upper courtyard with caution, knowing Davio's inner sanctum was just on the other side of the fountain. Upon reaching the circular fountain, I could see that the sun was setting among pinkish orange clouds against the broken skyline of the city. It would have been a breathtaking view under different circumstances.

The whole atmosphere was still, chilled. Not a soul was in sight. It unnerved me that it really *was* quiet. It occurred to me that this might have been orchestrated for my benefit, just to lure my ass forward. I had no doubt that Davio knew where I was at this very moment, and had ordered all his men to clear a path for me, straight into the lion's den.

I approached the immense circular stone building in silence, rifle raised, and I recognized the same tall oak doors from my most recent nightmare. They swung inward without a sound. Great. I knew in my gut that this was it. This was the moment that made me physically sick to my stomach, that I had psyched myself up for, for months. No turning back. I was long past the point of no return. I was almost pissed at myself that I was giving Davio what he wanted: a meeting with me. But it didn't matter. I was planning on murdering the bastard even if I perished in the process. We'd both go out in a shower of fireworks.

As soon as I took that first step inside the cold and darkened interior, a palpable terror descended upon my entire body, making my skin crawl. I felt a heavy inner heat, couched in dread, emanate from the core of my being into my extremities, causing my hands to shake of their own accord. My anxiety ratcheted up to immeasurable heights. I wanted to beat feet out of there, and it took every ounce of strength I had to force myself to press on. I was scared as hell; I struggled to get a bead on my surroundings. The warrior mindset that Mickey was always harping about had exited right out the oak doors I had entered, and I didn't have to turn to know that the doors were closing behind me.

I stepped forward, with each foot not quite finding solid ground. It could've been quicksand or carpet for all I knew in the low light of the single overhead chandelier. My mind was foggy, as if a blindfold had been pulled over my eyes with my brain intermittently firing circuits in a wave of erratic amnesia.

When I ended up in what I guessed was the center of the room, I stopped, glancing behind me quickly, my eyes darting to and fro, taking note of the floor-to-ceiling dark velvet drapes flanked by two marble pillars. The drapes spanned the entire width of the back of the room.

Remembering the 3D images from my grandfather's chip, I assumed the altar with the tome and the throne were behind the drapes.

I held my rifle at the ready, in unstable sweaty hands. I braced myself to face whatever emerged from the depths. I was not about to venture behind the curtain, but I would wait Davio out if I had to, doing everything in my meager power to emerge from this demon cave alive. I felt as armed as I would ever be, but then who is ever ready? I had the knowledge, training, and weapons I needed to succeed, and I hoped against hope that some sheer dumb luck would keep me in the game.

I held my breath as I watched the drapes slowly part down the middle. A leg clad in black slacks emerged as a man dressed in a black suit stepped toward me. I stared in silence. He was not very tall; he had black hair combed straight back, and he looked more like a handsome politician than a venomous dictator. There was a calm and confident demeanor surrounding him, which was throwing me off. If it wasn't for the ominous vibe in the air, I would've thought he was some game show host coming to shake my hand and welcome me to the contest. This was Davio? It was hard to believe that this man had initially forged peaceful relationships among many warring nations on his rise to power.

When he halted in front of me and we stood face to face, I felt an immediate subconscious warning that something was very off. I noticed a strangeness about his eyes. They were as black as a moonless night, but they flashed with some weird unearthly light. If you blinked, you missed it. The fact that I was leveling a laser rifle at his head didn't seem to alarm him in the least.

I was staring at everyone's worst fear. Before me stood the one sobering terror that wakes a man up in the middle of the night: an in the-flesh-encounter with the ruler of the earth, Davio himself. He sweet-talks a man into submission with promises of grandeur and riches, then swiftly destroys that man with no hope of escape. I stared at him as his deep red mouth parted in a low, deliberate smile.

"You expected me." I found my voice, not lowering my rifle for a second. I was scared out of my mind.

"Of course," Davio answered evenly, meeting my steady gaze without flinching.

I scoffed. "You're responsible for the massacre of hundreds of thousands of innocent people." My breathing was laborious within my tightened chest. "You are the epitome of evil. You murder anyone who doesn't bow to your commands. Your empty promises kill. You executed my friend . . . my team . . . my innocent, unarmed brother . . . ." I stumbled over the words, swallowing hard. "You are to blame for the miserable state of the world we live in."

Davio spread his hands, tilting his head. "Perhaps."

"Perhaps?" I was incredulous. He grinned again, his eyes flashing. I wanted to pummel him into the marble floor with the end of my rifle.

"YOU EXECUTED MY BROTHER!" I yelled, hoping to catch him off guard, my eyes still fixated on his evil eyes. Hate was coursing through my veins, distorting my vision, and contorting my purpose for being there. Intense emotions were messing with my clarity of mission, and somehow I sensed that he was counting on that. We stood before each other, watching . . . waiting.

Davio stared into my dilated pupils, unblinking, attempting to assuage my anger with a reassuring smile, but then his grin began to fade. An eerie consternation etched his face, and I felt an unseen force push my rifle down against my will. I strained against whatever otherworldly power was pulling the rifle from my fingers. I ended up shooting off a few lasers in the process, hitting Davio twice in the right leg. The shots had no effect.

Oh, my God. I watched in horror as my rifle broke free of my grasp and swung in a slow downward arc so that when and if Davio took hold of it, the barrel would be leveled at *my* head. I knew full well that once Davio acquired my weapon, it would mean the end of me.

In the nanosecond it took for the rifle to reach Davio's hands, I dropped to the floor and rolled to the left, jumping to my feet behind one of the pillars as temporary cover. When I peeked out from behind the pillar, I saw Davio grip the rifle with his left hand. He turned in my direction. Damn.

"Sheitan," Davio said in a level tone, summoning someone else to our little meet and greet.

A much taller man emerged from behind the drapery. He looked familiar. Where had I seen him before? His head was shaved smooth, and he had to be at least six and a half feet tall. He was wearing a long black robe of sorts, for lack of a better description. What I didn't expect was that instead of both men closing in on my obvious hiding place behind the pillar, Davio handed the rifle to the taller man, and I stared in amazement as the rifle vanished into thin air at the wave of the man's hand. WTF! Who were these men? Did ADF leadership really know who they were up against with these two?

Ash Sheitan made his way over to me as Davio looked on. Seemed his henchman did his dirty work, I smirked. I felt the atmosphere change with every step he took. The air was so thick with oppression I could hardly breathe. It was suffocating. Screw this; I made a snap decision to advance on Sheitan myself, leaving the cover of the pillar. He was not startled with my rapid movement. I pulled one of my two knives from my waistband and spun it in my hand, gripping the handle with three fingers, my thumb on the hilted top. Sheitan just grinned.

We circled each other, all of my senses on high alert, me waiting for him to make the first move. I matched his rhythm in order to assume the lead position. The wicked grin on his face spooked me, to say the least. His body language indicated for me to go ahead and take the lead; he didn't care. The confidence in the way he moved was unnerving. It seemed as though he was unarmed and had no need of any weapons, or maybe I was just hypothesizing in my hyper vigilant state. He showed no fear whatsoever that I was brandishing a weapon at him.

My mind raced—was he going to attack? Use diversion? Pull some terrifying magic stunt to freak me out? I focused on remaining calm but not relaxed. I was mindful of my breathing and of keeping my back and abdominal muscles taut. I concentrated on maintaining a 180-degree peripheral sight plane, watching my enemy through narrowed eyes. The knife in my right hand became an extension of my entire arm. I drew on every piece of training I had received and silently thanked Luc for being so hard on me.

I faked fear in my eyes and suddenly screamed at something just over his left shoulder, sending a palm heel strike to his lower face and thrusting my knife toward his mid-section in the split second it took him to react. The strike did little to stun him. He immediately cammed the knife away and grabbed my wrist in a stronghold, pulling my body against his left side. His swift, hard movement shoved me backward. I scrambled to regain my base and space. Simultaneously, he grabbed my chin, wrenching my head to the side away from him. At the same time, in one swift move, he kneeled, bending me over his left knee. My back was painfully arched over his knee as he shoved my face down even further. I struggled as he pressed my wrist toward the floor, causing my hand to drop the knife.

I gasped for breath in my unnatural position. He just laughed. I strained to see his evil face looking down at me, his eyes flashing in a similar fashion to Davio's. I saw my knife on the floor, still within reach. Why had he not kicked it away or retrieved the knife himself? I scrambled to get out of this hold, and fast. I took the chance to swing my right leg up, aiming for a snap kick to his throat or his face. He lunged out of the way, throwing me clear across the room. I slammed into the far wall but catapulted to my feet, mentally stifling the sharp pain shooting throughout my body. He had swiped my knife off the floor in the time it took me to get upright.

I retrieved my second knife from my waistband and circled him once again, knowing with a sickening dread that I was no match for this man. He was taller, more skilled, and quicker than I was. Maybe I could use his over confidence to my advantage somehow. However, I didn't kid myself into thinking I could outsmart this opponent or out muscle him. All the while, I kept well aware of where Davio stood in the background enjoying our cat and mouse game.

Sheitan held my knife pointed in my direction yet above his head. I kept both my hands close to my body, still on the offensive and prepping for my next defensive attack. He must have concluded this was a no-contest fight because this time, he lunged forward, attempting to slash across my chest. I made two neat cuts along his arm as my knife traveled up to his throat. He widened his eyes slightly, and I realized it was possible to catch this man off guard. I grabbed his arm in the process, rolling his body with all my strength and vice gripping his wrist. He shrugged free in an effortless shirk before I could slice his throat. Dammit!

He was visibly pissed that I had managed to get in some strikes after all, but I was waiting to see the welcome sight of blood flowing from his two impact wounds. When my eyes scanned his arm, all I observed was torn cloth and the absence of any blood. No blood was seeping from his wounds! I was positive I had felt my sharp knife penetrate his clothed arm—what the hell? Did he give me that move for free just to show his eerie indestructible immortality?

He circled me again, fully composed, and I lunged forward, attacking to the side, across the front of his chest, with him blocking my every move. Screw this. I faked to the side and sent a swift kick to his groin. He buckled slightly as I swung my knife in a high arc over my head, ready to plunge it into his heart. As the tip of the knife made contact with his chest, I fully expected the blade to sink into flesh, ribs, cartilage, and hopefully his heart. Instead, my hand was violently repelled backward, sending the knife flying. It was as if I had just stabbed a block of marble! My knife had merely ricocheted off his chest. I stumbled backward in horror, steadying my jarred hand with my other.

He grinned at me beneath hooded eyes as he advanced toward me, but I had managed to snag my knife from the floor and was flipping it over and over in my hand. I don't know why I even tried, but I had to do something, anything. I grasped the blade and hurled it as hard as I could at his head. He deflected it easily with the knife he had commandeered from me just moments before. The knife clattered across the marble floor, skittering toward Davio's feet. Sheitan and I faced off. I was now weaponless, out of options, and staring down the tunnel of certain death.

Chapter 36

"If you know the enemy and know yourself, you need not fear the result of a hundred battles."

—Sun Tzu's *The Art of War*

"Enough." Davio approached me with an air of commanding authority, motioning Sheitan aside. I couldn't tell if Sheitan was pissed because he couldn't continue sparring with me or if he was simply giving Davio a turn in this sick game of king of the hill. I lost concentration, my eyes shifting back and forth from Davio to Sheitan. My eyes settled on Davio's as he stopped in front of me. I guess he was cutting into my dance with Sheitan. I attempted to assume a fighting stance, but realized that I could not move. My extremities refused to cooperate. I could not lift my arms no matter how hard I tried. He made no move to fight me.

"You are in possession of something that belongs to me." Davio's every word was dripping with venom. "If you relinquish it now, I will spare someone's life . . . someone of your choosing, but only one." He accentuated his last words with his forefinger. "And there is no chivalry in saving oneself, I must protest."

He must have been unaware that the system was currently being crashed by Alex, and no one was storming into the room to tell him, either. I found that very odd. I was exhausted and wanted this daymare over with.

"What makes you think I am going to surrender?" I challenged him, grateful my voice worked, but still terrified as his mysterious hold over me had me weighing my options.

"Do you actually believe you have sovereignty over nations? Over nature? Over the world?" Emotions overruled me, and I was shouting. I wanted to break free and choke the life out of him, crush his windpipe with my thumbs.

Davio laughed derisively, even clapping his hands together.

"Tsk, tsk, tsk," he clucked under his tongue. My feet glued to the floor, I glanced to where Sheitan was standing near the curtain, and my mind raced with thoughts of creating another diversion. I don't know if making eye contact with Sheitan was a mistake, but he leapt into action, reaching me in three long strides. He wrapped one hand around my neck and lifted me effortlessly off the floor. Sheitan's death grip brought swimming red blotches into my vision. Damn. My arms did not work, and it'd be only a matter of minutes before I lost consciousness.

"Speak!" Davio commanded.

I saw his now humorless eyes flashing with an evil light, boring into my soul. This was the end. I might as well kiss my sorry-ass life goodbye. I had failed. Thoughts of my friends, my family, Mickey, Genesis, Zan, Josiah . . . flickered through my mottled brain. I opened my mouth to give in when I heard someone scream.

"Davio!"

The interruption sliced through the paralysis Davio held over me, and I took my shot. I plucked Sheitan's hand from my neck while simultaneously delivering a strong head butt to his face; he dropped me and staggered backward. I hoped I had broken his nose, but once again, I saw no blood. Undeterred and unhurt, he roared and lunged toward me, but Davio held up a hand, stopping him in his tracks. We all looked at who had screamed Davio's name.

I caught a fast glimpse of Mickey leaning against the back wall. He had entered Davio's sanctum unseen, unheard. I stared as Mickey slid down into a sitting position with his back against the wall. *Oh, my God* . . . . He looked butchered. It seemed he had been shot several times in the abdomen and left leg, making it difficult for him to remain upright. A lump lodged in my throat as my eyes began to sting.

"You piece of putrid scum." Mickey forced the words from his bloodied mouth. His angry eyes egged Davio to venture forward.

My eyes shifted to Davio, who stood his ground. He and Sheitan were so focused on Mickey that they seemed to have forgotten about me. Maybe they were confident I wasn't going anywhere. I took a step in Mickey's direction to test their reaction, and Sheitan grabbed me by my hair and yanked me hard backward. I hit the marble floor on my side, slapping the ground with my hand and twisting my body to absorb the impact. Sheitan thrust his boot down on my neck hard, keeping me pinned to the floor. I grasped his boot with both hands, trying to break free, coughing. I watched as Davio advanced on Mickey with a murderous look on his face. Mickey had succeeded in pushing Davio's buttons; insulting his pride and vanity must have done the trick.

Mickey slid something across the floor toward me and I caught it with one hand before Sheitan knew what was happening. It was a stylus flare. I activated it and stabbed the laser into the leg Sheitan had planted on my neck. He jerked his foot away, and I sprang to my feet.

I rushed Davio before he reached Mickey, slamming into the back of him in an attempt to turn his focus on me. It felt like I hit a brick wall. I rebounded off his back without getting any sort of grip on him. I staggered backward while Davio spun on me. With one look from him, I was thrown off my feet and sent sprawling spread-eagled against the stone wall behind me, my arms flung out in a crucifixion stance. I was affixed to the wall once again by some unseen force, paralyzed. All I could do was glance down at where Mickey lay slumped against the wall, just inside the double doors, his breath coming in labored gasps. I lifted my eyes to the ceiling, not holding the tears back. They streamed down my face in dirty rivulets. Everyone had grossly underestimated Davio and his second in command.

"Leave him be!" Mickey rasped in a loud voice. "It's me you want."

"NO!" I screamed in desperation, looking down on Mickey, helpless to do anything. What could I do?

Mickey threw his rifle to the side and his left hand plunged into his gear bag. He pulled out another stylus flare, activated it, and shone the harsh glaring light directly in front of him, flooding the room with light. Davio tore his eyes away from me and shielded his face from the flare. His hold on me ceased, causing me to crash to the floor.

I scrambled over to Mickey, who motioned for me to open his gear bag. I looked down into the bag and sucked in my breath as I saw the disarmed land mine! He had snagged it as a souvenir without me even knowing. In an instant, I knew what his plan was. My eyes locked with Mickey's.

"Get out of here!" He growled. I saw Davio advancing on us out of the corner of my eye, but it was too late for me to do anything. I was looking into Mickey's eyes as they went wide. Davio had reached Mickey in two quick strides and had plunged one of my knives into his heart.

"NO-O-O-O-O!" I screamed.

I delivered a strong front kick to Davio's chest, thrusting him backward with every ounce of hatred surging throughout my body.

I reached into the gear bag and pulled out the disarmed mine. I stared at Davio and Sheitan with dead, tear-filled eyes as they advanced on me next. I held the mine out in front of me, making sure they saw what I had and discerned what I was going to do. Davio's gaze paralyzed my limbs once again, just as he stopped Sheitan with an outstretched arm. Dammit!!!

"Go!" he barked to Sheitan, his eyes never leaving my face.

Sheitan didn't look like he planned on going anywhere. Davio took his eyes off me for a split second when he ordered Sheitan to leave, and I took my chance.

Everything happened in slow motion.

I twisted the top of the mine as it sparked on, glowing green. As soon as I hurled it into Davio's face, it would all be over. I would see Josiah again soon, somewhere in another dimension, another time, another place. All thoughts of this life dissipated from my head as I threw the mine as hard as I could toward Davio, who was turning his head in my direction at that very moment.

The mine spiraled through the air and hit Davio head on.

The room erupted in a brilliant light, brighter than the sun, hurling Sheitan sideways and throwing me violently backward through the chamber doors. I didn't know what was happening, and was shocked that I was not blown to smithereens! Why hadn't the mine ignited when I had made a move to throw it? I had been prepared to die! My mind whirled with questions as I struggled to stay in one place.

A strong, powerful wind rushed all around me, causing me to throw my arms over my head. My eyes were watering profusely as I shut my eyes against the blinding white light. I peeked through the broken doors and saw the pillars cracking and the velvet curtain wrenching from the ceiling. On my hands and knees, I crawled away from the impending deluge of collapsing stone walls and the ceiling's rain of marble.

I protected my face against the roaring of the wind, but forced myself to turn in Davio's direction, slitting open one eye. Davio was unrecognizable, a heap crumpled on the floor, but Sheitan was somehow still alive and seemingly unscathed from the explosion. How was that possible?

I caught sight of Sheitan assessing the carnage from the back of the room, his eyes darting around in confusion. He raised his hands high to the heavens then thrust them outward in one swift motion, bringing down fire from the sky. The ball of fire consumed what was left of Davio. Just as abruptly, he turned and ran.

Finally, I walked over to the burning corpse that was once the most powerful dictator in the world and shielded myself from the heat. Just then, the wind and flames subsided as quickly as they had come. I saw that nothing of Davio remained, not even ashes.

I glanced about at the mass destruction. One of the pillars had crashed to the ground, the drapes had disintegrated, and where the ceiling was before was just the sky filled with stars.

I picked up Mickey's rifle, which had managed to survive the blast, and I walked out toward a stairwell on shaky legs, numb with fear and emotion. I sucked in the night air as I looked down into the courtyard below. It was empty, but I heard fighting beyond the walls. I assumed the ADF and the SR were deadlocked in battle. I didn't want to know who had survived and who hadn't. I wasn't sure I could handle any more carnage.

I staggered down the staircase and tripped, falling down the length of the stairs. When I landed at the bottom, I got up, not feeling the pain from the fall. I walked the length of the courtyard in a daze.

I walked through the carnage of hanging bodies, not caring what happened anymore.

I saw that the huge main gate in the Dominion's walls was partly open. Walking through, I saw what was left of the ADF staving off the SR, firing their rifles from behind cover.

I stumbled forward, not caring if I was hit or not.

Someone grabbed me hard and yanked me behind a low wall. It was Genesis.

"Where have you been? What happened?" Genesis asked. Her eyes were wide with concern at my disheveled appearance.

"Mickey's gone . . . ." I faltered, not quite believing my own words. "And Davio . . . Davio's . . . dead."

"What was that explosion?" she asked.

"Where's Alex? Where's Cory?" I dreaded the answer.

I lowered my head. *Please, God.*

"Only a handful of us managed to get out of there alive. You know this, Goro."

"We need to go get the rest!" I shouted, ready to fall over from fatigue. I didn't want to admit it, but I was dreading going back inside. "If those jerks took Alex or Cory . . . ."

"How do you suggest we do that?" Genesis demanded. "We need to regroup, decompress, start over . . . . I'm sorry, Goro. It's over." She pressed a bandage to my head to stop the blood from a scalp wound I didn't even know I had sustained.

I then heard Luc yell, "Let's go, men!"

It took every ounce of strength I didn't know I had to lift Mickey's rifle and start firing on the remaining soldiers. It was strange that there were so few fighting us. Where were their so-called legions of armies? Davio never did anything random; there had to be a reason. We were outnumbered, but I caught sight of Cory and Alex behind the corner of a building, and a wave of incredible relief flooded my mind and soul. They were alive!

Using laser bombs and firing everything we had left, we crushed the few SR soldiers who had ventured out to confront us. When the last man had fallen, I collapsed onto the ground, face up. I saw the stars in the sky between my flame-seared lids.

I lay there for some time, thinking of the remaining team members, my friends, as prisoners of war. They would most likely be tortured. *That's why the SR didn't initially fire on us*, I mused. *They wanted POWs; probably wanted to serve the entire ADF to Davio for dinner*. Alex's hacking into the SR's network may have created an unpleasant diversion for them. They also wanted to preserve most of their soldiers, I presumed. In their book, we hadn't gotten the upper hand at all. Our ill-fated attack was just a game of tag for them.

I thought of Mickey, who had sacrificed his life for more than just us. I thought of Zan. I remembered Josiah, wiping my eyes. I couldn't save anyone right now. I could do nothing more at this point. It would have to be later . . . maybe. The ADF would rise out of this death once again, even if we had to start over from scratch. We would rescue our friends. I would find my family. I would hunt down and kill Sheitan if it took the rest of my living days. We would win this war, even if everyone I loved ended up dead, even if I crossed death's threshold myself.

Epilogue

I lost consciousness and awoke in a hazy fog, my head swimming in choppy, painful waters. Someone was leaning over me in the dark, talking in whispers to another person just outside of my peripheral vision. I could not decipher their cryptic words. Every muscle in my body burned with a low, throbbing voltage, and I would gladly name my firstborn son after anyone who'd be kind enough to bring me a cup of ice-cold water.

As I attempted to turn my head on the rickety cot, my eyes gradually sharpened into focus. I sensed someone leaving as I rubbed my eyes. I finally saw that the person who was hovering over me was Genesis. Where were we? I opened my cracked mouth, but she silenced me with a finger on my lips.

"Sleep." She stared down with kindness into my blinking eyes, gently brushing my hair off my forehead.

"What . . . how did we . . . ?" I struggled for words in my weakened state.

"You plus Alex plus Mickey equals Armageddon." She attempted to come off humorous, but ended up just shrugging.

"Huh?" I was lost.

"Okay, good news is, you crashed the system. Whatever magic Alex did, well, it worked. Identity chips are no mas. Bad news is, the masses are freaking out. It's cray cray. No one can do *anything* now. The public can't buy food, communicate with one another, nothing. It's mayhem outside."

I let that marinate for a minute while finally making it into a sitting position. I felt like an eighty-year-old man.

I sighed, running my hands through my hair. "Ow." My fingers had stopped short in my scraggly hair, not moving past the grittiness matted in it. I was embarrassed that Genesis was seeing me in this sketchy state. I glanced at her out of the corner of my eye, wishing on the down low that she would go away, actually. Luc made an appearance in the doorway just then, and Genesis left us, thank God, because I was sure that I stank to high heaven.

Luc sat down on the edge of my cot, crossing his arms and staying silent for a moment, looking at something on the floor with intense scrutiny.

"Sorry about Mickey," I mumbled, a sharp pain throbbing behind my eyes. I was still sore at him for our confrontation back in the Dominion.

"Life goes on." He swallowed. "It is what it is, son." He glanced up at me then, his moistened eyes giving him away. "He was always one to be self-sacrificial."

"It should have been me . . . ." I faltered in my speech.

"No, son." Luc glanced down, his arms still crossed. "It wasn't meant to be you," he said pointedly. "We need you. And, um, I need you, to be honest."

He looked back at me again, and it was then that I knew an understanding that needed no words had passed between us. I wasn't about to forgive him yet; his leaving Mickey and I behind may have cursed our entire mission. He got up and meandered out of the room, leaving me lost in thought. The letdown in the aftermath of our siege sucked. I wasn't prepared for how depressed I felt. Genesis came back in as I was trying to get up off the cot, and she rushed over to help me stand. She must have been loitering in the hall, either eavesdropping or waiting for Luc to exit. She threw her arms around my neck and rained kisses all over my face. Girlfriend was too much! I just hugged her back.

"I'm just glad you made it out alive," she whispered in my ear. I pulled back to look at her. "I mean, it sucks about Mickey, of course," she was babbling as if she was suffering from PTSD.

"To be honest, I wanted you to be okay, mostly. I know that's selfish, but, whatever." She finished in tears. I wiped them away, resting my forehead against hers.

Alex and Cory walked in then, and Genesis stepped to the side. The two of them took two strides and attacked me in a bear hug that crushed me. We all stood there for what seemed like forever, breaking each other's ribs until I broke the hold.

"It's all good," I sputtered.

"You badass hero!" Cory slapped me on the back. "I can't believe Davio is toast!"

"Bedtime story later," Alex chuckled at Cory as he motioned for him and Genesis to leave me be. As I watched them walking slowly down the hall, I thought of my family and what was next for us. I still needed to find them.

I ventured out of my room and down the hallway in the opposite direction, exploring my surroundings, finding a door, a window, anything that would take me outside. When I found an exit, I peered out and took a deep breath of semi-fresh air to clear my head. The daylight blinded my sight momentarily, and I thought I saw someone I recognized standing across the street. He was talking to someone just inside a doorway.

Was that . . . ? No.

I stepped further outside into the street.

The man turned in his conversation and I saw my father's profile. Was I hallucinating? I choked up. He sensed he was being watched, and he glanced in my direction. His eyes locked with mine in disbelief; joy lit up his face. Tears stung my eyes as he strode across the street and grabbed me in a hug. I embraced him tightly as hope filled me again.

A random quote rolled through my mind at that moment, something some dude from the "Stone Age" said long ago…

"Now this is not the end. It is not even the beginning of the end. But it is, perhaps, the end of the beginning."

—Winston Churchill

. . . . . . Continued in *TRIUNITY* . . . .

Ash Sheitan survived the attack on the Dominion, only to assume power as the new ruler of the Sovereign Regime. He is more cunning, more wicked, and even more merciless than his predecessor Davio. The identity chip program and data has been destroyed, but a new, virtually virus free system has been instilled in its place. More and more civilians have been persuaded to join the SR, and those who have resisted have been commanded to join upon pain of death. Goro, Luc, and the newly reborn ADF keep a low profile as they sift the city of LA in search of new recruits, all while planning to free their imprisoned team members, including Robbie. But when Goro's sister Stephanie is abducted by the SR for a far more sinister purpose than soldier training, Goro can no longer wait for the right time. He must act immediately or lose his friends and sister forever.

Acknowledgments

A huge thank you to my acquisitions editor, Terry, for giving me the surreal opportunity of having my first book in print. Thank you to my managing editor, Megan, for helping me navigate the complicated waters of publishing. Thank you to my rock star publication team, who became the creative sounding board I needed. Also, thanks to my marketing squad; without them, the world would never know.

They say that to teach is to touch a life forever; well, I sincerely thank every student I've ever taught. You are valuable to me, and you have purpose in this world! Over the course of my teaching career, you have taught me more than ever about persevering through the hard times in life and not giving up on dreams. ☺

Thanks to my kick-ass Krav instructors at KMW—kida!

I want to thank my favorite author OF ALL TIME, the one and only Michael Connelly, for miraculously helping me fall in love with

Los Angeles. If I hadn't picked up *The Overlook* that one fateful summer, I wouldn't be in the City of Angels today.

Thank you to my fantastic beta reader and close friend Robbie Johnson, who selflessly spent countless hours shooting the breeze with me over my crazy ideas.

Also, I thank my best friend, Stephanie van Belle; I will forever be grateful for your incredible kindness the first day we met so many years ago, as well as your continued presence in my life. I'd take a laser hit for you!

I wish to thank my incredible family, especially my brother for all his amazing hard work in assisting me on this exciting journey as an author. And last but definitely not least, I want to thank God, the Alpha and the Omega, for being my gracious rock and redeemer.